I0452538

A BOUQUET OF DILEMMA

Tayo Emmanuel

To Mzee's triplets

ONE

Who wouldn't remember her first kiss? Yes, I remember mine now. It was in form four, a week after I played Juliet in Shakespeare's famous romance tragedy in the school's end of first term fiesta. The boy who played Romeo had asked me to wait after classes so he could give me a gift for putting up a good show. The fact that he thought of giving me a gift was enough to make my silly head run in different wild directions and it made me feel very special. It was common knowledge that most of the girls in my set wanted a piece of him, for being so ruggedly handsome and streetwise. Even before I opened the gift, he had pulled me to himself and kissed me with such gusto I almost fainted. And of course, he knew I enjoyed it because he soon graduated to touching my breasts once we were alone in the class. And then he had kept pushing for more, asking me if we could meet after school.

Maybe I would have given in eventually, it always felt good and I thought it could only get better. But our romance came to an end towards the end of third term, when I made the mistake of mentioning to my friend, Maggie that the silly boy had jokingly threatened to stop seeing me if I didn't pass my Maths as he wouldn't want to be associated with a dullard. Maggie had lured him out into the playground and given him a showdown. He didn't talk to me for the rest of the term and I was heart-broken when he started seeing another girl within two weeks. That seems long ago.

It's amazing that the end of one journey is often the beginning of another, yet you start each one with so much relish as if its completion would be the most remarkable event in your life, only to get to the end and realise that you've actually just opened another page, leaving you wondering if it would ever end. That's how I see life now, an unending quest for different things at different phases of life. The next phase of my life is clearly defined even though no one had bothered consulting me. Like everybody around me, that would be another four years of study at the university, and then another one year at Law school. And then what?

Memories of the past five years float back into my head as I take another bite of the sausage roll; I remember the good ones like when I won the literary and debating award in form four and when my form three class teacher continually referred to me as a good role model; the bad ones like when my skirt got stained during my first menstrual period the second week I resumed school and when I fell face-flat during the one thousand, five hundred meter race in the inter-house sports; and the really terrible ones like when my two-timing boyfriend told me off in the presence of his girlfriend in form five and when a bus conductor almost tore my uniform because my purse got stolen in school and I couldn't pay my bus fare. I find every bit of all that amusing now.

I retrieve myself from the nostalgic reverie and focus on the party, which is turning out to be a carnival of sort. I haven't stopped wondering how Maggie had convinced her parents to agree to such a big party. Of course, they are very rich, but even at that. What would they do when she finally qualifies as a lawyer? Well, one good excuse is that she didn't celebrate her sixteenth birthday last year and they agreed to the party only after *GCE* and *JAMB* results had been published. We passed brilliantly well, especially with 'A' in Literature; and 'C' in Maths is not bad either. And we both got admission into the State University.

Positioning myself by the gate, I start welcoming our friends. I can practically see the expression of awe on their faces when they enter the compound. Most people in school knew Maggie was from a rich home, but no one knew how rich, especially when she tells them she is not in any way related to the famous Abiola family who also lives at Ikeja. When she introduces herself, Maggie would usually add, 'and my father is not MKO' so people would not bother to ask.

I revel in that look of shock and then admiration the moment someone steps into the compound. One girl takes some steps in, then retreats and asks me if this is a hotel or Maggie's house. By five o'clock on the dot, one of the servants comes to close the gate and I go to join the party at the garden. Maggie had said anyone who came later than one hour didn't deserve to be at her party. She is still inside the house, but people are mingling very well and apparently having fun. As the co-hostess, I need to keep on circulating to ensure everyone is okay. It's a cocktail party, so there are no chairs;

some have formed chatting cliques while some others continue to look around, eating, drinking or dancing.

Segun, Maggie's older brother emerges from the house and I quickly drag him to the dance floor. He's her exact male version; dark, handsome and slim with a muscular six-foot frame. Maggie and I call him stud (he doesn't know that), because he has a lot of girlfriends. As far as looks go, I wouldn't have minded him except that I would rather not fight for his attention beside the fact that we have a familial boundary, like brother and sister.

"Why do you want to dance with me, where is your boyfriend?" He asks smiling, pretending to be resisting my pull.

"I had to rescue you from your lonely state, bro, seeing that Maggie was mean enough not to invite any of your girlfriends. She probably got confused or have they all ditched you?"

"Not on your life. If you hear that a girl ditched me, it's because I want to help her keep her pride intact." He says arrogantly. "I'm actually hoping I would get a catch here tonight."

How does he manage to swing all those girls? "Thank God I'm not your girlfriend."

"You?" He looks at me with an enticing smile. "With a girl like you, who needs another girlfriend?"

"Hmm, I'm in love. You could have fooled me."

"By the way, why didn't you girls think of a pool party instead of this cover-it-all affair?" Segun asks. "I've told Maggie severally to leave party organising to the boys, she never listens."

By my reckoning, a lot of the girls are wearing the barest minimum while trying to maintain public decency. "You want them to come naked?"

He shrugs. "That would make me less confused as I am now. You could have done better than this, that's all I have to say. Which one of those girls would you recommend?"

"None, Segun you have no shame." I answer curtly. "Pitch your tent elsewhere. They could all pass for your junior sister."

"Don't be ridiculous, I'm content to have only one sister and I'm not related to anyone of your friends in any way." He shifts his eyes to scan the crowd. "Junior sister indeed!" He snickers. "Anyway, which one of these bores is your boyfriend?"

"Why are you interested?"

"So I'd know if you've learnt anything from me about boys."

"And who says you're the yardstick for romance?"

"You just said it." He laughs. "That girl is staring at me now, the one in pink top?" He is focused on someone ahead of me, but as I make to turn and follow his stare, he turns my head back. "Don't look now!"

"Hey, that felt like a slap." I wince, rubbing my cheek.

"Sorry, but I don't want her getting embarrassed, we've already made eye-contact."

"Are you going after her?" I ask, pouting. Silly question, I already know the answer.

"What do you think?"

Maggie elegantly enters the garden now with her latest catch. They've been going steady for about a month now and as usual, they are all over each other, laughing and touching. She looks like a life mannequin with her professionally done hair and makeup, especially the thick red lips and really, if not for her small breasts, she could have passed for Anita Baker's alter. Apart from country music singers, Anita Baker is the only other singer Maggie cares about, because of her stylish hairstyle. She is wearing a black clinging halter neck dress with silver sequins draped all over and matching red sequined sandals. Since her new found boyfriend is not from our school, some of the girls would be wondering where she hooked him up from, but I'm not doing any telling. She goes into her regular intro-dance-steps, one leg after the other with intermittent gyrating hips, head swinging and finger snapping in calculated synergy to the music as we all cheer her to the dance floor.

And the beat goes on…

People start cheering as someone comes in carrying a carton of what I guess is liquor. Even though their parents had forbidden it, Segun had insisted we needed the liquor to put the party in full swing and he had commissioned his friend to bring it in. The first time I took alcohol was with him and Maggie and somehow I knew I had lost control of some parts of my brain. So I steer clear. But not Maggie; she has her rascal brother to support her; my only brother is just like Daddy; an *effiko*. Otherwise, why couldn't he be at this party? He said he had his final project to defend, as if he is the only undergraduate. He's four years older than me, but at twenty two, I'm not sure he has ever had a girlfriend.

Segun and I break up our dance and go to help his friend unpack. Only then did I see the full profile of the tall, dark guy, dressed in stretch black jeans and white linen shirt. My heart suddenly skips, stopping me in my tracks. He looks at me deeply, causing me to flush inside. He is delicately handsome, hunky, penetrating eyes, dimples and lips to die for; the kind of guy you see on the front page of GQ. Segun nudges me with his elbow, "Have you guys met?"

I must look really taken, I don't utter a word. But he rescues me. "Hello, my name is Richard."

I could die for that Teddy Pendergrass' voice. I hold out my hand for a handshake before remembering that his two hands are occupied with a carton. "Er, my name is Tobi, I'm Maggie's friend." As Segun makes to collect the carton from him, I quickly pick a bottle from the stock, leaving immediately to look for Maggie and particularly in a bid to conceal the overwhelming feeling of self-consciousness that has suddenly consumed me.

Maggie and I are backing the wall subsuming the flow of the party. Those heels must be killing her by now and knowing her, she would make me suffer for it, because she would definitely ask me to massage her feet. She takes the last sip of the brandy directly from the bottle and places it behind a shrub where no one can see it. After making small talk for a few more minutes, she drags me along to chat with the guests.

I notice him, the one with the baritone voice gliding towards one of the girls, but our eyes meet and he seems to change his mind and heads towards us instead. My mind starts racing and my stomach starts churning left, right and centre at the same time.

"Birthday girl, the last time I saw you, you were this little." He says to Maggie, demonstrating her height and pulling both her cheeks.

She smiles and gives him a bear hug. "That's a lie, I see

you've been growing up too, even taller than Segun now."

"It's not my fault your brother stopped eating beans." He jokes.

"Thanks for the drinks, I knew we could always count on you. Segun said you came alone." It seems she intended that to be a question.

"Didn't all your friends come alone?" He replies gracefully. "It would be a waste if there are no dudes like me to cheer them up, you know."

"Hmm, true." She turns to me. "Richie and Segun were best of friends in boarding school, but he's the master of the game when it comes to girls."

"Tobi, don't believe everything you hear?" Richard makes a face at Maggie. "That's not a nice way to introduce a gentleman. I will do that myself." Did I detect a hint of arrogance in him?

"Oh!" Maggie exclaims, genuinely surprised. "Tobi, you know Richie?"

"No, no." I manage to slur before she gets on to any mischief. "We only just met today."

"Yes, that's like Richie, never a slacker." She has that mischievous smile and it seems she's thinking about what to do with the two of us. She leans forward to him and does a whisper.

Richard shakes his head and gives her a gentle push. "I'm sure your other friends would need you now, you don't have to monopolise Tobi."

"Common Richie." She urges with that voice she usually employs when she wants to have her way. He keeps on shaking his head, indicating a no. She shrugs and scurries away.

With Maggie out of the way, Richard turns to me with a smile I can only describe as alluring; his dimples are deep and hot! And my legs feel very heavy. "How do you ever cope with Maggie?" He asks. I answer with a shrug. "It seems you are the quiet one?" He asks again and I almost shrug a second time, but decide I should say something before he thinks I've gone mute because of him.

I count from one to three inside me and then I respond with as much calm as I can muster. "Only when there's nothing to say and I thought you wanted to catch up with Maggie."

"Can anyone ever catch up with her?" He is looking at her and shaking his head. "She has too much energy and always up to something." I notice Maggie disappear into the house.

"So, what do you think she's up to now?" I ask, trying to keep up the conversation. But more like trying to suppress the electric current racing throughout my body. If that swimming pool was not cordoned off, I probably would have jumped in. Why do I feel this way? I hope he can't notice.

"She's your friend, you should tell me."

"I'm not the one she whispered to." I mumble, more because I am curious about what Maggie told him.

"Oh, that?" He turns one hundred and eighty degrees facing me and brings his mischievous eyes back to mine. "She said you are her most precious friend, so I should handle you with extreme care, like glass and make sure you don't break into pieces."

"She said that?" The blood rushes to my face now. His eyes are scorching through my clothes right to my skin and his voice is captivating. What am I supposed to say to him? Get hold of yourself, girl, stay calm. "I didn't know I was that fragile."

"Actually, she didn't say that, do you believe everything you hear? I hope I didn't offend you?" I shake my head, not sure of what to say. I don't want to look stupid in his eyes any more than this. "In that case, I need you to tell me if you are fragile or not?"

"I'm not sure I know what you mean."

"You used the word fragile, although I must admit you are really pretty and you do look very precious."

I think it would make sense now to simply ignore this trend of conversation since I don't know what he's driving at. "Thank you, why don't you get on the dance floor while I go get a drink?" Maybe I can breathe better if he leaves, seeing that my own legs can't do any walking now, lest I trip.

He ignores my suggestion and chooses rather to expatiate on what Maggie said. "Actually, Maggie said …"

Neither of us saw Maggie as she flashes back, holding a bowler hat. She whispers to Richard, again. He starts protesting, but she is insisting and as I look on, trying to fathom what the argument is about, she drags him to the middle of the dance floor and puts the hat on his head. He looks back at me helplessly, shaking his head continuously. He adjusts his shirt and the hat and then starts Michael Jackson's moonwalk dance. It had happened so swiftly and I had been so consumed with his presence, I did not realise when the music changed to *Billy Jean*. Everybody stops dancing to form a circle and watch him do the dance. I have watched the Billy Jean video over and again and watching someone of his age and physique do the whole song and not miss a beat gives me goose pimples.

When the song ended, he takes a bow and throws the hat in my direction, but the girl standing beside me reaches out to catch it. The applause is reverberating as someone pushes her towards him and she almost falls but he catches her on time and they go on dancing, naturally, as if it's a scene he had rehearsed severally.

Soon enough, the show is over. Everyone goes back to dancing or chatting. Someone manages to hook me on the dance floor. Thankfully, I am breathing normally again and my legs are working perfectly. Well, almost. The guy I'm dancing with tries to talk to me, but I keep pretending I can't hear him because of the loud music, so we continue dancing. Yet dancing with him does not take my mind off Richard and I peek at him dancing with the other girl with a tiny twinge of jealousy. He is so astonishingly gorgeous; effortlessly and casually. Those penetrating eyes and tempting luscious lips are my undoing. What if he goes for her?

Strangely, I feel his eyes on me; almost boring a hole in my skin. I peep at him again and our eyes meet. I feel the blood rush to my face for the umpteenth time. If what they say about light-skinned girls is true, my face would be all red by now. In an instant, Richard swings the girl away from him to my dancing partner and I find myself dancing with him. How did he manage that?

"May I have the pleasure of this dance?" He asks in the most seductive voice. I nod, not that I have a choice; he already has me in his hands.

The only thing I feel is inadequate after watching his dance manoeuvres. "I hope you won't be disappointed, I'm not near as good as you." I mumble. He simply smiles and he continues to hold on to my hands, twirling me with him. When his right hand moved to my waist, I feel a shiver inside me and I suddenly step on his toes almost losing my balance. That pushes me closer to him, but he pretends not to notice and we go on dancing. I hope he wouldn't think that was deliberate. I need to get a grip of myself. After a while, without saying a word, he guides me to a secluded corner, right at the end of the pool and on impulse, we both sit on the floor.

"I warned you about Maggie, didn't I?" He asks.

"Maggie is the perfect mastermind, but we all enjoyed the flavour you added to the party."

"So, now I am the flavour." Richard laughs. "Anyway, thanks for the compliments. You dance well."

"Who, me? Thank you, but no thanks because I don't believe you." I reply. Why does he think he needs to be nice about that? Why can't you just take a good compliment, the other voice replies. But I know he's either trying to be nice or he's mocking me, dancing is not near the top on my list. "And where did you learn to dance like that?"

"My mother told me I started dancing three months before she gave birth to me." We both laugh. My body is beginning to relax, but I still feel internally hot. "You know, I have this feeling that we'll go a long way together." He holds my hands in his, caressing them. I should pull my hands away, but I don't, pretending it's the most natural thing in the world. "Your hands are very supple." He turns my palms up and stares at them in admiration before pressing them against his face.

"You know I have a feeling I'm not going to be one of your

girls." I reply, trying not to sound easily beguiled, yet I leave my hands with him. Like Maggie said, he is not a slacker at all, but I don't intend to make it easy for him now that I have found my voice.

"My girls? That's the problem with having a reputation." He makes a face which looks more like a contorted smile. "But I like you all the same, and I know you like me." He stares into my eyes and I feel he's trying to force me to admit that I like him. For sure, I liked him from the first time I saw him, but that Maggie's introduction just kind of threw in a spanner.

"How can you be sure I like you?" I ask in a low-pitched voice, looking aimlessly at my feet. All too soon, I have become rather self-conscious to meet his probing eyes.

"I know because I read bodies, like I'm reading yours now, and don't even try to hide under that 'girl playing hard to get' lie." He says self-assuredly and flirtatiously as he begins to turn my right palm up, but I withdraw from him. His touch is light, but electrifying. Well, whether he read me or not, I don't have to reveal that I am inwardly swooning over him, although that is taking a lot of effort on my part.

"I think we should get back to the party. I wouldn't want you to miss all the fun and I need to take care of the guests."

He pulls me back. "I'm sure the guests can take care of themselves, or are you trying to avoid me?"

"Why should I try to avoid you?" He shrugs. Putting me on the defensive seems to be his subtle way of stopping me from leaving. Yet I can't make sense of why I am staying. "What would you like to talk about then? Maggie said you are master of the game, so you can take charge." I say sarcastically. "Maybe we should talk about girls. Definitely you must have your hands full."

"I have some." He nods. "But I guess you keep looking until you find what you really want."

At least he is sincere, although I wish he was more modest. So what does he really want that he hasn't found on campus? That's where most men fish from these days and from what I've heard of universities you can find any type of girl there, from the most ludicrous to the most serious? Then he goes on to tell me about himself. His full names are Richard Adebola Aro. He had to leave home after secondary school because money was tight; he is twenty three, lives all by himself; lost his mother when he was quite young, his father lives in Ibadan and is married to his fourth wife; he has one brother, one half-sister and a lot of step sisters and brothers he hardly sees, although they are all on good terms; he rarely goes to church, he was lucky to get a job as a sales clerk immediately after moving to Lagos, he used to work as a DJ a while ago, he has an old blue Volvo he drives about town; he drinks a lot, but doesn't consider himself a drunkard; yes, he likes girls, and that has put him in trouble because he has a two year old daughter from a girl he doesn't care so much about; he wants to go abroad in search of greener pastures; life has not been easy at all, but he's determined to make the most of it and enjoy himself.

Without any written handbook, I have seen enough around me to know that every young Nigerian contends with a lot of social constraints in the nineties. When your relationship with the opposite sex begins to take a more serious dimension, things could be quite tricky. There are a lot of informal rules that could make nonsense of the most prospective relationship. First you had to consider the tribe -Ibo, Hausa, or Yoruba;

then the religion -Christian, Moslem; and then the socio-economic and cultural status -educated/non-educated, polygamous/monogamous, poor/middle-class/rich.

This is not to mention the subordinates that come with these parameters. For instance, it would not be enough just to know that he is Yoruba, you had to confirm if he is Ijebu, Ekiti, Egba, Ijesha; and if he is a Christian, you need to know if he is Pentecostal, Anglican, Catholic, Jehovah Witness to mention just a few. Believe me, all these have nothing to do with the individual's personality or value system, but some myths and cultural practices passed down from one generation to another based on some long forgotten events and the sources of which no one is clear about.

I am Yoruba -Ekiti, Christian -Anglican, from an educated monogamous, middle class family. My mother always talks about marrying well if I wanted to live a really good life. Apart from being Yoruba, every other thing about Richard's profile looks like it's far from where I want to be heading in a relationship; I should sensibly get up now and leave. But I go on to tell him about myself anyway. My name, Oluwatobiloba Amanda Bolade; where I live – a three bedroom flat in one of those government-built estates at Ogba; how many we are in my family – four; what I would be studying at the university – Law; my father – a lawyer; my mother – a teacher; my brother – an engineering student, my friends – Maggie and a few others; I don't drink or smoke, I go to church, I don't have any obvious talent, I like country music and literature and I would like to be a successful lawyer, marry a rich man one day and have two children like my parents.

"So will you marry me, when I become rich?" He cups my

face in his hands, gently stroking it.

In the shadow of the looming night, I look longingly at him, not knowing what to search for, I just want to reach his soul and feel the depth of his emotions. I am not one so easily taken in by boys, but somehow Richard feels different. In spite of his background, his escapades and his uncertain future, my soul and body aches for him. "You would have to get rich on time then."

He doesn't respond, just reaches forward to kiss me, so passionately, I dare not stop. It's a kiss like no other; more matured, more playful and more soulful.

TWO

I first met Margaret Abiola in the students' waiting room when both our mothers went to the bursar's office to complete our admission process. Co-incidentally, we had both been transferred from different private schools by the second term of form two, because our parents concluded we weren't doing well in Literature in our previous schools and we hit it off almost immediately. Maggie and I have some things in common, we both like country music, we both have one older brother and we both wanted to become lawyers.

Yet, we are of different stocks. She is rich; I'm middle class -that's my father's classification of not being unbearably poor; she's kind of bossy, I'm compliant; I'm reserved, Maggie is a buzz; she takes the lead, I follow; she's often factual, I'm mostly emotional; she's dark-skinned and slim (amazing, with all the sweet things she guzzles), I'm fair and just a little short of fat, but tall – thank goodness; the only conservative thing about Maggie is her hair style which she keeps short in the typical Anita Baker cut, while I go to great lengths fixing long weaves or braids. With all sense of modesty, I can say we are both good looking in our different ways.

Maggie ditches boys as if they were toys. She started dating in form three, but once she's kissed a boy nine times, she was ready to move on. Oh, yes, she counts the kisses and her philosophy is that the tenth kiss would make the boy too comfortable and might make her cross the line. "Tobi, when we're gonna have sex, it's not gonna be with any small boy in this school." She had said in her wanna be tone in form four. That was not an advice, it was a directive. On the last count, she's had four kissing partners; one lasted two terms, the other ones lasted just one term, but by the time we were leaving school, we were both boyfriend-less.

Maggie's house is an architectural myth-buster by all means. I used to believe Daddy's story that land was in short supply in Lagos until I got to her house. The house, built on a massive plot of land at Ikeja, is on three floors including the basement, so from the streets it looks like two floors. There are six bedrooms, three living rooms; one for her father, one for her mother and the last one for Maggie and her brother with their friends. From the entrance gate, you could either take the stairs down into the extended garden or towards the small front garden which ultimately leads to any of the three living rooms – up, to the father's big living room; middle, to the mother's; or down, to the general living room which opens into the garden and the V-shaped swimming pool at the extreme end. There are two big rooms on the top floor, two small rooms and the main kitchen on the middle floor and two rooms and another tiny kitchen on the basement floor. Maggie's room is on the middle floor while the other room serves as a guest's room. Her brother occupies the basement apartment and their parents, the top floor. Almost all the rooms have private balconies and staircases that take you from one floor right to another. I would agree it could be quite confusing.

At a time when most houses are floored in terrazzo, Maggie's house is tiled from wall to wall. She had to explain to me that only the living rooms are tiled with granite while the other areas are tiled with ceramic, even though I never could tell the difference; all I know is that the floors always look glossy. Mine is floored with rug. The first time I visited the house was in the company of my mother and even she couldn't hide her surprise at such splendour. I teased her that if not for me, how else could she have seen such a beautiful house and she responded that if she hadn't changed my school, I definitely wouldn't have met Maggie.

Maggie's house is also a constant reminder of an enigmatic normalcy in modern day Lagos; opulence co-habiting with poverty. Putting it in my grandma's words, the charcoal pot has the honour of cooking the white pap. How else would you describe this beautiful magnificent house buried behind a village, which explains the high wall and the barbed wire fence encompassing it? The way to the house is lined with a number of pretentious houses which are actually huts, built with muds and covered with thin layers of cement, some of which have fallen off. Ironically, these are the houses where the original landowners live.

Indigenous landowners have a culture of polygamy and having several children, including not schooling or working since they live off sale of their fore fathers' land. Naturally, once they've finished selling all the land, they are more impoverished than ever, and then they send their children to work as servants for the same people who had bought land from them. To me, this is the epitome of Voltaire's position that *'the comfort of the rich depends upon an abundant supply of the poor'*.

The particular street on which the house is located gets heavily flooded during the rainy season because there is no drainage for water to pass through. According to Maggie's father, he had tried to organise each house owner to construct drainage in front of their houses, so they could chase away the floods, but some people had refused, claiming that it was the government's job to provide drainages as long as they pay their taxes. Afterwards, he had tried to solely finance constructing the drainage, only for the local government to tell him he needed official approval to do it. That was the end of the matter; Maggie's father couldn't fathom why he had to bribe local government officials in a bid to help do their job. So the road keeps getting eroded with each rainy season. Thank God it's the August rain-break now, and the pools of flood have dried a little.

The morning after the party, Maggie and I are lounging in the general living room with Segun, in between snacking, purposelessly watching a musical video and discussing the highlights of the party. The garden is getting back to normal gradually as the servants are tidying the place. Talk about being richly spoilt, if I ever held a party in my house, which is highly unlikely, my father would make sure I spearheaded the cleaning.

"What if that boy had fallen into the pool? You girls should know the limits of your friends next time you are thinking of a party." Segun tries to admonish us as if it was our fault one of the boys had had too much to drink. Except for the drunken incident, the party was 'solid as the rock' as some of the guests had commented. Apparently, the boy had started taking off his clothes and announced that he wanted to take a swim. He had to be restrained by two others boys before they got hold of Segun and one of the servants. "I'll keep reminding you, that you need lessons on party planning, Maggie. But your strong head wouldn't let you listen."

"Big brother, remember we had concluded our plans, until someone came and volunteered booze. Tobi, can you remind us who that is?" Maggie responds with a smirk on her face. She would never accept defeat lying low.

"Segun!" I submit, pointing to him. "Probably because he wanted to get some girls drunk, so he can pull a fast one, unfortunately that didn't happen." The joke is on him now. Maggie and I laugh. But he just sniffs his nose at us, smiling and then he starts whistling.

"Or did you?" Maggie's eyes widen in surprise as the import of his whistling hits her. "No, you couldn't have." Maggie should know better. "*Sege bobo,* who is the unlucky girl this time? You are just impossible. Those girls are my friends." She says with as much indignation as she can express. It appears she has mixed emotions, one of admiration for her brother and the other, disdain.

Segun moves swiftly to her settee and blocks her mouth with his right hand. "Shush, there's a girl in there." He whispers.

"A girl? What girl, where?" My goodness! My eyes are wider than Maggie's now and I stare hard at Segun, hoping my thoughts are wrong. Why am I surprised at the stud? It's common knowledge he has a reputation with anything in skirts. But which girl would have stayed overnight and what will she tell her parents? Is it that girl in pink he mentioned? I can't even recall who the girl is. How could he have managed to sneak a girl in without us noticing him? "You sure know your trade, I must say you break the scale!"

"For your information, I won't leave here until that girl comes out." Maggie whispers, but loud enough for all to hear, except the girl in the room. There's a sound of anger or disappointment or perhaps embarrassment in her voice, I'm not exactly sure which. She may have to wait for quite a while if she really meant that. All the rooms in the house have inbuilt bathrooms, which makes everyone comfortable without venturing out a whole day, except to douse hunger pangs, catch up with friends or watch TV. This is some limits for me. Does this have anything to do with a phase of life, I wonder. But Segun is extremely different from Lami, even though he's only older by a year.

"What's your problem girl? Has anyone tried to stop you from sneaking in with the boy next door?" Segun asks, unrepentant.

"You should be ashamed of yourself." Maggie pouts.

"There's something called mutual consent, sis, freely given, freely taken." He sniggers at her and takes a sip from his teacup. "By the way, you, what were you doing with Richie?" He asks, right from nowhere and looking in my direction.

"Me?" When did this conversation shift to me?

"Yes, you or did you give him room to cosy up to someone else?"

"This conversation is not about me, so leave me out of it."
I frown and try to hide my shyness beneath the frown and
calm voice. I get up and head for the fridge to get a bottle of
coke; that gives me some breather.

Segun patiently waits for me to return. "It's about you
now." He insists. I look at Maggie for support, hoping she
would say something to rescue me, but she meets my gaze with
a nod, in agreement with him. For some reasons, I had tactfully
avoided mentioning my dalliance with Richard at the party and
she hadn't mentioned it either, probably she had been too busy
to notice us together. I scratch my head to think. Why is it
difficult to answer?

"Er, we were talking, we danced and we sat by the pool to
talk, just generally enjoyed the party." I hope that sounds
casual enough.

"Just talk?" Maggie probes. "So what is the big deal, big
brother?"

"You call that just talk?" He retorts. He puts a biscuit in his
mouth and stares at me intently in between munching. It's an
uncomfortable stare, but I say nothing. "You practically
colonised Richard. I'm sure I saw you kiss."

"Who, Tobi, you kissed Richie?" Maggie shrieks and then
smiles naughtily. That sounds like a reprimand, not a question.
"Richie boy." She gloats over the name with an uncanny
admiration. Her mouth is still open to say more I think, but
she changes her mind and keeps quiet. She shakes her head in
disapproval all the same.

"What's the fuss about? That's not as bad as Segun has
done." I say defensively.

"Tobi, do you like Richie?" Maggie asks. "Silly me, that's

obvious, isn't it? Not like you go about kissing boys anyhow. I should have known I couldn't trust him with you."

"Hey, what's the problem here? Nobody committed murder, it was just a kiss." I manage to say still wondering what the fuss is about. Why are they trying to persecute me or Richard for that matter? "He didn't do anything untoward with me."

Segun looks at me with amusement all over his face. "My dear sister, Richard is not your type, so steer clear if you don't want your heart broken." He pulls his left ear, like you do when you tell someone to listen carefully.

"And why would he break my heart?" I gawk at him.

"Because he's a bad boy." He stretches the bad for emphasis. "A long way out of your league."

Maggie comes behind my seat and starts massaging my back as if I needed consolation. I gently push her hand away, but she remains there.

"Thank you, but no thanks." I say defiantly. "Since when did having a boyfriend become a lifelong commitment?"

"Tobi, if you don't want a boyfriend like Segun, then you don't need Richie." Maggie advises in a gentle voice, her hands back on my shoulders; I let them rest there this time.

"What's that supposed to mean?" Segun snorts.

"But Maggie said he's your friend, how can you talk about him like this?" My voice pitches a bit higher, getting some reprieve from Segun's discomfort.

"Tobi." He responds. "Richie is my friend, but you are like my sister, I would blame myself if you got involved with him, he's a player. And I intend to tell him to keep off you."

This is so unfair, what right does he have to treat other girls recklessly, yet trying to be protective of me? If this is what it feels like to be on the hot seat, then I'm there now and it's not a comfortable place to be. I'm flushed, exasperated, but afraid that there may be some truth in what they are saying.

"It was just a simple kiss, why are you trying to make me feel guilty?"

"You girls are so naïve, God!" He laughs and shakes his head in frustration. "Richie doesn't kiss for simple sake, he follows up. Good girls shouldn't be mixing with bad boys."

"Tobi, I think you should listen to him. I've known Richie since they were in secondary school and just like this boy here, he changes girls like this." Maggie snaps her fingers after pointing accusingly at her brother. Perhaps I'm different; but I dare not say this. He's told me all there is and I still like him. But I guess there's no need to argue with them. Maybe they know much more than he's told me. I wish life isn't so complicated.

Segun chooses to ignore Maggie. "And just so you know, girls are like a game of numbers for us. The more girls we have, the more macho." He flexes his biceps arrogantly. That sounds condescending. "And he has a daughter, so he's got his hands full." He says, staring at me. Something tells me he thinks he has dropped a bombshell, but I guess he's disappointed at my reaction.

"He told me." I murmur. Now they are surprised.

"He told you?" Maggie and Segun chorus and exchange glances. I nod in agreement and everyone goes quiet. Segun gets up, shakes his head, takes his teacup and goes to the bookshelf where he had stacked the remaining drinks – behind some books – where their parents wouldn't see them. He pours some brandy into the teacup and comes back to his seat. Maggie seems somewhat restless; she snatches the teacup from his stool and gulps down some brandy. Maybe I should take some too. Segun scowls at her and clenches his fist as if to punch her, she sneers at him with her tongue lashing out and goes back to her seat.

"Richard told you he has a baby?" She asks, squinting. I nod. What is wrong with these people?

"Well, that's a first." Segun says. "He usually doesn't reveal that part of himself to any girl, least of all on a first date. Maybe, just maybe …." He doesn't finish the sentence, but keeps on nodding in a reflective stance, and then he shakes his head. "I don't think so."

"Okay, let's try to rationalise this." I raise my hands to quieten the two of them. "Segun, you always say the experience of dating many boys is good for us. Right?" He nods. "So, why are you concerned much about me dating Richard if I can add him to my pool of experience? Meaning, this is a non-issue, I'm just eighteen and it's not like I'm getting married tomorrow."

"Girl, are you hard of hearing? Richie is not the kind of guy you practise with because he is far too smart for that. He definitely would have gotten under your skirt before you even know what hit you. Is that what you want?" Segun asks. "And for the records, you are three months away from eighteen." He adds jokingly, trying to defuse the stiff atmosphere.

I should try to change my tactic if I'm going to get these people off my back. "How come we are not talking about Maggie and her boyfriend?" I ask, praying it works.

"I don't know that boy from Adam, if he messes around

with my sister, I'm going to beat the living daylights out of him and he would never talk to a girl again." Segun threatens.

"Just mind your own business and let me mind mine." Maggie sneers at him.

He ignores her. "But I can't kick Richie's butt for anyone, because he's my friend." And he stares hard at me and if I'm to read his face correctly, it says, 'a word is enough for the wise'.

THREE

My father makes the ordinary things of life seem like luxury and he has all the right answers to justify it. For example, he wouldn't buy a video player because watching video was a waste of productive studying time and he has already proven that owning a TV was bad enough; we didn't have parties because it was a terrible way of wasting food in the midst of hungry people; we didn't get so many clothes because investing in books would empower us to get more clothes in future; not to talk of designer labels because people who didn't know you shouldn't affect your life so much; we didn't need to move to a bigger house because you could only sleep in one bed and one room at a time; we didn't need two cars because travelling together was a good way for the family to bond even though riding with him was almost like lecture time, I never looked forward to it; and he didn't need to be very rich because riches didn't exactly make one happy, although I don't know how it could make one sad either, since I don't notice any sadness in Maggie's family.

My mother, who is from a fairly liberated background, would complain to no end about his austere outlook to life and how it negatively affects the entire household. When she realises he wouldn't budge (which is more often than not), she would go ahead and do whatever she could afford under the circumstances, which is how she bought her first car. They are so different and sometimes, I wonder what else they have in common beyond giving their children very good education.

One can never be too sure of Mummy's stance, though. Sometimes, she's the reliable confidant; other times she goes on and tells Daddy everything she was told in confidence. I know my mother enough not to mention anything about Richard to her. As far as my parents are concerned, messing around with the opposite sex when one wasn't ready for marriage was taboo. By their reckoning, I needed to finish university even before I started considering dating, by which time I should be at least twenty one years old. I never quite understood that logic, if dates serve me right, Lami was born when my father was about twenty one and my mother was nineteen, and my grandmother must have been about sixteen when she had my father.

The difference between Maggie's parents and mine are definitely too much to begin to mention. Once, I tried to reason with my mother that Maggie's mother had told her she could discuss boyfriend issues with her when she turned fifteen, my mother was shocked. "That's definitely not going to work for you." She had said. "I hope that woman knows what she's doing. Does she want to ruin that girl's life?" So far, I can see the girl's life is on track. And I think that's one of the reasons Maggie is closer to her mother than I am to mine. In fact, I've learnt more about boys and sex from Maggie's family than from mine. Fools' paradise is what I would call where my parents live as far as boys and me are concerned. Although, sometimes I think it is Lami's docility that gives them the impression that all kids should treat life like a serious project.

Apart from these, there are other reasons Richard is an unlikely candidate to discuss with my mother: (one) he wasn't from a good home- that's my mother's conclusion about polygamy or single parenthood; (two) he wasn't getting an education – which is the only way my father believes one can get ahead in life, and (three) I am almost sure this crush would pass like all others.

To make matters worse, Maggie and her brother are still not sold out to the idea of me dating him. They keep telling me that even though he is nice, he is way too matured for me; he is known for flings, too easy going, no sense of commitment to anyone or anything and he has too much unpredictability about his life that would do me no good. And as usual, I wonder why they think I didn't know that already. And how on earth was he different from Segun for that matter?

So in spite of all the yearnings of my heart, I try to push Richard to one obscure place and focus my mind on the novelty and possibilities that life in university would open up to me. Since the house phone isn't working because Daddy wouldn't pay the unsolicited bribe to fix it, there is no way Richard could reach me, except through Maggie, who isn't keen on being the go-between. And if I don't go to her house, I wouldn't be tempted to use her house phone to call him at work. So really, it isn't so difficult avoiding Richard. At least until Segun conveniently came to the house with him under the guise of looking for Lami.

"Hello, Tobi." Segun says with a mocking smile. "Won't you invite us in?" I look back into the apartment to see if Mummy has come into the living room. No! I don't even bother to look at Richard. Shocked, embarrassed? Whatever it is, I am totally caught off balance. Segun practically pushes me aside to stroll in with Richard tagging behind. "Uncle, are you home?" He yells out for Lami. Uncle is Lami's nickname in school; I guess everyone felt that was better than calling him any other bookworm-ish name.

Richard grabs my hand. "Are you avoiding me?" He whispers in his guttural voice. If he was a singer, he would have girls flocking him for that voice alone. What a waste. I shake my head.

Mummy comes into the living room and Richard quickly drops my hand, although I'm almost sure Mummy noticed. Richard and Segun curtsy as they both chorus. "Good afternoon ma."

"How are you, Segun, didn't Tobi tell you Lami went out?"

Obviously, Segun wasn't expecting Mummy to be home at this time and he fumbles to answer her, dropping his naughty enthusiasm. "I thought she was joking ma."

"Oh." She glances at me. "Tobi, are you okay?"

I nod, not sure why she's asking me.

"How are your parents and Maggie?" She turns back to Segun. "What have you been up to since you came back from service and who is your friend?"

"I'm sorry ma, his name is Richard. I'm starting work in Daddy's office next month." Richard curtsies again.

Mummy acknowledges his nod. "Hmm, it's good your

father decided to give you that opportunity. I hope you won't bungle it. You have to be serious with it, so you can properly earn your place. Don't let people label you *Oga's* son" Mummy advises, even she suspects Segun has a streak of playfulness.

He manages a smile. "Thank you ma, I won't disappoint him." Just then Lami comes in.

"Hey, Segun, you are here, good afternoon Mummy."

"Did you get the medicines?" Mummy asks.

"Yes ma." Lami searches his pocket and gives Mummy the medicines for her cold and she goes back in.

Relief!

"Lami, meet Richard, Richie for short." Segun says.

"Tobi's Richard?" Lami glances at me as he extends his hand to Richard. I want to disappear right now.

"Yes, Tobi's Richard." Segun stifles a laugh. "I brought him to see her."

Mummy comes out, ready to go out. "I hope you people are not going out." That is a directive, especially with Segun around. "Your father is likely to come back early. Segun don't you want anything to drink?"

"Tobi was just going to get us drinks ma. Thank you, ma."

I disappear into the kitchen. Phew! Why on earth should Segun do this to me? He's apparently having fun at my expense. He it was, who said he couldn't trust Richard with me? And Lami calling him my Richard is another matter altogether. Unassuming Lami, did he have to be so plain? I only told him I had kissed Richard because I found him the most irresistible male at Maggie's party. Does that now make him my Richard? Boys!

Seeing Richard had suddenly brought back that

overwhelming feeling of desire and under another circumstance I would have mugged him with a tight embrace. I had felt like floating when he held my hand. If Mummy hadn't been around, I'm not sure what would have happened. I just wish they would go. I don't know what to tell Richard.

Why am I so mixed up and analytical about him, why can't I just go ahead and have fun with him like Maggie is doing? Because I'm afraid he would have sex with me and run away. And then, what? Sex would happen eventually, won't it, why not with Richard? Because he can't commit to you. Who says? He would have to commit to one girl someday too, won't he, why can't that girl be me? Fool yourself, he would move on to another available girl as soon as he's done with you.

"Lami said I could come and talk to you." The rich baritone voice cuts into my thoughts, suddenly he is behind me in the kitchen.

"My own Lami?" That is rather unusual as even Lami had said I should forget Richard if I knew what was good for me. "What did you do to the real Lami?"

"I only told him I've been finding it difficult to breathe since the last time I saw you, and he believed me." He is his usual charming self. "I'm sorry for barging in on you like this. I needed to see you. Segun said you'd strangle him alive, I really had to press him hard before he agreed to bring me here. Tobi."

"Okay, so you are here." He takes a bow and pulls me close against his body, humming and almost wiggling to Stevie Wonder's *I just called to say I love you*. I shake my head and pull away. "What do you want with a plain girl like me, there are lots of girls out there who would give you more fun, I'm not that kind of girl."

"What kind of girl do you think would suit a fine boy like me?" He smiles, but I don't find it funny.

"Richard, I can't be one of your toys. I don't compete very well in that area, please."

"Who are you competing with?" He looks around the kitchen. "There are just two of us here, Tobi. And I can never treat you like a toy, you are special, I only plead that you don't judge me by the past. I've made some mistakes and I'm not so proud of myself, but there comes a time when a guy wakes up from his stupid slumber." He makes to hold me again. I pull back. I can't allow him touch me if I'm going to talk to him sensibly because every time he touches me, my knees go weak? I can't even look him straight in the eyes.

"How many girls have you used that line for?" Me and my big mouth! I didn't really mean to say that, but it's out.

He shakes his head. "Baby girl, I have many vices, but lying is not one of them, so I don't lie to girls and neither do I make empty promises." I look at him quizzically. "Honestly, I don't spend so much effort on girls like you would want to believe. But I'd rather not talk about that now, please."

"That doesn't sound modest at all, Richard. How proud can you be?" I wish I could get angry with him.

"I'm sorry, I didn't mean it like that. What I mean is I don't really chase girls like you think."

"Is that because they chase you instead?" That's not a question I need an answer to. This conversation is not going well.

"I think it would make sense if we don't talk about other girls for now." He says quietly. "They have no role in this discussion."

"So you want to add me to your statistics. Sorry, I'm not interested." Even I don't believe that.

"Statistics? You think I want to add you to my statistics. There's no award for laying around, Tobi." He says contritely.

"But you have a lot of girlfriends, you told me that yourself."

He pauses. I think I notice his eyes narrow a bit as if he's thinking. "Yes, I have friends who are girls, but none comes close to special."

Special, that sounds good. But why should I believe him? "What makes a girl special?"

"To tell you the truth, I don't know. I hope you are not disappointed. What makes gold special? Let me see." He's thinking again. "I think it's the effort that goes into cultivating it, refining it and then the value we decide to place on it." He sighs. "I want to cultivate you and place a high value on you. I don't know how else to say this. But you've been special to me since that first time I saw you. Could you just be my friend, I won't try to push you, I would only plead with you, don't close your heart to me."

"Right now, I think I should guard my heart from you. I can't stand broken hearts, especially if it's mine."

"I'm not that bad, I've been like any other regular guy, we all do stuff and I can't say I'm proud of all that, but I want to put that in the past."

"I'm afraid Richard, you can't simply wish the past away like that."

"That's true." He says reflectively. Finally, he has accepted defeat. But will he just leave it at that? That's not what I want. I open the fridge and bring out a bottle of water. I'm praying in my mind he would say something before we get to leave the kitchen. What's he thinking? I leave the bottle on the counter, not trusting myself to take a drink now even though my throat is dry. "I know I can't wish away the past, but I can rewrite my future and that's why I'm here."

Thank goodness, I thought I had lost him there. "What will be in the future you want to rewrite?" I ask quietly, pretending not to be too enthusiastic.

"You, Tobi, I want you in my future, please. I'm not messing around with you. You have a place in my heart and I want to be close to your heart too. I may not look like what you want right now, but I can be, just believe in me and give me some time. I think we have something special, don't throw it away, please." A loud silence! He goes on. "I know you are probably not ready for this, but I don't want to lose you. Could you just give me a chance?"

He holds my hand again, pleadingly. This time, I don't pull away, he moves closer and kisses me. He doesn't have to say another word. After a while, he pulls away and starts humming Lionel Richie's *Penny Lover*. I don't know if I've truly captured his heart, but I know he has captured mine!

FOUR

Life in university is a potpourri of sorts; so much freedom in the midst of so many constraints. Of course, you are free to do whatever and go wherever because your parents are not somewhere breathing down your neck. But, you also have sole responsibility for your own welfare; keeping house, cooking, studying, attending lectures, keeping fit and socialising. Life, they say is about balance, and I guess university is one of the places you learn to keep on juggling to find the equilibrium of life. It is not just about getting an education; you are advised not to pass through the university, but to also allow the university pass through you. As a *Jambite or fresher*, you are barraged with invitations to countless parties throughout the first year, and you need some level of sanity to keep yourself in check.

There are four categories of students in the school. The first group manages to attend all the parties they forget to study and by the end of year one they have acquired so many Fs, they are advised to withdraw; group two socialises selectively and manages to pass by a hair's breadth and are put on probation, group three are the majority who hover between the safe grades of Bs and Cs and group four consist of the one per cent studious students who face their studies and leave no time for socialising, hovering between straight As and Bs. I think my brother belonged to group four while Maggie and I conveniently slip into group three.

University is the real world, where boys and girls have the audacity to exercise their rights – vices and virtues alike. It is where you make real choices; like falling in love, getting engaged, having sex, getting married and sometimes, starting a family. If one doesn't have a boyfriend or girlfriend before the end of the first semester, then something must be seriously wrong with the person; he or she is one of those one per cent who is after a first class grade or probably a member of the Scripture Union, (including any other religious fellowship) or have an inclination to be one. So much freedom, so much pressure and so many choices!

The first month at school is a flurry of activities; payment of fees, sorting out accommodation issues, meeting course mates and other *Jambites*, registration, followed by the matriculation where you are formally inducted as students; an induction where one is not fully told what to expect, leaving one with a lot of high expectations and hopes for a bright future. Immediately after this, comes the selection and de-selection of courses based on their compulsory or elective status, but more particularly based on gists from some of the senior students and some equally ignorant *Jambites* about the pass/failure rate of the course or the disposition of the lecturer.

Through referral from the Student Affairs office, we were lucky to find two vacant rooms in one of the flats at Vintage Lodge, a block of four three-bedroom flats at PPL – either twenty five minutes' walk from school if you choose the shortcut via the back gate or thirty minutes' drive manoeuvring through buses and human traffic and the un-tarred zigzag roads. The kitchen is well furnished; built-in cupboards, a four-footer fridge and a gas cooker with oven; the living room is furnished with three pieces of two-seater fabric settees; and a wooden centre table; and each room comes with its own toilet and bathroom.

Being Maggie's friend comes with some benefits. Of course, my parents had advised me to get a more basic and cheaper accommodation, but Maggie's mother persuaded mine into agreeing to share the flat with Maggie, at the same rate I would have paid otherwise. Sometimes Mummy can be a darling. The only current occupant in flat four upstairs is a year three English student named Biodun. Tall, slim and black ebony beautiful, she is extremely pleasant, even though deliberately reserved. She helped us unpack, cooked for us the first day, and gave us some unsolicited advice about the neighbourhood, campus boys and general life in school.

The fun part starts from the second month when we get invited to welcome parties usually organised by some Associations or by older students (especially boys). The first party we attended took place in the common room of Jungle, a boys' hostel on the exact same street where Vintage Lodge is. Biodun brought the IVs the following day we moved in and told us we could just take a stroll to the party and we could leave at any time if we were bored; since it was on our street, and we didn't need any pick up or drop down. Apparently, most girls in the compound would also be attending the party. Welcome to freedom!

*

The girls at Vintage Lodge start leaving at about midnight, hoping to catch the party in full swing. Partying at this time of the day is a first for me, not Maggie; she has sneaked out severally with her brother to night clubs and numerous other night parties. We are all dressed in jeans and tops in varied forms of cuts, colours and genre. As we near the Jungle, we see a lot of people outside; some smoking, some drinking and some simply chatting or *toasting*. People are already making out at different spots under the twilight; some couples are pinned to the wall, while some are creatively crouched on the pavement. Making out is not really a strange phenomenon to me, but the intensity on which some of these folks are riding, it is likely that sex might happen there and then. I whisper my concern to Maggie.

"Oh, that would be quite romantic." She says.

"So you wouldn't mind?" I quiz, not exactly surprised, but wanting to confirm all the same.

"Tobi, I wouldn't mind at all, sex can happen anywhere for all I care. I think you need to get rid of all that M and B sublime romance plots we read in secondary school. This is the real world." Maggie replies with a patronising smile. With the way she talks, you would think she is more experienced than me.

The music is good, but reverberatingly loud, I can almost

hear the *gbam gbam* in my heart. The dance floor is filled up already, hectic and heated up. We sit a while to feel the party; it's a real swing. We continue chitchatting, shouting over one another's heads, so we can hear ourselves. I scan the room to look at the prospect of a catch, but almost all the guys are engaged with one girl or the other. After some time, Biodun points us to a side of the room, where we can get drinks. I wonder how many times she has attended parties here. I pick a bottle of Maltina and for some strange reason, I struggle to open it.

"Let me help you." I see the hand before hearing the voice. A guy takes the bottle and opener and *voila*, gives me the drink. He must feel really proud for this accomplished feat.

"Thank you." I look up to see my saviour as much as the dark disco lights would allow me. He looks somewhat familiar, I probably have seen him on campus but I'm not quite sure. Anyway, it wouldn't matter since almost everyone here, if not all would be from school.

"I'm Furo." He shouts over the loud music once again and offers his hand which I shake without ceremony. "Would you like to dance?" He asks.

"I was told that's one of the things you have to do at a place like this." And I follow him to the dance floor, still with bottle in hand. At least holding the bottle will not make it so obvious that I can't dance so well.

The music drones on and we dance on. Talking is almost impossible with the volume of the music, so Furo gives up after two attempts and me pretending that I couldn't hear him. No wonder a lot of people are outside. The music is good and I think I'm beginning to catch the dance bug. As I look around me, I realise that I am not doing badly at all. Maggie and Biodun are doing their thing with some other guys too. Maggie loves to tease and you can see it in the way she's dancing right now, wriggling her tiny waist and pushing out her bum while backing the guy she's dancing with. The guy is holding her waist and gyrating to the rhythm of her dance. Biodun is dancing slow motion, keeping an arm's length, if this is how she dances, she might as well be sleeping at home. Unless, she just wanted to take us out.

As we dance on, I take another look at Furo. He is tall alright, but not as tall as Richard. Ah, Richard, he suddenly invades my thought as he had been doing since I met him. I inch closer to Furo, slightly pressing my body against his. Maybe he can distract me from Richard. At least he is in school and should be a better prospect. He takes the cue and moves closer, slowing the tempo of the dance. Where will he be right now, what will he be doing? Probably clubbing or partying too or making out with a girl. A dash of jealousy rushes through my veins at the thought of that. I wouldn't trust him to sleep through a Friday night. Richard, why isn't he just a regular guy, with no sordid past or unsuitable profile?

As much as I wanted to, I have not been able to get him out of my mind. Even though the school activities have been consuming, somehow, he manages to creep into my mental space. I have never felt like that about anyone before in my life and that is why it's difficult to articulate what the feeling is. I know I want to see him, I want him to hold me, touch me, kiss me, hum in my ears and tell me everything would be alright. I want to play with his dimples, feel his lips and just feast on his lithe body, I want to trust him and encourage him that life could indeed be better in spite of everything.

'... So much confusion when it comes to loving you."
As if the DJ is part of my thoughts, this song by Nu Shooz is
right on cue. Truly, Richard and I are very different and there
are more reasons to stay apart than to be together. Should I say
yes? I don't know. Should I say no? I don't want to! I really
wish I knew him better, beyond his escapades. Which do I
listen to between my heart and my mind? I haven't been able
to decide about Richie boy, as they call him. Maggie and her
brother had suggested that I hold on till we get to school, since
I am likely to meet better prospects and would definitely get
distracted from Richard. It's too soon to tell, I guess. Maybe I
should go with the flow.

"Are you okay?" Furo asks. I think I must have looked lost
in thought. He inches even closer. "Please can we go outside?"
I nod and he leads me outside. A breath of fresh air has never
felt so good. I look at the time, it's past three, already. When
do people get to sleep? There are more people outside now
than when we first arrived. I see Maggie, walking down the
street with a guy. Is she going home? No, she wouldn't leave
me without notice. I have a feeling Biodun left already, because
she had disappeared from the dance floor a long time ago and
she's not outside. Could she be with someone, in his room?
Hmm, that's a possibility.

"I think I've seen you before." Furo cuts into my
meandering. "Are you new, did you register for GNS?" I nod.
GNS is the General Studies course for all new students. "I'm
new too. I'm Furo Cookey." He introduces himself again, just
in case I didn't hear the first time.

"I'm Tobi. Tobi Bolade." Do people still remember

surnames these days?

"Lovely name."

"Thank you."

"Have you been to Jungle before?" I shake my head, no. "I live here, would you like to see inside, away from all these people?"

Just like that? Would I like to see inside the Jungle? No, not me, thank you. Didn't you give him the green light, I chide myself. "No, thank you, I like watching the stars sometimes. Can you see that one, it's very bright."

He follows my pointed finger and nods. "Yes, brighter than the others." He says tensely.

"Is it true that those stars signify human beings? They say the brighter ones represent the important people in society."

"I think it's just a myth." He replies. He is not really bad looking, even though he has no dimples. Maybe I should start with him and get my mind of Richard.

"I'm in Law faculty, what about you?" I volunteer.

"Political Science."

"Are you interested in politics?"

"My father is a politician. Where do you live?" He asks, changing the subject. He seems to have suddenly become fidgety.

"Vintage lodge."

"Oh, just down the road. Can I come and see you then. I'm sorry, I may have to leave you. Please, I need to fix something inside." He says quietly and politely, yet hurriedly. Is he walking out on me, what could be so important? Oh, maybe he has a girl waiting for him. But he invited me in before. Well, tough luck. So what do I do now?

"Okay, we'll see in school." I say graciously and start walking back into the common room to wait for Maggie. Maybe another guy will fish me out. What a night!

*

I started seeing Furo after that night and he was endearing in his own little way. For sure, being a student in the same uni would have scored him an A with my parents. But there was something about his personality that I just couldn't place a finger on. Sometimes he would be extremely calm and withdrawn, at other times he would be so chatty I would want to get a padlock to shut him up. As intelligent and nice as he was, it was incomprehensible to me that Furo would be skipping school and if I asked him where he had been, he would just look at me with his sometimes blank eyes and a shrug.

I put the pieces together when he asked me one day if I had ever smoked and if I would like to try weed. That put paid to our near-relationship.

The first negative impression I had of weed is that of a boy who ran mad in our estate, which my mother attributed to use of marijuana and some other drugs. And then she went on to explain how that was the singular reason she didn't like my father's only vice – listening to Fela's music.

"That Fela has destroyed so many destinies in this country, with all those innocent children following him up and down and taking marijuana like it is food." Only parents call weed marijuana.

"But Mummy, how can you blame Fela for the

waywardness of other people's children?" Lami asked.

"Truly, Mummy, that doesn't sound fair." I added my voice. "Is it not the parents that are responsible for training a child in the way that they should go?" I got that from Proverbs in the bible.

"I know a parent has the responsibility of training the child, but you know children belong to the community, so everybody is involved in how a child turns out. And Fela wields a lot of influence in this society."

"Mummy, Fela is just one person, why is the rest of the community not being blamed for the weed-smokers. And Wole Soyinka, his cousin also wields a lot of influence, why don't people follow him like they follow Fela?" Lami queried again, always trying to pick a hole in Mummy's hypotheses.

"It's the music, my dear. Music is effortlessly potent."

"But he is not the only one singing. Onyeka Onwenu is a singer, okay, maybe because she's female. What about Sunny Ade, why can't people follow him?" I asked. It's always a pleasure arguing Mummy to a standstill; she is the only one we can argue with anyway since Daddy doesn't discuss with anyone.

Lami picked up from where I stopped. "My own conclusion is that those parents have failed in bringing up their children, and then we want to make Fela a scape goat. Do you even know that Fela's son doesn't smoke?"

Mummy was surprised at that piece of information. "You see what I'm telling you now, that man is going about making other people do what he won't allow his own son to do."

I shook my head, wondering why Mummy would not accept the truth for once. "Don't you always tell us that each person is responsible for his destiny at the end of the day? Anybody that chooses to join Fela in smoking should just accept responsibility and besides the Fela you are talking about hasn't gone mad."

"Hmm, so you think a man that marries twenty seven innocent girls in one day is sane. It's not everybody who wears clothes that is sane. He doesn't even wear clothes anyway. Do you know there are different degrees of sanity?"

"Mummy, Fela is not mad, he's just innovative." Lami almost screams.

"It's the poverty in this country that makes it difficult to tell who is mad from who is innovative. It's that same poverty that is pushing people to identify so much with his illogical philosophy of social freedom and power. Even your father believes in that nonsense. Tell me, has it changed anything since?"

"Maybe if all the people who claim to be sane try to fight the government like Fela is doing, things would have changed, but everyone sits in the comfort of their world pointing accusing fingers at the person that even tries. I think it would do us good to have more people like Fela in Nigeria." Lami defends.

"More people like Fela promoting marijuana, would never be taken seriously. And that is why I don't like your father listening to that afro beat nonsense."

Surprised, Lami and I look at each other. "Do you think Daddy will ever start smoking weed?" I asked. Lami and I started laughing. The thought of Daddy with a cigarette, not to talk of him rolling weed into one tiny sheet of paper was hilarious. Mummy gave us that look that said the conversation was ended and that was it.

But that discussion was forever lodged in my head, and anytime I see a madman, the first thing that comes to mind is weed, so when Furo mentioned weed to me, it sounded like a hint that insanity is just a block away.

After Furo, Abubakar got on my case. Not so tall, rich, charming, baby-faced, stainless mulatto. Abubakar was a no-no as far as I was concerned; Fulani and a Moslem to start with. But Maggie suggested I should live life for its own sake and try to play around a little instead of dwelling on a faraway future.

"Must you have marriage at the back of your mind every time a guy talks to you? Besides, you've always wanted a rich guy, so maybe this is your break, you may not get everything you want girl, just cherry-pick." Maggie had said.

So, we cherry-picked Abubakar. But behind all that charming facade was an arrogant spoilt child whose only problem is having too much money at his disposal, much too much that he had hangers on where he was supposed to have friends; he smoked pot tobacco when boys smoked cigarettes; he forgot to say please or thank you and had no inclination to study neither flair for self-enlightenment. He was in school to get a degree, not an education and it seemed to me that the only way he was going to pass out of this school is to buy his way through, which he had already started doing, by fraternizing with the lecturers and paying some students to do his coursework for him. As if those were not bad enough, he believed his money could buy him anything and anyone, including me. Even Maggie had to eventually write him off as an empty show-off who would depend on his parents forever. I told Maggie we needed to reclassify my preference; a self-made rich man, not just any rich man.

FIVE

I wake up to the distant melody of a trumpet-like sound. When it comes to musical instruments, I can't tell an eagle from a vulture, it's possible that the sound is from a flute or horn or any other wind-blowing instrument; trumpet being the first thing that comes to my mind, since it sounds like a hymnal from church. The timid light trying to penetrate through the curtains confirms that the day is just breaking. Between wakefulness and sleep, I may have been dreaming about the trumpet, as there's no church around us, besides today is Saturday, so I make to go back to sleep. But the sound keeps on, getting closer and louder.

Now I'm fully awake and I turn to lie on my back, glancing at the clock, it's a few minutes past seven. Who would be doing this at this time of the day as if he's a rousing town crier? As the sound gets closer, my mind follows the rhythm subconsciously and I realise it's a 'happy birthday' tune. Happy birthday? No, it can't be! What a coincidence. Today is fifteenth of November, my birthday. The sound gets closer and stays below my window. The trumpet or whatever it is goes on playing different tunes, still below my window; the sound is coming out loud and clear now. Is it possible that this is for me? No, of course not, maybe the town crier missed his way.

Suddenly, the trumpet stops, just as I am beginning to enjoy it. Finally, the town crier has recovered himself. I get out of bed, stretch and quickly take off my hair net and I fish out the tee shirt I wore yesterday, hoping to catch a glimpse of him and his trumpet with which he has chosen to disturb the entire neighbourhood on an otherwise quiet Saturday dawn. Maggie comes into the living room at about the same time I got out.

"Did you hear the sound, what was it about?" I ask. She shrugs and keeps clearing her eyes with two of her left fingers. We both make to go to the balcony, but Biodun comes through the exit door with the albino town crier right behind her, and his instrument proudly hung around his neck.

"Tobi, he's looking for you." Biodun announces. "Happy birthday."

The town crier curtsies and without saying a word, starts playing the happy birthday tune again.

I look at Biodun and Maggie, lost. I don't recognise the guy from anywhere and he doesn't look like a beggar; stylishly dressed in black suit, white shirt and black bow tie. By the way, how would he know today was my birthday unless one of my friends put him up to this? Interestingly, very few of them know my birthday. What's this all about? I look at Maggie again. Could she have organised this? She raises her brows, shrugs and shakes her head. No! Then, who?

"Happy birthday, Tobi, I'm Blackman Sax." He introduces himself and offers his hand. "Richard sent me. Do you have any song that is special to you?"

Richard? I have not seen him for about a month. And he remembers my birthday? "Richard sent you to sing for me this early morning?" I ask him. He nods. Biodun motions him to take a seat, but he shakes his head, professionally poised with his trumpet to play at the snap of a finger.

"Richard sent you?" Maggie asks too as she takes a seat now, fully awake. "This is what I call romantic."

This is absolutely mind-blowing, I'm lost for words. My first birthday outside my father's house and this is what I get. Nobody has ever made me feel this important. My mind is trying to take it in and even though I appreciate Richard's gesture, the fact that it's early in the morning and the high pitch of the saxophone as Blackman pointed out, makes me self-conscious. There is no way the other house residents would not be disturbed.

"Thank you, Blackman, I really appreciate it, I think you've played enough. I don't want to wake the entire building." I say apologetically, not wanting to hurt his feelings, but his look betrays his disappointment.

"It's too late for that." Biodun says. "Your guests would soon be arriving."

As if on cue, two girls from the flat downstairs peep in through the front door, "Happy birthday, Tobi." They chorus as they come in. Blackman resumes playing his sax without waiting for me any longer. More girls come in and soon enough a party begins to form. This is becoming interesting.

Shortly afterwards, in the thick of our unplanned party, there is a knock on the door. I quickly go to answer, thinking it would be Richard. I'm disappointed to see the lady from the snack shop down the road. She's carrying a big box and before she says anything, I immediately guess it to be from Richard. "This is for Tobi." She says. Of course she doesn't know any of us by name. I collect the pack from her and thank her. Inside the pack is a twelve-inch cake decorated in peach and cream icing on which is inscribed 'Happy Birthday Tobi.' God, I don't want to wake up from this dream.

Maggie and I come back from the market late in the evening to meet Richard waiting in the living room, watching TV. As far as the TV goes, it might just as well have been another piece of table for us girls; it would be happy someone gave it attention today. Thank God Biodun was at home to open the door for him. I had stopped expecting him to come when he didn't show up by four. It was a struggle concentrating on anything after all the girls left as I twitched my ears for the sound of a horn or a slight knock on the door. Our mini-party lasted about two hours and we had some girly, gossiping fun time after Blackman left with his saxophone.

The girls teased me about my secret lover since none of them knew Richard apart from Biodun and Maggie. He had only been to the apartment once since we moved in. More so, I couldn't exactly call him my boyfriend. Apart from the fact that he had told me he wasn't used to chasing girls, Segun had gone ahead to warn him to steer clear of me, after that fateful trip to my house. So Richard had decided to give me my space and said we should allow things take the natural course. I wonder how that was supposed to happen if we weren't seeing each other.

"Hello, Richie." Maggie says excitedly. "When did you

come?"

Richard gets up to pull Maggie's cheeks. "About fifteen minutes ago, what have you been up to?"

If anyone had told me a guy could look good in pink, I would have argued vehemently, but seeing Richard in pink short-sleeve linen shirt and black chinos clad to his body totally knocks me off. He leaves Maggie and hugs me tightly. "Happy birthday, baby." He draws back, stares at me hard and hugs me again. "I've missed you so much."

"I've missed you too. How have you been? Where have you been? Why didn't you come earlier? Thank you so much for making my day. Thanks for the cake, everything, thank you. I was pleasantly surprised. I didn't even think you'd remember." I blurt out, uncoordinatedly. I hope I'm making sense. I'm so surprised and glad to see him. I look up to him, he's all smiles as his dimples start to deepen, and his eyes meet mine intensely. The only thing I want to do now is to kiss his curvy lips, but he doesn't move, appearing to be intent on smiling at me. Maggie excuses herself and goes into the kitchen to drop the shopping bags we brought from the market.

Richard gently seats me on a settee and takes his seat opposite me. "So tell me about your day." He turns off the TV and puts the remote control on the centre table.

I clear my throat and try to steady my breathing. "I think you know more about my day than I do, since you succeeded in waking me up. No you woke us all up. Thank you for that. We all had fun. All the girls in the house came up to dance. And the cake was served as breakfast, Biodun made tea for everyone. If we had known, we would have bought coke. That guy, Blacksax or Blackman is very good. You made my day,

Richard, thank you."

"I wish I could do more." He whispers graciously with his deep voice.

"Oh, how much more? I've never had such a great time in my entire life. And to think that I wasn't expecting it. You blew my mind, I have to admit."

Maggie returns from the kitchen. "Richie, something to drink, should I get you a stout?" She asks him.

Richard shakes his head. "I'll take water, thanks dear." He turns to me as Maggie goes to the kitchen to get a glass of water. "Biodun said to tell you she went out."

"Oh, I'm so sorry, I thought she was in the house, she left you here all by yourself?" I say apologetically.

"I told her I would be okay, I'm just happy to see you."

Maggie comes back with the water and puts it on the table. "I'm sure you two don't need me for now." She says, retreating to her room.

"Thank you Maggie." Richard says smiling. "I will call out for you if Tobi wants to strangle me." Once she was out of sight, he delves into his back pocket to bring out a small beautifully wrapped gift. "This is for you."

"Me, again? But you've already done enough. What is this? This is too much Richard."

"I'll do anything for you Tobi, as long as I can, and as long as it makes you happy." He shoves the gift into my hand. "I hope you like it."

"Oh, thank you, thank you so much." I gently un-wrap the gift, self-conscious that his eyes are on me and hoping my hands wouldn't shake. It's a metallic Sony audio cassette. Although I'm not such a music enthusiast, I've heard a few things about metal cassettes including the fact that it's rare and expensive and used to record special high quality music. I caress the cassette with the same gentleness I wish I could caress Richard.

"It's a selection of country music, Kenny Rogers, Jim Reeves, Billy Ray Cyrus, Don Williams, Dolly Parton and some others you may not know. I mixed it myself. I hope you like it."

"Of course, thank you so much." Maggie would be green with envy. "We've been talking about me since, what about you. How have you been? How is your work?"

"Oh, work is okay, it's just the usual bit. Today is your day, so we need to see how we can spoil you some more. Would you like to go out and celebrate? You can ask Maggie if she wants to come." I thought I already had a party in the morning. Now I know Richard is a master planner and I am curious to see what more he has in stock. Without asking Maggie I'm sure she would be willing to go anywhere as long as it is called 'out'.

"Where do you have in mind?" I ask. Maggie would be particular about dressing appropriately for wherever it is, even though I don't care, as long as Richard doesn't mind.

"We can go to Niteshift, if you feel like dancing." Richard suggests.

"Oh, that would be good." I respond excitedly, jumping to my feet to get Maggie. I've been itching to go to a night club since Maggie shared her experience with me when she sneaked out with her brother. Niteshift would definitely not be a bad idea. I've heard it's one of the classiest nightclubs in Lagos where you often meet professionals and highly placed people in the society. Students don't usually go to Niteshift, maybe because it's far from school or probably because it's more expensive as I heard. Anytime I pass in front of the coliseum on my way to Maggie's house, I usually wonder what the inside would be like.

Maggie seems to be sleeping already, so I tap her gently. "Are you really asleep or just pretending?" I ask. She opens her eyes and yawns, covering her mouth. Only Maggie remembers to cover her mouth every time she yawns, even when waking up, it's unbelievable.

"I think I dozed off." She glances at her watch. "Is Richard gone?"

I shake my head. "No, he's still here. He wants to take us out."

"Again, to where? She says in between another wide, muffled yawn.

"Niteshift."

"Really, are you serious?" Maggie's face brightens as she sits up. I nod. "Count me in. I think you've got yourself a boyfriend girl. What did you give him to eat?"

"Maggie, it's so difficult not to love him, you know."

"I can't argue with you. Honestly, nothing compares with what he did this morning and then he shows up when you least expect him. That's the kind of guy you want to have around you."

"That's cool, coming from you." This is a new perspective to Maggie's opinion of Richard.

"Well, truth has to be told. I think he really, really likes you. How much is what you have to find out." I sigh. It doesn't seem fair that life should always come with conditions. "And we may all be wrong for all you care." Maggie adds.

As Richard speeds on the expressway towards Ikeja, I wander between sleep and consciousness. Staying up late is not one of my strong points, even to read, but missing this opportunity to be with him is not an option. Maggie fills the void that would have been by continually teasing him. I think they must have been playing this teasing game for long, because they both have a good hang of it and neither is backing down for the other. There are very few cars on the road and the cool breeze of the night is good for a clear head. I glance at Richard without being obvious about it and I try to reflect on how my day has been so far.

The last time I celebrated my birthday was when I turned ten, I was not privy to how my mother had managed to convince my father to allow that small party, but we had it all the same and I felt on top of the world because everyone around then had made me feel like one special angel. Subsequent birthdays had been marked with ordinary jollof rice, chicken and coke for the whole family, nothing more. For my thirteenth birthday, Daddy had promised to take us all out and he had lived up to his promise. He drove us to the SOS Motherless Village at Isolo where he took us through the moral narrative of cultivating an attitude of gratitude since we had the opportunity of having and knowing our biological parents, unlike the children at SOS. It was a lesson I would never forget.

Definitely, by all standard today has been explosive compared to the past. Nobody has ever made me feel so special, not even my parents I dare say because all I got from them was a bulky book titled 'The Making of a Righteous Woman' – highly predictable. If Richard would do all these for me with the little he has, then I must mean something special to him. That song plays in my head again, *'Should I say yes?'*

Why shouldn't I say yes? Every reason I had revolves around his background and past; the girls, the baby, his family, his education. But common sense should tell me that people don't have a say in the family they come from, neither in the way they are brought up. So if a guy has had a rough start in life, what is he expected to do? I wonder. I know life can be cruel sometimes, but everybody deserves a second chance at life. Should I say yes? I don't know. Should I say no? I don't think so.

We reach Niteshift in less than an hour. There's just a tiny bit of crowd outside doing different things. A slim girl, with big breasts shooting out as if they were not part of her body dis-entangles from her friend and walks up to Richard, ignoring both Maggie and I. She is wearing micro mini jersey skirt and a large top, which is about two inches shorter than her skirt. For some reasons, her heavily made-up face and painted false nails bring up the image of Jezebel in the bible to my mind. She hugs him tightly and catches my eyes with a smirk on her face. "Richie boy, long time." She says loudly.

Richard does not hug her back, but pushes her away, gently. "How are you? My friends." He gestures to us, we nod and she nods back. Then he holds me and starts walking. She moves to his other side.

"Oh, I see." She ogles at him. "I haven't seen you for a while. What's *gwam*?"

"Just chilling out. I will see you later." He says dismissively.

Even though I'm happy that he's not giving the girl the attention she craves, I can't but put myself in her shoes. How would I feel if I am being discarded in the presence of some other girls? But the expression on her face doesn't reveal that she minds in the least.

"I'll see you later then." She mouths a kiss to Richard, rolls her eyes at us and goes back to her friend.

He leads us into the coliseum after greeting the two imposing stocky gentlemen at the entrance familiarly. He explained to me that these are bouncers who kick out trouble makers from the club. But it doesn't seem like he would explain the girl to me. Even with the semi-darkness, it's easy to tell that the place is magnificent, not that I have anything to compare it with. The feel of the floor against my rubber-soled loafers confirms that the floor tiles are rich and the walls illuminated by various shades of neon lights look and feel very plush. Despite the loudness of the music, the atmosphere appears unobtrusive.

He holds my hand as we climb the staircase and Maggie tags right behind until we take our seat close to the dance floor since Maggie said she wanted to see all the dance moves. I settle down to look around; it's really a nice place and the people here are a mixed breed of young and old, some look respectably dressed like Maggie and I, I suppose – patterned cotton shirts on black trousers. A lot of the other ladies are simply outlandish – outrageous colours of satin and silky tops with leggings or short skirts, and short dresses, some are even wearing high leather boots like those girls who ply the streets. I think I saw somewhere at the entrance that jeans was not allowed, not quite sure now, but I can't see anyone wearing jeans.

A waiter comes to take our orders. Richard requests for soda water, while I order two cups of chapman for Maggie and me, but she asks for two shots of brandy in addition. "How can I take only a soft drink on your birthday?" She asks mischievously across the table.

"Oh yes, we are celebrating, maybe you should try some." Richard suggests as he clasps my hand in his. I shake my head.

"Thank you, but sorry, if you're trying to get me drunk, it's not going to work."

"Sweetheart, a shot of brandy doesn't get anybody drunk." He says. I like the sound of sweetheart on his lips.

A funny looking guy wearing a red afro wig walks up to our table and hails Richard in a rather loud voice, slapping him on the back which seems more to me like someone looking for a fight than a form of greeting. 'Richie rich, where have you been? *We no dey see you for club again, wetin gwam?*" He asks in pidgin.

"*I just dey busy boy, na im, nothing spoil.*"

"*I trust you, I dey wonder whether you don shift base go another side.* Hello ladies, I'm Jazzman Craze." He bypasses Richard and shoves his face and hand forward. He didn't have to announce that he was crazy, he looks it every bit. All these guys and their musical appendages; the first one I met this morning (that should be yesterday morning now) is Blackman Sax, now this is Jazzman Craze.

"This is Tobi." Richard pauses and Jazzman takes my hand and brings it to his lips with a curtsy, he does the same to Maggie. "And Maggie." Just Tobi, I thought he would introduce me as his girlfriend. The two boys retreat from us for a while for some catching up boys' talk, I guess.

"Enjoy yourselves ladies. *Make I dey go*, old boy, *I dey yonder* if you need me." With that Jazzman Craze merrily disappears.

"A jolly good fellow." Maggie giggles, rather loudly; I hope the brandy hasn't started taking effect.

"That's the house clown." Richard volunteers. "If you see him in broad daylight you would hardly recognise him. He has an office job and does this just for the fun of it."

"Are you serious, so what's his real name?" I ask.

"Trade secret." Richard says smiling.

"How nice."

"And what's he like underneath that crazy heap of clothes and the wig?" Maggie asks.

"You would have to wait until morning to catch a glimpse of him." Richard smirks. "That's another trade secret. It would be my pleasure to introduce you to him when he is normal."

The club is getting fuller as more people come in. Richard seems to be quite popular here, because every now and then someone waves to him and he goes on to tell us who the person is. The waiter comes and serves another round and more brandy for Maggie. The dance floor is also filling up rapidly, with flashlights and smoke billowing all around, and the music is beginning to take on a faster tempo. Maggie is swinging in her seat and singing along while watching the dancers intently.

"Why are you taking soda water?" I ask. When I met Richard, he had been the organiser of *shaks* at Maggie's party and I know he drinks heavily and regularly because Segun has told me that apart from girls, no one tries to beat Richard at *shakking*.

"It's a long story, I shouldn't bore you with it?"

"Try me, you never know, I may find it interesting."

He pauses for some seconds and appears to be giving it some thought. "Well, Segun and I had a bet to stay away from some things for six months, alcohol, being one of them. And I intend to win his money."

"Are you serious?" My eyes are wide in amazement, the things men do. Before he responds, he spots a guy across the hall, who is walking towards our table now. Richard gets up and they both pat each other on the back while shaking hands.

"Richie boy." The new guy says fondly. "Long time no see. How have you been?"

Richard smiles and actually hugs him, "My guy, up and about, just trying to make ends meet. You look good."

"Trying to catch up with you." The guy glances and nods at me and then Maggie. "I saw Jazzman Craze back there, he told me you were here."

"Would you like to join us?" Richard offers. The guy shakes his head.

"My guy, I came here to dance. I need to get some weight off this body." He pats his stomach affectionately, which is where most of the weight is trying to settle in, compared to his whole body. He looks at us again. "So who is going to dance with me?"

Maggie jumps up, one would think she had been waiting for that question. "I hope you are up to this, I don't stop until the music stops." She warms up to him as if they have been friends before.

"Richie do I have your permission to flaunt my dancing prowess or I should pity her?" He asks, taking Maggie's hand.

"I wouldn't want her to take it out on me, so take it easy." Richard urges them to the dance floor.

"Your friends are very warm." I remark.

"I wouldn't call them friends, really. We only meet here once in a while and that is it, I've known some of them for about two years or three. When another club opens in town, we tell each other and we go check it out, but we always come back here. It's cosy, isn't it?"

I nod, my mind drifts to my family. Lami would definitely be in his bed somewhere in Port Harcourt and my parents would be at home, likely snoring off now. Sometimes, it's good for life to be predictable. My father is the most predictable human being on earth. Work, home, work home, church on Wednesday and Sunday. If he hasn't left home by seven o'clock or come back by six thirty in the evening, then something terrible must have gone wrong, which rarely does. I wonder if he knows that the rest of the family plan our lives around his predictability. What will my mother think if she learns I was at a nightclub? Her first reaction would be to call me *Ashewo*. Certainly, she could never have been to a club, yet she would know that only *Ashewos* go there. Then she would give me a history lesson on how a notorious armed robber was arrested at a night club in the midst of several *Ashewos* back in the days. I love my family.

Richard snaps his fingers. "Hey, why are you smiling?"

I didn't know I had smiled, but now I smile deliberately, still remembering some of the fun things that happen in my house. "I'm just thinking about home and wondering what my mother would say if someone told her I was here."

"Fortunately, I don't think your mother's generation comes

here."

Scanning through the hall, I see a very popular actor that used to be a regular feature on the NTA operas dancing with a young girl probably about my age. The actor should be closer to fifty than forty and definitely closer to Daddy in age than the girl he's dancing with. I point at him. "What about that man?"

Richard follows my lead. "Ah, that's uncle T, oldies like him are rare anyway. That man loves life, I wish to grow up like that."

"Chasing young girls?" I make a face at him suspiciously.

He shakes his head, laughing. "Are you jealous?" He grabs my hand. "You have to promise me you will ever remain young, so I don't get tempted. You know I love to boogie."

"Do you think you can ever be faithful, Richard?" I had asked that before I even realised the thought was in my head. On reflex, my hand goes to cover my mouth, too late. And to make matters worse, right at that instant a girl turns up at our table, pats Richard on the back and practically drags him up without as much as a glance in my direction.

"Hey, Richie, long time." She hugs him tightly for what seems like eternity and whispers something in his ears, disappearing immediately in her skimpy skirt and long shapely clean-shaved legs. Of course, her DD cup breasts had brushed against his chest. I am uncomfortable and cling on to my glass of chapman, but say nothing. There has to be something about Richard and big breasted girls. Unconsciously, I glance at mine; thankfully, I am not disadvantaged in that department at thirty four D. Is that why he was attracted to me in the first place? I wish I could just open his mind and see what's going on in there. There is so much I don't know about him, I muse ruefully.

"Sorry about that." He takes my hand again as if nothing happened. "Where were we?" Silence!

"Are you angry?"

"Why should I be angry?" I snort, feeling hot all over.

Unexpectedly, he drops my hand and laughs as if a joke is on me. "Exactly, what she wanted you to feel and you play right into her hands. Tobi, you shouldn't concern yourself with every girl I talk to, because it's likely to happen a lot." That doesn't sound encouraging. He retrieves my hand. "If I haven't told you before, let me tell you now. My roving days are over and I've got eyes only for you?"

"Because I don't know if I can trust you. I don't want to get used to girls rubbing their bodies against my boyfriend and flaunting it and I have to keep wondering if you are still going out with them or not." I whisper.

"Did you call me your boyfriend?" He asks with a bright look of victory on his face. "Baby, the only way to trust me is just to trust me, we can work through this if you allow me."

"I don't want to get hurt."

"I will personally shred anyone that tries to hurt you." He embraces and kisses me on the forehead. I thought he would kiss my lips. An intoxicating sensation runs through my body. "Would you like to dance?"

I shrug. "If you want to." He takes me by the hand and I follow him to the dance floor, where we take a convenient position to dance. Maggie and Richard's friend are somewhere in the middle of the dance floor. She always looks at ease teasingly wriggling her bum when she's dancing. It's no news that Richard is a natural dancer, so I just follow his steps, hoping I can match him and I think he deliberately slows down so I don't look or feel amateurish. I don't care. I think I love this guy. I lose myself to the rhythms of the music.

And then Evi Edna's song. *'Hoo yeah, I wish you happy birthday, hoo yeah, very many happy returns.'* The music blares on. Is this another coincidence or do birthday songs get to be played normally? I've never been to a nightclub before, so I don't know the protocols.

How and when did we get to the middle of the dance floor? I only realise when I saw the circle forming around Richard and I and we are in the middle of it on a slightly elevated platform, people are dancing and cheering us with the birthday song. Is this for me? How did it happen? When was it planned? Here, how? I look at Richard, and he is naughtily grinning from ear to ear. Happy birthday, he mouths as his voice is drowned in the song. I stare at him, in amazement. How could he have pulled this off? People start clapping as the song comes to a slow stop.

Jazzman Craze is beside us with a microphone and urges the crowd on. "Let's give it up for Tobi Bolade." He lifts my hand, as if people can't already see enough of me. Another round of applause! I look around the hall, all eyes are on me and right now I simply wish I could disappear. I've never been under such intense attention, either positively or negatively and at a place like this, all in one day; it's becoming much more than I can take.

How many girls has Richard done this for? Even in my naiveté, I know he can't be doing this with every girl that comes his way. And he is calmly casual about it, like it's something he does every day. I feel lucky and special and a sense of triumph over the two ladies who had previously assaulted him with their femininity. I glance at him for the umpteenth time in one night and an affectionate kind of warmth washes over me. How can you not love a guy like Richard; tall, funny, caring, carefree, handsome, dimpled, painfully sincere, creative and yes, sexy? How can I not love this guy that has turned my world inside out in one day?

"Please come." Jazzman Craze takes my hand. I follow him semi-consciously to the side of the stage. Who knows what else they have planned. Pop, comes the sound of the cork of what I think is champagne. A waiter brings a tray with three narrow glass cups and Jazzman Craze pours the champagne for the three of us and returns the bottle to the waiter, who I think goes about serving as many as can be served. I stand there like a zombie staring blankly ahead of me, too overwhelmed to know what to say or do. After what seems like a very long time, Jazzman Craze raises his glass and requests the house to make a toast to a wonderful lady - Me. "Hip hip hip!"

"Hooray!" Chorus from the house.

Richard intertwines his hand in mine and gulps down the bubbly white drink. I follow suit. I know champagne has alcohol and I don't know to what level but I'm too happy to start analysing what effect it would have on me. Besides I feel safe with Richard. Yes, safe. The waiter comes back to collect the glasses and everyone cheers again. The music resumes and Richard leads me back to the dance floor to dance to the song written specially for me by Don Williams. I feel like a queen, a light-headed one. And indeed I would love to be a gentleman's wife which I'm not sure Richard is, just yet.

Every girl dreams about meeting a knight in shining armour. I think I just met mine. His name is Richard Aro.

SIX

Richard had beaten everyone's imagination with his total dedication to me. He exhibited a high level of maturity that I found lacking in the boys around me in school. He promised not to impose himself on me and said I could have my space. "To discover myself", he had said. Eventually, I discovered that all the boys in school also had their own share of baggage and I was much more comfortable with him than anyone of them. In spite of my experiments with boys, he had remained committed to me.

We started dating officially on my birthday. Who could resist all that shower of attention, especially the way he was casual about the whole incidence as if he wasn't expecting anything in return? We left the club just before dawn and he got us back to Vintage Lodge in less than an hour. It would definitely be one of the most memorable days of my life. When we alighted from the car, he made to leave, but Maggie and I insisted he stayed until full break of dawn. It was only when we got into the flat that I started considering the sleeping arrangement. Not that I had any scruples about him sleeping in my room since it was a regular occurrence in most of the hostels, I just wasn't sure I could share my bed with him without having sex. As randy as I was, with all the tingling sensations rioting in my body, I felt it was not the right time or place. Richard saved the day by volunteering he would sleep on the settee in the common room.

Maggie looked at us and shrugged. "That's your business." She left us there and went into her room. I chose to stay on the settee with him, but instead of sleeping, we ended up talking about my *toasters* and family, his work and his future plans. When there was nothing more to talk about, he reached out to kiss me and we started cuddling until the day got bright and he was ready to go.

Life with Richard was good. He introduced me to a whole new world of fun I only hear about from Segun or watch on TV and in films; restaurants, night clubs, beaches, the theatre, cultural carnivals, musical shows and gift shops. He could find all the exotic spots in Lagos, he knew the day each night club was open seven days of the week, he was in touch with the latest trend of fashion and cars, he had friends like him who were fun to be with, he was familiar with a lot of actors and musicians who have a way of making me extra special when we are with them. As far as I was concerned he knew everyone, everywhere and everything that made life unpredictably exciting and he always had me there with him.

*

"How do I look?" I ask Richard. He is waiting for me in the

living room. Except for the *environmental sanitation day* restrictions, we spend Saturdays together from early morning before he eventually drops me off at home in the evening. We're going to the international trade fair and even though Richard had said he wasn't sure it was a good idea for him to go to the fair with me, he also didn't want to miss spending time with me.

He looks at me for about five seconds. "Ugly."

"Liar!" I fling a throw pillow at him. "Why can't you say the truth?"

With a smile on his face he looks at me again, "Hmmm, pointing boobs, lovely eyes, sexy legs, fine dress and beautiful make up. On a scale of hundred, I think you should be on 99.99." He pulls me to himself. "I've told you a million times that no matter what you put on, you always look great."

"Thank you, please don't make me blush."

"And, I don't understand why you are making such a fuss about dressing up for the trade fair. With all that crowd, who would notice you?" Richard asks, still smiling.

"Have you forgotten the Boys' Scout motto - Be prepared."

He shakes his head. "I hope you are comfortable in those shoes, Tobi, because you have a long walk at the fair. Do not say I didn't warn you. Why do you girls give yourself so much pain?"

I look at the turquoise shoes, it's medium height and shouldn't give me much discomfort. We bought the shoes two weeks ago and I've been itching to wear it since I got the matching polka-dotted black and turquoise top yesterday at the boutique opposite the school. Nobody is going to talk me out of wearing these today, not even Richard. "But, you bought these for me, why are you complaining?"

He shakes his head in disagreement. "You picked the shoes, I only paid for them. I'm not complaining, I'm only concerned for your comfort. I don't think you should wear them for long walks, but it's up to you."

Anytime I'm going out with Richard, I always like wearing the things he bought for me. Somehow I know it makes him feel good, even though he tries to be modest about it. "Don't worry, I will be okay. No pain, no gain."

"Please before we go, can we agree on the other things you would like to see apart from the dress?" Richard changes the subject suddenly. He had promised to buy me a dress at the fair.

I shrug. "I don't know, when we get there."

"That's not going to work this time." He brings out a notepad and pen from my bag and makes to start writing. "I'm waiting." He says.

"I'm definitely not going to make a list, we are going window shopping." I pout.

"Maybe we should definitely not go then."

"Are you serious?" I believe he's trying to avoid the kind of incident that happened two weeks ago when he accompanied me to Balogun market on the Island. I can't blame him.

"Dead serious!" He nods.

I have to scratch my head for this. "Okay, clothes, shoes, bags, books, kitchen stuff, cars." This is not working. "Really Richard, I don't know, the point of going to the fair is to see latest trends, that can be anything."

"Can we agree to leave there by three then?"

That should be about four hours. I think that's a fair deal. I nod in agreement.

I read somewhere that an average of five hundred thousand people visits the seven-day International Trade Fair daily. Lagos, being one of the biggest commercial cities in West Africa welcomes people from all over the country and from neighbouring countries to take advantage of good bargains and promotional sales, and to catch a glimpse of latest launch of products and services into the market. But it's not just a trade fair; it also has the reputation for being a tourist attraction and an entertainment arena. It's a place where you run into friends you haven't seen in a long time or even strike new friendship and where you can day dream about living big when you become rich. If you are like me who likes to shop with or without money, you can spend the whole day wandering from stall to stall and you still wouldn't have covered all the grounds.

At the home section, I notice a new kind of blender that could perform many functions including mixing cakes. There are lots of ladies hovering around the blender, admiring it and asking questions about the wonders it could achieve. The Sales Manager goes on to explain that the appliance is an advancement of the regular blender, made with a new kind of technology and called a food processor because of its ability to perform multiple processes based on the fact that the blades and disks are interchangeable.

"Apart from using it to blend peppers like the regular blender, you can also use it to mix cakes and knead bread, chop and slice vegetables, grind hard nuts and it doesn't need as much water as a regular blender." The Sales Manager cheerfully enlightens his teeming audience while illustrating with the different blades attached to the processor.

Maggie and I love baking; in school, we sometimes bake cakes and pies for our friends and they always compliment us, but the hassles of manually mixing the cakes forced us to stop baking altogether. "Can I buy this Richard?" I ask.

"It's up to you, either you buy this or you buy a dress." He looks at the price. "But it's okay, at least you have no more excuse not to cook for me."

"Thanks dear, does that mean I will still get the dress?"

"If they will sell on credit, why not?" He says casually, hands in pocket.

"Okay, let's go." I make to leave the stall but he pulls me back.

"Oh, no, you can have it, I was just joking. Of course you can still have the dress, as long as you can find the one you like today."

"Let's see if we can get a better deal. I'm sure there would be some other places we can get it, I don't want us to be short-changed."

"Tobi, if you want it, why don't you pick it now? What if you don't get another one?"

"Then I'll come back for this."

"Are you sure we'll come back this way?" He asks. I pretend not to hear him as I go on ahead of him. He starts humming under his breath and follows me out of the stall. My feet are beginning to hurt, but I dare not say anything lest he makes fun of me. My only reprieve would be to get to the restaurant just ahead of us so I can take off the shoes, at least for a while. That takes us about fifteen agonizing minutes, waddling through the hoard of shoppers.

The restaurant is big, but the number of people who have finished eating and refused to leave makes it difficult to find a suitable place for two to seat. I ask Richard to order some snacks and drinks at the counter while I go to find a seat; I need to get these shoes off as fast as possible and can't imagine staying on the service queue for another ten to fifteen minutes. It takes me like three minutes to get a space at the extreme end where a couple are just about getting ready to vacate their seats. I stand beside their table to indicate I am waiting for them and under a different circumstance, I would have classified this action as rude, but right now, I can't be bothered. The man gives me an understanding nod and gets up almost immediately, but the lady takes another two minutes, struggling to wear her sandals and tie the strings. Why do we do this to ourselves, really?

I thank them as I watch them go, drop into one of the seats and hurriedly remove my shoes. Great relief! Richard comes with two plates of fried rice with a pack of orange juice and a bottle of soda water. He is really bent on winning Segun's bet. I remove my bag from the seat to make room for him.

"Are you okay now?" He asks as he takes his seat opposite me. I nod, while my hand impulsively goes back to my small toe, massaging it to relieve some pain. "Bring it, let me help you." He says, referring to my toe.

"You want me to place my foot on your leg?" I ask, not exactly sure he meant that. He nods. "Here?" I look around the restaurant to see if there are other lovebirds like us. Plenty! Even though they seem to be consumed with whatever they are doing, eating, conversing or glossing over the fair's brochures. Richard ignores me and places my left foot on his leg and starts massaging it. It actually feels better, but I'm self-conscious about this display of affection in broad daylight. What if Mummy happens to chance by or any of her friends, or Daddy for that matter? No, Daddy would never come to the fair; he doesn't shop, just hands over the money to Mummy and gives her a list. I keep my reservations to myself and go on eating the rice. It's delicious, for mass-produced food. Or am I hungry? Richard keeps massaging my foot and sips on his soda water.

"Your food will get cold." I remind him.

"Hey, Richie, is this you?" A girl shouts over my head. Richard shifts his gaze from the food and I turn sideways to see if there's another Richard behind me. A bespectacled girl in pink silk blouse with frills round the neck bypasses me to Richard. I notice she is almost flat-chested.

"Excuse me, Tobi." Richard manages to say as he drops my foot gently on the floor and stands to greet the girl who has almost tipped our table in her excitement to get to him. He smiles and stretches his right for a handshake. "Hello." He says quietly. She beams and grabs his hand, shaking it expectantly, and then hugs him. Richard stays calm.

"It's been a long time. How have you been, where have you been hiding?" She asks and she looks towards the counter, as if searching for someone. "Flaky would be very happy to see you. Richie, what happened?" Am I the only one that calls him Richard?

He ignores her question. "Please meet my girlfriend." He stretches his hand to me. "Tobi, this is Lisa."

She turns to me, acting surprised as if she had not noticed I was there all along. I make to get up to greet her, but she raises her brows and meets my eyes with her inquisitive look before summing me up from head to toe. "Oooh." She drawls.

I decide she doesn't deserve the courtesy I was going to extend initially, so I sit back and nod, muttering a hello.

She turns back to Richard and I turn back to my food, poised to hear what they would talk about. However, she disappoints me by drawing close up, whispering to him. Then she draws back and waits, but he only smiles and says nothing. After what seems like forever, she decides to speak. "What happened then, you just disappeared like that?" She snaps her fingers.

He shrugs. "Life happens. How have you been?" He pulls back to examine her and eyes her playfully. "You look good." He surmises.

The compliment changes her mood immediately. "Oh, thank you." She pulls him by the hand. "Come, let me take you to Flaky."

Richard resists. "That won't be necessary." He gives her a gentle push. "Say hello to her for me. And be a good girl." From the corner of my eyes, I see him wink at her with a smile and she pouts her pink-shaded lips and leaves. Whoever suggested pink lipstick to black ladies under the pretext of matching colours must be extremely wicked. He sits down and sighs. "I'm sorry about that."

I remain mute and continue to pick on the rice without lifting the spoon to my mouth. There's a discussion going on in my head right now. Would there always be a girl lurking around anytime I'm with Richard? At least he acknowledged you as his girlfriend, that should give you some assurance. And then he says he's sorry, what am I supposed to do with that?

Accept it. Why? Because he means it. Why does it have to happen in the first place? You already know he had a lot of girlfriends. So? Anyway, obviously, she's not his girlfriend. Who is Flaky then? Ask him. "Who is Flaky?"

"Someone you shouldn't concern yourself with, someone in my past."

"How many pasts do you have, Richard?"

He lets out a deep breath. "You don't want us to go into that now, baby. It's just a coincidence, don't let it spoil your mood, please." He takes my hand. "I have eyes only for you, girl." He stares into my eyes.

"Thank you, but no thanks. What didn't she want me to hear that she had to whisper?"

"Is somebody jealous here?" He teases, tickling me.

I flinch. "That's not funny, I don't like the feeling that I'm doomed to meet your girlfriends every time we go out."

"For the record, you didn't meet my girlfriend, that was her cousin." He spoons some rice into his mouth and gnashes his teeth, shaking his head. The rice is cold by now.

"So what did she tell you?"

"You don't want to know."

Is he trying to hide something from me? "Try me." I insist and fold my arms across my chest expectantly.

He starts rubbing his brows. "She asked me if you are better in bed than her cousin."

"What?" My whole body heats up in embarrassing shock at the likelihood of me being the topic of a sex dalliance with Richard. At the same time I feel my nipples tingle as the thought of sex with him unconsciously excites me, I hope he can't notice. I raise my two hands to my face and starts massaging my cheeks in rhythmic motion to calm my nerves. I don't know what words would suitably describe how I feel right now.

"Tobi, please don't let any girl distort what we have. I'm serious. I've said my goodbyes to all those ladies and I don't mess around again."

I should be happy. He keeps professing that he loves only me and truly, I believe him, I just wish I don't have to continue meeting his girls. Then you have to stop going out with him, one of my voices says quietly. Do you want to stop going out with him, the other voice screams. I stifle the 'No' by secretly and gently biting my lower lip. I wish I had some boys in my past to help me even with Richard. You are not exactly innocent too; the second voice comes back. What if your other boyfriends had insisted? I push the thought of the boys I've kissed from my mind. Especially Romeo, I would have regretted sex with him for the rest of my life.

"Are you not bothered?" I ask.

Pondering, he shakes his head. "No, since I can't turn back the hands of time. Are you?"

I nod, then I shake my head. "Seriously, I don't know anymore. How would you feel if you kept meeting my exes?"

"You really want to know?" He asks, smiling and I nod yes, curious. "I will break their necks."

"Oh, would you?" I gawk.

He smiles and strokes my face, I look around, but nobody is minding us. "You've got to trust me, Tobi. We can't go anywhere without trust."

Easier said than done. "I trust you." Yes, I do trust him, especially when he looks so effortlessly sincere with his dimpled smile. I sip at the little coke remaining, continuously drawing on the straw, even when the coke had finished. I take a breather. "By the way, how do you get rid of those girls without hurting them? I'm just curious. I would hate for you to tell me off, you know." It had suddenly occurred to me that such a fate may befall me if he meets someone else.

After sipping his drink, he lifts up his head, still smiling, "Trade secret." The confused or is it scared look on my face makes him laugh. What does he find so amusing? "Tobi, I'm not a mean person. I simply stop going to see them, and I make myself unavailable. It's not easy though, but I've managed thus far. And by the way, I spend most of my time with you, so if you want, you can cut me some slack." He glances at his wrist watch. "We had better get going if you still want to shop for a dress." He pushes the table aside and unexpectedly stoops to help me place my feet into my shoes one after the other. "Now, shall we." He dusts his hands and pulls me up.

How can I stay crossed with him?

I have heard it said severally that everyone without exception has one thing or another that he or she is crazy about. For me, that could be anything, as long as I consider it trendy – clothes, shoes, bags, perhaps cosmetics and maybe books too. The only place Richard decides to visit is the electronics centre. He's particularly enthralled by the Bang and Olufsen musical system; I can see the excitement all over him, as if his body would start shaking. I try to show interest for his sake, so I look at the label on one of the equipment and I am shocked to see the price. I pick up another one, hoping the previous one was a mistake, alas no. I am ready to leave, but he stays on, asking all kinds of questions from the Manager. The way he is ogling and caressing the equipment, one would think they were made of gold.

"What is with you and music?" I ask him, when he eventually manages to prise himself from the shop.

"Music happens to be the food of love,…" And he continues humming, wriggling his head to dance as we keep on walking.

"I give up." I shake my head and increase my pace. Shakespeare must have had him in mind when he wrote in All's Well That Ends Well, *'Why, he will look upon his boot and sing; mend the ruff and sing; ask questions and sing; pick his teeth and sing.'*

"That's by Musical Youth, 1982." He announces after catching up with me. Until I met Richard, an artist's name had never been of interest to me, but he prides himself on knowing the artist, the album and the year of release. I wish there was a way he could make money with that wealth of information.

"I hope you know it's originally Shakespeare's." I reply.

"What does Shakespeare have to do with music, baby lawyer?"

"Shakespeare it was who said, 'if music be the food of love, play on'. That's in Twelfth Night or What You Will." I got used to cramming quotes from secondary school literature class when we used to compete on who said what, to whom, when was it said and why, but I'm not sure Richard is down with that, I would have told him Duke Orsino said it to the musicians at the opening scene because he was obstinately in love with Olivia. Am I obstinately in love with him?

"Why are you smiling?"

"Am I?" I relax and smile the more. "I was just playing the scene of that quote in my head, it's very funny."

"Do you carry all those big Shakespeare's books in your head?" He looks at me with admiration.

"I think it's the same way you carry all those songs in your head, and I mean that as a compliment."

"Hmmm." He mutters as we continue to wade through the sea of people all around us.

Whoever planned that the fashion section be positioned at an extreme side of the fair must have only one thing in mind; that ladies would at least pass through all the other sections, knowing fully well that they would not get tempted to leave without getting to the fashion section. What was not considered is that by the time you get there, if you do get there, it would be likely late and you would be terribly tired. Richard is awfully bored and I am horribly tired and my feet hurt so bad, coupled with the pressure on my calves now. After making fun of me, he had suggested that we buy a pair of slippers, which we haven't gotten so far. He had also suggested going back, but that wasn't an option for me.

So here we are trying to buy a dress. "Which one do you like?" I hold out two dresses for him to make a choice.

"You are the one to wear it, which one would you be more comfortable in?"

"If I wanted to decide, would I ask you? Please, pick one, I'm going to be wearing it for you anyway."

He pauses for a moment, collects one of the dresses and places it on me, his hand brushing my breast in the process. I feel my nipples rise, and at that instant, a hundred thoughts flood my mind. I peep at him shyly but he doesn't seem to notice that he had evoked any feelings. Or is he deliberately avoiding my eyes? "I think this orange one looks like you."

"Hmm, why do you think so?" I look at all the dresses back and forth. "Why not the black one? I can wear that for court attendance once in a while."

"You asked me a question, I gave you my opinion, but it's up to you." He responds.

"Yes, I know." I say glumly, I'm not really sure I like the shade of orange as much. "Why did you pick it?"

"Because orange complements you, but if you want the black, it's okay too."

"Do you have this in another colour?" I ask one of the sales assistants. She goes into a back store and brings out a purple and red for me. I place all four dresses against my body one after the other and ask Richard to choose again. He keeps shaking his head one after the other.

"Orange." He says again.

"Not even this red?"

"Tobi, if you don't like the orange, why don't you just leave it and pick the one you want?"

"But I want you to choose for me."

"You have a funny way of showing it. Okay pick the black."

"You don't like the red?"

He stares hard at me now, but softens immediately and starts humming. "Hmm, I think the red is cool too, my lady in red." He pauses thoughtfully. "You know what, let me try and get you a pair of slippers." He disappears instantly into the crowd before I can protest, leaving me to make my own decision.

I had forgotten about my hurting feet. On second thought, I hope he's not going out there to look for that Flaky girl. That's not fair, I chide myself. But, why can't he pick a dress and defend his choice? I only wanted his opinion. Soon enough, he comes back with a pair of basic flat slippers. God bless his soul, although, I think he could have done better than these Dunlop slippers.

"Have you decided now?" He asks.

"I think I will take the purple one."

"Good, can we pay now?"

"Yes, if you want to."

"I want us to get out of here." He glances at his watch, pays the assistant and collects the packed dress.

"Do you think I got a good bargain?" I ask him, suddenly unsure.

"I think you got a dress you like. Now we have to get out of here."

"Why? Where are we going?"

"What do you mean where are we going? Home!"

"But we haven't finished looking around." I glance at my wrist watch. It's nine minutes to four. Does that mean we've spent almost five hours here?

"If you still want to look around, then I will wait for you in the car. You are not tired?" He asks, hurrying ahead of me.

I look around the fair; the fashion section is still sprawled so long before me. If I hadn't picked this dress, I'm sure he would have allowed us look further. I try to catch up with him.

"We have to go that way to pick the food processor." I remind him pointing to the home section.

He stops in his tracks. "Please could you repeat exactly what you said?"

"The food processor, we haven't bought it."

"Are you serious, you still want the blender?"

Why is he acting surprised? "Yes, didn't you notice that the other vendors didn't have one as innovative as that?"

"Sorry girl, I warned you." He brings out his purse and gives me some money. "You know where the car is parked." And he begins to walk away.

"Are you going to leave me here?"

"Sometimes, adults have to bear the consequences of their actions, don't you think, Tobi?" He mockingly blows me a kiss and disappears into the crowd. Phew!

SEVEN

Why is it that anytime I have something important to do a lecturer comes up with an impromptu tirade of morale boosting? Mrs Fash, our Contract Law lecturer decided to give us extra tutorial this morning, of all days when every other sane human being is loafing in their hostels. And two hours on, she doesn't seem to be rounding off one bit, probably because it's Saturday and she's not eating into anyone's time, except mine. Ordinarily, I should not blame her, since it's about three weeks to exams, and she had promised at the beginning of the semester that she would pass as many of us as possible, if we were equally willing to put in more work.

About ninety per cent of us failed her course last semester including my humble self and I guess she felt slightly responsible and overwhelmed with the number of students that had to retake the course in addition to the current students. Rumour also has it that the VC or the HOD (whichever one it was) had reprimanded her, that it's either she couldn't communicate effectively with her students or she hadn't spent enough time on her lectures, which somewhat places the onus of passing on her rather than on the students. She had better do her best not to have a repeat performance this semester. It's five minutes past eleven now, I look about the class, a lot of people are yawning, but Mrs Fash doesn't seem to notice. I pass a note to Maggie that I would be leaving the class in about five minutes and she responds.

Why?

Because Richard is coming.

Oh, I forgot. Maybe Biodun would let him in, or he would wait.

I don't want to keep him waiting, he said he's coming with Faith.

But this is important, Mrs Fash would notice you leaving.

I might as well be going to the toilet, so I will leave my bag here for you.

Is Richard taking you out?

No, I don't think so. I just want to meet Faith.

Good. Could we go to Chuks' place together, then? Richard can drop us on the way.

Okay, I think so.

If you leave now, then I have to walk home alone? And carry two bags.

Will it be the first time? Anyway, you can get a ride if you are nice to someone.

If you leave, I won't give you my lecture note.

Definitely, Maggie is as bored as every other person in this class. A two hour tutorial, already dragging to three hours, especially with Mrs Fash would make anyone feel sleepy. If I keep responding to Maggie, she wouldn't tire of it. I check the time again, another nineteen minutes have gone past. It would take me about twenty five minutes to get back to the hostel if I walk, which is the most reasonable thing to do right now because of the traffic build-up on the road. I rush out of the class as Mrs Fash talks on, hardly noticing me.

I reach Vintage Lodge just in time, Richard's car is there, but he is not; he must be at Chez-Amis bar around the corner. Chez-Amis is owned by one of the big boys in school and frequented mostly by the students living around PPL. I hope he didn't take Faith to the bar. Faith is Richard's love child and she lives with her mother, Bibi. Richard had consistently mentioned that he wanted me to meet her and try to get along with her because he wants to be actively part of her life.

I go to Chez-Amis. There's a reason the bar is a choice hangout for students; it's the only small bar at PPL that is fully air-conditioned apart from the fact that it's owned by a student too. It usually starts filling up from evening, so Richard is the only one there, hugging a bottle of big stout at arms' length. The last time we talked about it, he had said he was giving up alcohol totally and switching to soda water. Seeing him with stout gives me some kind of concern.

"I'm sorry, I'm late, Mrs Fash decided to do make-up class. I hope you're not mad at me."

"It's not a problem." He responds curtly without bothering to look at me.

"Are you okay? You don't look very good. Where is Faith?" I can't see the girl anywhere.

He removes his hands from the bottle and rubs his brow back and forth. That's what he does when he is upset or confused. "I think Bibi is up to some mischief, when I got to her house, she wasn't home, and she had left a message that

97

she took Faith with her to her father's place even after we had agreed I was coming to pick her today." He's still staring at the bottle.

I take a seat opposite him. "Is that why you are drinking? You can always bring her another time, why are you so uptight?"

"I'm not drinking. I just wanted something to hold. It's becoming rather regular and I feel kind of helpless about not being able to see my own daughter."

I notice the crown is still intact. "Has she done that before?"

"Oh, many times. I don't know why she wants to keep the poor girl away from me. She's always telling me she sent her to visit one family member or the other, I'm worried." He looks at me now. "Would you believe I've not seen her for about six months now?" I don't know if I'm supposed to answer that, but I keep quiet, so he goes on talking. "I'm always worried about her. How can I be a good father to her when I can't even see her? I don't know if she's well fed, if she's healthy, if she's growing well. I keep giving Bibi money and every time I see her, I think she lavishes the money on herself rather than take care of my baby. I'm sure she can't take care of Faith. You know this is one of those times I wish my mother was alive. I would have taken custody of that girl."

This is another Richard, so sullen and downcast. I feel for him, but how can I help? I take his hands intimately and bring it to my face. "Don't worry my dear. Maybe it's coincidental and she's not doing it deliberately."

He shakes his head. "You don't know Bibi, she's very vindictive. I'm sorry, I really don't want to say such things about her, but that's the truth. She just wants to show me she's in control and that if I don't want her, I shouldn't want her baby. But Faith is my baby too."

Why don't you leave the baby for her then and let her wallow in her foolishness? I keep that thought to myself. "I'm sure everything would sort out soon, maybe she'll get tired of playing out." I pause a while for me to think of a solution, Richard is apparently not in any thinking frame of mind. "Maybe you should try and talk to Bibi's mother to reason with her or maybe you should threaten to stop giving her money if she doesn't let you see Faith." I hope I made sense.

"Forget Bibi's mother, she doesn't like me at all and she supports Bibi in whatever she does. I've threatened to stop giving her money several times and then she would tell me, she would stop feeding my baby."

Is this not what one would call a catch-22 situation? "What about her father then?" I ask. There has to be a way around Bibi.

"You know her parents don't live together, and I don't know her father's house." He replies. His voice is sounding better, I guess that is what talking does. "That girl is soon going to be three, and I have to start thinking of enrolling her in school. Because I can't trust Bibi to do that, she collected school fees from me last month and then told me I was foolish. Am I a fool Tobi?"

"Don't even think that, I think you are doing the right thing, you only need to find a way around Bibi. Maybe you could be nicer to her."

"How?" He stares at me as if I said a forbidden word. "You want me to have sex with her again? That's not going to happen. I think we should talk about something else." We both keep quiet, the air-conditioner humming on. Thankfully, two guys come into the bar and nod at us as they walk to the counter to get some beers. I smile back and wave.

"I think I have an idea." I look at him excitedly and pat his thigh. "And I hope you don't think I'm crazy. Why don't you take a drive there early tomorrow morning before everyone wakes up, and wait it out?" Now that I have said it, it doesn't sound like a smart idea after all. What if Bibi doesn't even spend the night at home?

He ponders over that and shrugs. "Hmm, why not? Anything is better than not having something to do." The two guys who came for the drinks are leaving now. Richards looks in their direction and gives them his witty dimpled smile as if he just noticed them. Only one of them smile back at him and gives him a left thumbs up before disappearing into the scorching sun. "I think I need to use the toilet now." He gets up and exits to the back. My eyes trail after his well-sculptured body, casually tucked into blue Levis jeans and grey check shirt, I can't help but desire him as I feel a rush of warmth inside me. Right now, I want him to hold me tightly and kiss me like there is no tomorrow or Bibi or Faith; just the two of us, living happily together.

The bartender brings two bottles of coke to the table. "Would you want something to eat?"

I collect the two accompanying straws, and shake my head; no, I don't want to eat anything and ordinarily I wouldn't be sitting here by myself at such an odd time. I thank him after he opened the drinks. I start sipping the coke and my mind shifts to Richard. What is our married life going to be? Has he asked you to marry him, I ask myself. So, what am I doing with him? Ah, well! All the same I wish his life wasn't this complicated; a string of ex-girlfriends and a baby seems to sum up to an uncertain future for us. Of all the men to settle for, I picked the one that comes with the most baggage. Yes, he is dashingly handsome, confident, hard-working, caring, extremely protective of me, and life with him is unpredictable in a happy way, but…

The bartender is in front of me, with a finely designed red paper bag, which he stretches out to me. I raise my head to meet his gaze, and question him with my wide, starry inquisitive eyes. He smiles. "Mr Richard said to give you this."

Mr Richard? I look towards the back door, but he's not anywhere in sight. Is he at the toilet really, or did he go out to get this? I collect the bag from the bartender and he curtsies. "Oh, okay, thank you. Thank you very much." I'm confused, I sit back to open the bag and find a small creamy, fluffy pillow on which is inscribed, '**I ♡Tobi, Richard**' in bold orange. I cuddle the pillow like I would Richard. I love it already. Cream seems such an unusual colour which makes it uniquely beautiful. Just what I was thinking about Richard, he is the master of unpredictability and I love him for that, and sometimes I wish I could match him.

What can I do to shock him? Maybe sneak into bed with him? How? The guy avoids touching me like a plague when we are alone together. I could rape him then? That sounds exciting, but I would need help to achieve it. Hmm, what else? Ah, yes, two can play at this surprise game. I beckon at the bartender and tell him I need to get something around the corner, after paying for the two bottles of coke, one totally untouched. It's his turn to stare at me, but he doesn't ask any question as I pick my pillow bag and walk into the street, heading back for Vintage Lodge to wait for Richie boy.

Thankfully, Biodun is home.

About ten minutes later, Richard bumps into the apartment looking ruffled. Good for him, he always seems to be in control. "Why did you leave like that?" He asks, making an attempt to act angry. It probably took him some time to realise I wasn't coming back to the bar.

"I got tired of waiting." I give him a shoulder shrug and remain seated, coating my nails with a red polish. "What took you so long?" I blow on my nails, lift my head up waiting for an answer. He keeps quiet and stays standing, looking at me, askance; also waiting for me to say something he wants to hear. "Don't you want to sit?" I nod him to sit.

"Tobi …" He starts.

"Hey!" Biodun barges in with the pillow bag. "Tobi, did you leave this by the door? Oh, hello Richard." She has refused to join the Richie bandwagon. He looks at the bag in Biodun's hand and then turns to me, more confused than ever. I keep on blowing my fingers while shaking my head, signifying plain ignorance.

"Richard?"

He rubs his brows. "That's the bag I gave to the barman. Didn't he give it to you?"

I raise my brows. Biodun shoves the bag to Richard. "It's yours then. I came back to pick something. Where is Maggie?" She heads for the kitchen.

"She's still in school." Thank God I escaped on time.

He stretches the bag towards me. "Why did you leave this

by the door? I got it for you."

"It's for you." I pull the pillow from behind me excitedly and show him. "You got this for me, not that."

"Oh." Now he is surprised and excited. He opens the paper bag and brings out the Discman that I had put there for him. Only yesterday, I had followed Biodun to one of her friends' shop at Alaba market. The man had just taken delivery of some new model electronics and he gave Biodun the sleek Sony CD player, explaining how it works. Richard immediately came to mind and I got one too.

"You got this for me?" He brings out the CD player from its pack while stealing glances at me intermittently. He fiddles with the buttons, feeling it and examining it at the same time. Of course it needs batteries to function.

Biodun comes back in from the kitchen with a plate of cake slices which she places on the centre table. "That's lovely." She comments.

Richard winks, caressing the Discman gently. "Thanks." He says. Was that to me or to Biodun? I can't tell, because he's still fixated on the toy in his hands.

"I'm going out now. Richard, see you later then."

"Bye." I chorus with him as Biodun dashes out of the flat. Richard jumps to his feet like he had been waiting for her to leave.

"What should I do with you?" He murmurs with gleaming eyes. He pulls me gently to himself in a cuddle and starts humming in my ears, rhythmically moving our bodies in slow motion. Maggie comes into the flat, without knocking. Why would she knock, she has her keys? Why did she have to come now? Kill joy! She coughs falsely. Richard ignores the cough and continues humming Bryan Adams *Everything I do, do it for you.*

He pulls away when he finished that beat and turns to the door to acknowledge Maggie. Maggie gives a clap and Richard takes a bow. These people won't kill me.

"I hope you didn't stop because of me?" She yawns and heads straight for the kitchen. I realise now that I am hungry as well. "Tobi, can we still make it to Chuks' house?" She calls out from the kitchen, clanking plates and spoons. Richard squints at me quizzically. I had quite forgotten about Chuks. Chuks is Maggie's final year virgin boyfriend, smart but very withdrawn. She was initially interested in him because he was an A-class student, and he agreed to give her tutorials at the library, of which I also became beneficiary. On investigation Maggie discovered he had been cruelly ditched by his course mate, who started dating another guy in the same class. Soon enough, Maggie started hanging out more with him and despite his insistence about not wanting to date, he had kissed her before he could walk away. When Maggie told me he was a virgin, I almost tripped on our way to school. I didn't know any other boy virgin of his age. Except Lami, my brother of course!

"No wonder the girl ditched him." Maggie had said, "Who wants a straight boyfriend?"

Her initiation into the world of sex was by Malik, a boy we met at one of those freshers' parties. Malik, a Year three English student and smooth talker had a famous reputation for his size and prowess in bed and girls struggled for his attention. What amazed me is how such a reputation was built in the first place, but Maggie was fascinated and that got her into bed with him. Her plan almost failed when Malik discovered she was a virgin. "You should have seen the expression on his face, Tobi." She hissed. "That boy is pompous. He said he couldn't be stressed to untie a knot and didn't want a crying baby in his hands. Except that he was far too gone to stop himself and you know when I want something, I get it." She had said with glee and pride of accomplishment. "Otherwise he would have broken my heart. But, Tobi, he is good, very good." And I could sense the energetic flow of lust all over her body. In less than a month, and about ten lessons in passionate, steaming sex, they were over; Malik had fulfilled his mission and Maggie had achieved her goal.

Her other relationships were just as sensational. One minute she would be all over the guy, revelling in the attention and the sex romps, within one or two months, she was out cold and bored, looking for another masculine quest. After, Malik, she dated three other boys in school and broke up with them complaining that they didn't challenge her intellectually. I wonder too! Then from nowhere, she announced that she wouldn't bother anymore until she found real love. And then, she met Chuks (Chukwugozie – I wonder why parents keep giving their kids long names, when they would still conveniently shorten it) at the library.

At the outset, I had thought Maggie wouldn't last with him, because she kept on sneaking to parties with the rest of us since Chuks was not a party freak. But, here they are, four months on and still going strong.

Chuks is the kind of guy you describe as cool; tall, sturdy athletic body, extremely light-skinned (I tease Maggie that their first child would likely be an albino), polite, confident, reserved (but when he does talk, he talks) dresses well without drawing attention to himself and from a middle class family like mine. Chuks is the guy that suits predictable, steady, focused and loyal. Richard is it for erratic, romantic; carefree and creative.

*

Chuks' family house is at Festac Town, the town developed in nineteen seventy seven to host the All African Festival. It's a very big housing estate and is segregated along all the categories of social class; low income, medium income and high income. But when people say they live in Festac, it's easy to assume that they are all posh and rich, just like when one of our class mates told us she lives in Apapa and we assumed it was mainstream Apapa until someone sighted her with her mother at Apapa-Ajegunle, one of the poorest, dirtiest and most populous slums in Lagos bordering the small, rich Apapa Wharf.

Richard drops us off and we take the stairs to the second floor flat where Chuks lives with his parents and two sisters. I am sincerely praying, just as Maggie that Chuks' parents would not be home. Being the only son and first born, Chuks had warned Maggie that his mother, a nurse at the General Hospital, is kind of protective of him. The only reason Maggie opted to come to the house is because Chuks had not been in school since Wednesday after telling her he wasn't feeling well and he couldn't be reached since his house phone is suffering the same fate as mine. I agreed to follow Maggie to give her moral support and make her a little bit comfortable.

Baby, the younger of the girls lets us in eagerly. Chuks had told us that in some parts of Ibo land, children are christened about three months after they are born, and they are called baby before the christening. In some rare instances, Baby sticks as the nickname. That is the case with Chuks' younger sister. Beaming with excitement, she hugs Maggie and welcomes us into the living room. Compared to Maggie's house, the living room looks like a playpen, yet it contains a lot of unnecessary decors which makes it look smaller than it ordinarily should be and choked up too; figurines, flowers and pictures (ranging from when Chuks' parents wedded up till when he matriculated) all over without order. Thankfully, the air-conditioner is on, that's a relief from the still air and heat we've had to endure in Richard's car.

"You are welcome. Chukwugozie mentioned you may come. Is this Tobi?" She asks Maggie as she leads us to a three-seater settee. Maggie nods. Obviously, Baby adores her.

"Yes, I'm Tobi, how are you?"

"Very fine, I like your trousers."

"Thank you." My black trousers is a high-waist culottes, aka Keep Lagos Clean, newly in vogue. Maggie had decided to wear a simple black knee-length dress, for fear of over or under dressing; you can never go wrong with a plain black dress.

"What about Chid?" Maggie asks still looking around the living room, trying to take it all in. Chid is the older sister. "And Chuks?"

Baby leans towards Maggie and whispers. "Please call them their full names, Mummy doesn't like us shortening names." Then she retreats and goes back to normal pitch. "Chukwugozie went to Satellite town with Daddy, they will soon be back."

That didn't sound very encouraging.

"I will tell Mummy you are here." Baby goes on. "What shall I get for you?"

"Water!" Maggie and I chorus. Baby leaves and apart from hearing her call out for Chidiebere, all we can make out are hushed voices.

"Just stay calm." I mutter and I place my hand on the right leg she is stomping as she does when she is restless or anxious; quietly, but steadily. We had not bargained for Chuks not to be home.

"I don't know why I even bothered." She says while the stomping continues, apparently, the leg is moving of its own volition now.

"You have to get over this one way or the other. By the way Chuks is passing out in less than two months. How else will you get to see him?"

She smiles and rolls her eyes at me. "Better call him Chukwugozie."

"Na me wan marry the boy? Abeg o."

"I thought he was seriously ill, if he's well enough to go out, then he's okay." Referring to Chuks, Maggie hisses.

"Maybe he got well yesterday." I try to make light of it, Maggie gawks. "And you know there's a nurse in the house."

"Well, if he doesn't come on time, that's his cup of tea. We are not spending more than one hour here." She looks at her watch. "And that's less than twelve minutes already."

"It's your call. Just make sure you don't break anything before we leave." We exchange glances and laugh quietly, amused at the figurines, titivating the dining table, the centre table and a wooden side stool.

Baby comes back carrying a tray with two glass cups and a bottle of water. She pulls a side stool and places the tray there. "Sorry, the water is not too cold, there wasn't light until about thirty minutes ago." That's the story almost everywhere in Lagos, electricity outages fifteen out of the twenty four hours in a day. The Military promised to fix everything when they seized power, but it seems they are fixing it backwards.

"Thank you." Maggie pours the water for two and gulps hers down while Baby looks for the TV remote and switches it on.

"Would you like to watch a film?" She brings out some video tapes and starts perusing the titles. "Chidiebere is still sleeping, she went for a vigil yesterday." Unable to make up her mind what to watch, she hands over the tapes to Maggie. Chuks' mother comes in, removing the apron she must have been wearing and gives it to Baby who gets up and goes back to the kitchen. The woman is beautiful; smallish, spotlessly fair and looking very well groomed, she could pass for Chuks' sister. One look at her and the living room arrangement begins to make sense. For someone coming from the kitchen, she looks too impeccably unruffled. Maggie and I jump to our feet, almost tripping the table over.

"Good afternoon ma." We both chorus, curtsying.

"Good afternoon, how are you, sit, sit." She gestures at the settee and takes over Baby's seat by the TV. We sit back and Maggie puts the video tapes on the stool beside the tray. "I'm not sure Chukwugozie knew you were coming, he would have mentioned it."

"We came to see him because we learnt he's ill." I respond.

For the first time, Maggie is tongue-tied.

"Oh, that's very kind of you, he's okay now. I'm sure it's all that junk food he eats in school. I don't understand why he won't eat healthy food." That sounded like an indictment on Maggie since she makes soups for Chuks, although sometimes she stuffs him with too much cakes and pastries. Another moment of silence. "Which one of you is Maggie?" She asks.

"I am ma. And this is Tobi." Maggie quickly adds.

"Who is your father?" She faces Maggie intently after the introduction. That did not sound nice at all.

"Abiola ma, he's a lawyer."

"Abiola?" There is a hint of surprise in her voice. "Where are you from?"

"Ogun State ma." Maggie's voice is totally subdued and I'm sitting there like any other piece of furniture.

"Is that the same Abiola, MKO?" She queries further, her face is becoming unbeautiful gradually. Maggie shakes her head to signify no. On an ordinary day, this is one question she wouldn't bother to answer. She gets annoyed when people talk as if there's only one Abiola in the whole of Nigeria, and that's why she usually adds that her father is a lawyer in her introductions, but Chuks' mother had failed to pick that up. "These English names can be so deceptive. To be honest with you, I thought you were Ibo when Chuks mentioned Maggie. That would be Margaret, right?"

Here we go again. Just to check up on a sick boyfriend and this is where we are. But if she is a nurse, she should be educated enough to live above this tribal nonsense. Where is Chuks for goodness sake?

"Yes ma."

Chuks' mother sighs and crosses her hands on her stomach in deep thoughts. "Do your parents know Chuks?"

"He's met my mother ma." Maggie answers demurely. I don't have an idea where this conversation is heading.

"You know Chuks is our only son, his father is a red cap chief and he would soon be one too. Did you know that?" Chuks' mother continues. Maggie shakes her head again. "Even if we ignore that fact, he still can't marry you, so I don't know what you are doing with him. Your mother should have told you that?" That's like saying your mother didn't give you home training.

Maggie shakes her head again. Her face is turning red and it seems she might be developing a headache. I notice Baby, looking sadly aghast, hiding behind the curtain. "There's no way my only son would marry a Yoruba girl."

We might as well leave now. This is the most humiliating discussion I've ever sat through and I pray to God it should be the last. Somebody, someday has to explain this silly undercurrents of hatred between the different tribes in Nigeria which has spanned generations, especially when it comes to the issue of marriage. I keep hearing the Yorubas betrayed the Ibos, no one bothers to explain how. If Maggie's mother was here, she would have torn this woman to pieces. And right now, I feel like Maggie's mother.

"Ma." I raise my hand instinctively like we do in class to signify that I have something to say. Maggie starts pinching me not to talk, but I ignore her. "Please can you tell us why the Ibos can't marry the Yorubas?" I am surprised as much as the two of them that I asked that question.

Chuks' mother turns to me for the first time since she

started talking, now acknowledging that I am not one of her chinaware. Did I really think she was beautiful? "Are you asking me that question? If you parents won't tell you, what is my business?"

"But ma, Chuks said you are Catholics." That's as rude as I can get now, Christians are supposed to be charitable and Catholics are expected to be more pious than the rest of us. Why does she keep referring to our parents by the way?

She ignores me and turns back to Maggie. "That's another reason my son can't marry you, you people don't have respect for elders. An Ibo girl would never talk back at me." She hisses.

Maggie clears her throat. "We're sorry ma." She apologises. Sorry for what? I wonder.

"And ma…" I continue, but Maggie quickly covers my mouth. I feel like shouting at her that I never talk back at my parents, and that is because they are never this rude, nevertheless I mute myself based on my friend's instruction. She gets up and I follow suit. "Thank you ma, we'll be leaving now."

Thank you ma, my foot. I muster the last iota of respect I could have for a human being. "Bye ma."

She hisses again and shouts out for Baby, probably for her to come and lock the door behind us. I wish I could have told her my mind.

EIGHT

One of the advantages of having a steady boyfriend is that it helps me stay out of trouble when I'm otherwise idle, and I have somewhere to go when others are looking for weekend exploits on Fridays. I have my own key to Richard's place, so going there is like going home, especially since it's closer to school. He lives in a one bedroom apartment that was converted from a servant's quarters in Surulere. It's incredible the things you can arrange in a room if you have no space. His room is just about the same size as mine at home, yet he's been able to squeeze in a bed, a one-seater settee, a fridge, a TV stand (which compartmentalised all kinds of Pioneer-branded musical appliances), cassettes and CDs, and a mobile wardrobe.

"I got it, thank God you are here. I got it Tobi!" Richard rushes in, with excitement written all over his face. I had been asleep in the room for about one hour. He pulls me up and swirls me into a dance. Then he brings out his passport and gives it to me, only for him to grab it back and flip through to the visa page. "The future starts now!" He hugs me tightly.

And he begins to hum Luther Vandross' *'Here and Now'*. Will this humming ever end?

I'm sure the kind of excitement raging through my body is far from whatever is going through his mind. He is excited about his visa. I am excited for him, but it's more about my body against his; my whole body is tingling with a burning sensation and what he's humming is different from the song I am hearing in my head; *'Tonight is the night'* – that Betty Wright's song every infatuated girl is excited to sing in secondary school when day-dreaming about their first sexual encounter.

This is an eventful day. Richard hardly ever touches me when I'm in his room because he says he doesn't want to mess around with me. He always insists on the need to avoid the alluring temptation of ending up in bed. When he does decide to make out with me, it's often out in the open where I'm too self-conscious to ask for more. Sometimes, I wonder if he's having sex with other girls, but he said he has been celibate for a very long time, probably like since he met me.

By the time he opened his mouth to speak, his voice has gone husky, mine is almost lost, my eyes are moist and my legs are weakening. I can feel his bulging groin against my body, and I'm secretly thrilled. "Why don't you say something?" He asks quietly.

"Like what?"

"Anything, just say something."

I guess this is the part where I say congratulations. "Congrats."

"Thanks, Tobi, I love you so much. I couldn't have done it without you." I'm not sure what I did exactly. Maybe just being his girlfriend brought him luck. I sit on the settee and he goes to slot in a tape; '*I wanna be rich*' by the Calloways. He's still excited and I am gradually slipping out of that romantic mood. He brings out a bottle of non-alcoholic wine and the only two glass cups from the fridge, making a toast to the future.

"So, what's the plan now? I ask with my now rasping voice.

"I already called my brother and he said if I could come in before Christmas, it would be easier to get a job, because a lot of people abscond from work due to the cold and the festivity." Today is twenty fifth of November, meaning he intends to travel in less than a month.

"You mean …" The words get stuck in my throat. Even though he had been talking about this London trip ever since we met, the reality of him actually leaving had remained vague in my head. Today has changed all that. I should be happy for him, I scold myself.

"I'm sorry, my baby." He comes to kneel in front of me, clasping my hands. "It means I have like four weeks. Benji said if I wait till January, it would be more difficult settling in. You know ….." There's a knock on the door cutting short whatever he is saying. Richard looks at me with a who-could-that-be-now surprise look. I shrug. I should be asking him. He answers grudgingly. "Yes, just a minute." He turns off the tape and goes to the door, but he doesn't let the person in immediately. He tries to shut himself out, however it seems to me the caller is not having that. It's a girl's voice and there's a kind of struggle until eventually he opens the door and lets them in.

Without any telling, I know it's Bibi, Richard's ex and Faith (I always wonder if they had not intended that to be Fate). I recognise the bleached-skinned Bibi from a picture Richard had shown me where she was carrying Faith at the christening.

From the way she's dressed, it doesn't seem like she has learnt her lessons about boys. She's wearing a black mini skirt and a grey see-through chiffon blouse which subtly reveals her big breasts trying to break forth from her black bra. For sure, Richard is consistent with D+ cups. Really, she would have looked prettier and younger if her face isn't so heavily buried under make-up.

Nothing ever prepares you enough for life's real experiences, especially the unpleasant confrontations, irrespective of whether you are at a vantage position or not. When such things do happen, you can only wish they did not. This is one of such events I wish never happened. Of course, Richard had been planning for me to meet Faith one day, but Bibi was never in that picture. Maybe this is what Segun had anticipated when he told me dating Richard was way out of my league. Now here I am and there is nowhere to run.

I say hello and in response Bibi looks me up from head to toe and hisses. "Is this the stupid girl you've been running around with?" Holding Faith with her left hand, she points at me with her right, as if I am a piece of rag. I am too stupefied to respond, frozen, I feel like I've floated away from my body and I'm watching this scene as an onlooker. Indeed, *'hell hath no fury like a woman scorned.'*

"Bibi, there's no need for you to insult Tobi." Richard is fuming and trying to get things under control, even though I don't see how. Bibi looks ready for a fight, which I'm not willing to give. The only time I was ever involved in a fist fight was in primary five with my neighbour and the street fight had been over a form two boy we both had a crush on. We had just started the scuffle which I thought I would win amidst the cheer of friends, when my father got there, ordered me into his car and drove me home. I left ashamed. Never again!

"Oh, so she has a name." Bibi sniggers.

Faith starts crying, trying to untangle her right wrist from Bibi's tight grip. She is tapping Bibi with her free hand. "Mummy, please." She drawls.

I pity the poor girl, a victim of circumstances as they would say, not fully comprehending the circumstances of her birth or what is even going on right now. I pity Richard; he looks like the world should come to an end here and now. I pity Bibi; saddled with a child at such a young age, I can't begin to picture a bright future for her. Something tells me she must have felt like she was the best thing to happen to Richard at one time and I sincerely hope that she finds true love, and I pity myself, how will I get out of this situation before it gets sour?

I've never seen Richard so upset since I met him. Ever cool, cheerful, self-assured, footloose and fancy-free Richard does not look cool right now and I'm praying to God that he wouldn't have to beat up his ex on my own account. Bibi releases Faith who hastily runs to Richard rubbing her freed wrist. I need to get out of here.

"Look here." Bibi is pointing at me again. "I hope you know he's going to jilt you once he's done with you. That's what he did to me and to the others, and don't go thinking you mean any special thing to him. The only person he loves is himself."

Richard drops Faith on the bed and grabs Bibi's arm. "You had better stop this nonsense you are up to."

"Or what will happen?" She shouts back. This might be the

only opportunity for me to get out of here. As I make to pick up my bag from the floor, Faith stoops to pick it up for me. Children! Bibi grabs the bag from her and throws it on the floor. The poor girl starts crying again.

"Bibi!" Richard yells, but he manages to hold himself. By this time I am already by the door, into the compound; and I am out. I must have probably held my breath for fear that Bibi would come after me. Luckily, she doesn't. It is at times like these that I appreciate the value of fresh air even if it is diluted a bit with generator fumes.

My mind is preoccupied and actively confused. Is this how stupid mistakes haunt people for the rest of their lives? He said they had sex about four times, no five times I think. What am I getting myself into? Surely, this relationship could get me nowhere. Why should I be with Richard? Why not? After all, he had said it was a mistake and he had been forthright about it. Serves him right, anyway, he should also have a taste of the bitter pill. But what if he dumps me like Bibi said? Could he, really; could he not? No answer! My bag is still there. I can live without the bag I guess. What will I tell Maggie? What should I do about him? Oh, God help me. So, what should I do now? Shakespeare's quote in A Midsummer Night's Dream flashes through my mind, '*The course of true love never did run smooth.*' How true. Maybe this is true love then. I keep walking, just keep walking.

I'm at the bus stop now, but there's no bus in sight. Where are all the buses today? Maybe I should keep walking. I continue to pray silently that Bibi doesn't have enough acidity in her to come and beat me up at the bus stop. So I keep walking, the dusk-setting breeze fanning my face is liberating a little. It's surprising how you could get so familiar with a place, yet unaware of everything. Now, I notice the small shanty shops and scarcely equipped stalls lining the streets where Richard's house is, manned by ill-fittingly dressed women and men. Their patrons are a mixed breed; some look middle-classed like my mother, some look just as poor as the vendors and I guess the ones who are rich are those who would pack their cars beside the stalls and order whatever from the comfort of their cars.

Keep walking! I walk past the man running a phone booth, he is the same one selling audio and video records and cassettes with blaring loudspeakers on the side of the streets; I see the row of women selling fruits and vegetables; I see the woman selling books and some other writing materials, with children loitering around her table; I see the man selling second-hand clothes and shoes, all strewn on a floor mat; I see the mobile tailor who sits under a shade just in front of the woman selling fabrics – the sowing machine on the rickety table is the only advertisement he needs; there is another row of women selling fish and then men selling meat followed immediately by the women selling peppers and tomatoes. In this small informal business community daily powdered by freshly produced dust from the un-tarred road, it seems specialization is defined. I see people, discussing, haggling, stalling, walking or running as if what they are doing at that moment is important to them. I wonder if anyone can see me too.

I keep walking. Everybody is in their own world, with different issues to deal with right now. The vendors have goods to sell, house rents to pay and children to send to school; the buyers have their own issues, probably last minute shopping to fix the family dinner; and I have mine, my issue right now is what to do about Richard and his baggage of fate. Faith indeed!

But I keep walking. And then I feel Richard's presence, he is beside me now and everything else pales into oblivion once again. How did he manage that? What happened to Bibi and Faith? But I don't ask him any question, I just keep walking. And he keeps telling me how sorry he is, how confused he is about dealing with Bibi because he wants to be a good father to Faith, how he regrets his past lifestyle and just wants a chance to do things right. I keep walking, with him beside me. Then we start walking in circles until we walk right back into his compound, into his room and I walk into his arms. I didn't realise I had been crying and he had been crying until he sweeps my hair to the back and starts wiping both our eyes, kissing my tears amidst our sniffles. Soon enough we are kissing and fondling. I am clinging to him tightly, praying he doesn't stop as the world around me blurs gradually and the only thing left is the craving to be loved and made love to. I've never ever felt so much pleasure in the midst of so much pain. His touch is gentle and soothing, making my body shudder with pure undiluted desire.

He is singing into my ears now. It's Boyz 2 Men's *I'll make love to you.* That's the only thing he needs to do to keep me going. My breathing becomes heavier as I remove his shirt and my clothes. He goes on kissing me and humming at the same time. My hands and mouth are all over him with sheer hungry passion, caressing, kissing, fondling. I feel his erection, yet he is not hurrying me, in fact he is trying to slow me down, but I am past that point of no return. I am afraid if I stop now, I will never get around it with him and I want him so bad.

My whole body is taut and tingling and sultry; how do you ever find the right words at this moment. I am on the bed, naked and ready; he manages to extract and wear a condom before lying down next to me. He is still humming, more quietly, when I feel him inside me. Gently at first, then getting bigger and pushing deeper. Must pain and pleasure always go together, I wonder. It's a sticky burning sensation, it's consuming, it's liberating; I'm crying and shouting his name and he is shouting mine too and it seems like I am about to faint, but I don't. I feel some more stickiness, then silence.

"I love you so much, baby."

"I love you too."

NINE

I open my eyes gently, coming out from my sleep. Is it
morning? I wonder. The multiple-coloured bulbs in his room
could never let me tell whether it's morning or night. I feel
Richard breathing softly. I make out his face in the semi-
darkness; he looks calm and peaceful. His lips are parted.
Those lips, will I ever get over them? Unrestrained desire
rushes through my body and I wish I could melt into him.
Now I feel the soreness in between my legs and the moistness.
Somehow, it feels like he is still inside me. I try to recall if I
read anything in Every Woman about having sex for the first
time, nothing comes to mind. But I remember Maggie and
Biodun saying the more you have sex, the better it gets. I feel
week and woozy, yet the sight of his body next to mine makes
me want to have sex again. He stirs a little and turns towards
me, his outstretched hand lands on my breasts; my hormones
begin to revolt, all leading to below my navel. I need to make a
mental note to find out why my nipples are terribly sensitive.

He awakens with a quiet gasp, and traces my face. "Tobi."

My name always sounds special on his lips. He leans on one elbow and raises himself to meet my eyes. "I'm sorry. Are you okay?"

"I'm okay. And you?"

He nods. "I'm okay, I'm sorry, I didn't mean to …" He wants to apologise. I bring up my hand and place a finger to shut him up.

Why does he want to make me cry? "It's okay Richard. I love you very much."

"I love you too." He says. He reaches out to kiss me and I embrace him tightly, not letting go until he starts caressing my body and we start all over again. And this time, I take time to savour all the things he is doing to my body and I wish he would never have to stop until I drift back to sleep.

"Will you come with me to see my father?" Richards asks me. I'm seated in a cuddled position on the bed, my hands wrapped round my raised knees. He is on the settee struggling to fix something in the equaliser. After, bathing and dressing up, he had mentioned something about bad sound quality and had pre-occupied himself with the appliance he called equaliser. Apparently, food is not on the agenda this morning since he doesn't have a private kitchen where I can cook.

"Your father, are you joking?" My eyes widen in surprise and confusion. Where did that come from, why would he want me to meet his father? After my experience with Chuks' mother, I would not be in a hurry to meet anybody's parents, Ibo or Yoruba, I don't care.

"Well, I wanted to go see him today and since you are here, why not?" He says that as if it's everyday a boy takes a girl to meet his father. "I need to let him know I will be travelling."

"Is that how you take girls to meet your father, just like that?" Somewhere in my head is this belief that you take a girl or boy to meet your parents only when you are sure you want to marry them.

He raises his head from the appliances and drops the cables in his hands. Is he angry at what I said? "Come here." He beckons. I uncoil cautiously and move to the edge of the bed. He cups my face in his hand and looks deeply into my eyes. Anytime he does that I feel like melting. "How else do you want me to tell you that you are special?" He kisses me on the forehead and turns back to his equaliser. "The only other girl my father has met is Bibi and that is because of Faith."

"But he won't be expecting me, what if he doesn't like me?" His father lives far away at Ibadan and travelling to meet him impromptu does not sound like an appealing idea to me at all, maybe if he had told me earlier, I would have mentally prepared in case he does decide to tell me off.

"He doesn't have any business liking you or not liking you. You are my girlfriend, not his." He says confidently. "Anyway, he is a liberal man and he generally minds his own business."

"Please, what do you say to your boyfriend's father when you meet him?" I ask, trying to make light of the situation.

"You curtsy and then you keep quiet until he talks to you or asks you any question, which you try to answer as sincerely as possible. Don't' worry, he won't ask you that many questions." He slots in a tape into the player to try it out.

"How do you know, if you've never taken any girl to him?"

"Hmm, let me think." He plays at being in a thinking mood and responds. "To tell you the truth, girls have always been part of our lives growing up. My father never made an issue out of us bringing girls home even when we were in secondary school. And when I took Bibi home, he was not upset or shocked for that matter."

"Are you serious?" I ask in amazement. We are both from entirely two different worlds. Even now that Lami has graduated, he still hasn't brought any special girl home. Although since he went for his youth service, I think something must have snapped in him when it comes to girls.

"Oh, yes." He shakes his head reflectively. "I don't think we should talk about that part of my life now, it was crazy."

"Why not? You would have to tell me one day, you know."

He sighs deeply and turns to me. "I started having sex when I was thirteen. Anti Kefi was our maid at the time and maybe about twenty years old. She had been with us before my mother left and married her other husband."

"Your mother married another husband? I thought you said she died."

He sighs again. "I know it's kind of complicated. My mother left for about two years and married someone else. But the man died and she came back with the daughter she had for him."

"And your father accepted her and the baby?"

"I guess that's one of the reasons I would always respect him, no matter what." He takes a deep breath. "Anyway, my mother went with Anti Kefi and came back with her the second time and she was with us all through my mother's battle with sickness till she died. Maybe she had some expectations from my father, because I think she turned to me when he started ignoring her after he married wife number two."

"You had sex with your father's mistress?" I almost shout, my eyes practically bulging out in utter shock.

He shrugs and continues. "It's just a suspicion. And truly, I didn't know any better then. I had just started getting attention from girls in school, but she was the one who initiated me and then it became almost a daily affair anytime I came home from school, until my step mother sent her away. And sincerely, I think she was also having a bang with Benji. I guess that because when she left we both went haywire with girls. I was too young to understand it all. And for me, she had created a void I thought I needed to fill immediately. When she left, I thought I would die, you know she was everything my mother could have been, and even more." He rubs his brows back and forth, while shutting his eyes intermittently. "That's it, I've never told anybody about it until now." He looks at me intently. "Say something."

My mouth is wide open, yet no sound would come out. I am absolutely speechless. How could a thirteen year old boy be having sex regularly under his father's roof?

"Tobi."

What is the appropriate word to say at a time like this? "But why didn't you report her to your father?"

He chuckles sardonically. "She threatened me never to tell a soul, and don't forget she was also our mother figure, so I couldn't even conceive of going against her wish. Then after a while, I started enjoying it and looked forward to her beckoning. But all that is history now."

All that is history now? How could he be sure? I'm trying to process this information even as my mind is actively rejecting the image of a thirteen year old Richard humping away at a faceless twenty year old cradle snatcher. Thirteen years old? The thought is extremely repulsive to me.

"And your father didn't do anything?" I ask quietly.

"I'm not exactly sure whether he knew there was anything going on between us and the girls. He was always too busy, either with his business or with his women and he wasn't home most of the time, so he may not have noticed so much." Richard's voice is painfully solemn. His hand goes to his eyes. "He must have loved my mother in his own way, because it was after she died that he totally lost it. Even when she left for another man, he used to tell us she would come back to him. I remember we used to be one happy family, despite the fact that they fought a lot over his drinking." His voice is quaking now. I touch his shoulder to console him and it feels very cold. "Now that I think about it, maybe we weren't so happy after all, maybe she just shielded us from the ugliness of everything, I'm not sure she was ever happy herself."

"I'm sorry."

"Thank God one of my aunties came to pick my half-sister some months after my mother died, so she wasn't exposed to all that. I think my father was relieved. Benji left one year after secondary school, shortly before he turned eighteen. And that is exactly what I did too."

This is too much information for me to digest in one day and I am intensely confused with a lot of questions plaguing my mind. How did I get myself into this? If this is what he has been from thirteen, can he ever be committed to me? How is his lifestyle different from his father's, now that he has started this path with Bibi? I know he is trying with Faith, but can he actually be a better father than his own father? This news about his mother having two husbands is even more disturbing.

What a family. Now I feel ashamed that I've always taken for granted the fact that Daddy always comes home after work.

Richard and I are totally different in a lot of ways, oh God help me. One of my mother's sayings -that everyone deserves a second chance in life -creeps into my mind. Is it then fair to judge him based on his past, after all he didn't choose to come through this family? If I had gone through what he went through, will I be any better? And he still has it in him to respect his father? I shake my head, I don't think I could do that. Well, maybe it's also not his father's fault, I wonder how many men can cope if they lost their wives, definitely not my father. I try to picture the last maid we had, luring Lami into her bed when he was in form two, but the picture would just not come together.

"Tobi." His deep voice cuts into my thoughts.

"How is your relationship with your father now?"

"So, so." He shrugs. "I don't begrudge him for anything, I'm sure if my mother hadn't died, he wouldn't have married another wife, I don't think he ever got over her death. The second wife was terrible to us for no reason. Maybe she hated children because we couldn't understand why she left even her own children behind. And then he had to marry another wife again, and that one left too. I know my family doesn't sound like a normal family, but we try to keep up with one another. I'm sorry. Not that I could have helped any of it anyway."

My mind drifts back home again. How would Daddy cope if Mummy suddenly drops dead? God forbid! I rarely see any display of emotional affection between my parents and sometimes Lami and I wonder if they have sex like normal couples do. Lami pointed out that we are a testimony to the fact that they must have had sex sometimes in their marriage. Would Daddy snap if Mummy wasn't around? It's a difficult question to answer. Richard said he was eleven years old when his mother died. Even at nineteen, I can't imagine how I would cope if Mummy was suddenly not around.

"You look distant. Did I shock you?" I nod, no use lying to him. "I'm sorry." He takes my two hands and starts caressing them. "You've given me so much reason to be a better person and live a better life. I promise you everything is going to be alright. I didn't know what love meant until I met you. I love you my baby and nothing is going to change that." He sounds like a father who has just found his lost daughter. And I feel like that daughter who is looking up to her father for assurance that he would always be there.

Despite all the un-answered questions raging in my mind, I feel loved and safe with Richard. I pull him to the bed and kiss him, he kisses me back and I gradually lose myself to the all-consuming passion of his touch and his love making. Any form of doubts I had in my mind about us fades progressively, until I can't remember anymore.

*

Maggie is in the common room when I got back from Richard's house, reading a novel and snacking on a pack of chocolate. Of course, we had to postpone the trip to his father's because I didn't feel up to it after that bit about losing his virginity to their maid. Besides I hadn't told Maggie I was going to spend the night with him and I didn't want her to be worried much.

"Finally, you are back." She jumps from the settee and glances at the wall clock immediately I opened the door to step in. "You got me worried, please don't do that again." Then she yawns. That is as angry as Maggie gets with me; cool but with force. She must have been pretty worried for her to stay in the common room all by herself, waiting up for me I suppose. Biodun hardly spends any weekend with us, so Maggie would have probably been all by herself. Except if Chuks came around.

"I'm sorry, I didn't know I would have to sleep over."

"Hmm, like you didn't plan it." She scoffs.

"Honestly." I say without any inflection. I'm feeling an aching sore and I'm overwhelmingly exhausted. I sink into the settee opposite Maggie, pulling the coverlet she had left there over my body hoping to get some comfort and just stare at the ceiling.

"Are you cold?" Maggie asks, looking at me suspiciously. I stare at her emptily, and shake my head. "Are you tired?" She prods further. I nod. She offers me the chocolate. I shake my head. "Water?" She points at the bottle of water on the centre table. "Why are you tired? You should be thrilled; I can smell sex all over you."

"Maggie!" I almost scream, turning to face her now. Why can't she just keep quiet for once?

"What?" She snaps back. "Did you or did you not?" She is almost gloating over me for a response.

"Yes, I did." I confess quietly.

"Why are you trying to be casual about it? Didn't you like it? And what's tiring about it, every girl gets an after-glow after their first time with someone they love." She looks at me for a reaction. None. "Did he force you?"

"No!" I screech. How could she even think that about him? "Richard would never do that to me."

She opens her hands in exasperation and sits back, looking at me intently. "So what is the problem? Are you afraid you'll get pregnant and end up like Bibi?"

"He used a condom." My mind flashes back to when he brought out the condom and I realise that even if he had not I would still have had sex with him. Now I understand how Bibi got pregnant. Blind, irrational passion! That is after the fact.

"At least he has sense on that."

"Maggie, please don't make me feel worse. It's not just about the sex, it's about if we can actually have a future together."

"What happened?" Once Maggie wants to have a conversation, she doesn't understand the phrase lay off.

I heave a heavy sigh and place my crouched legs on the floor so I can sit up, but I retain the coverlet. "It's so many things at the same time. He's gotten his visa and…."

Maggie cuts me short and her face brightens up. "Finally!" she exclaims and claps. "That's good news."

"That's the good part of it." I say and that calms her down now. "Bibi almost beat me up. And seriously, I'm beginning to have doubts about his capacity to remain faithful." I don't think I should tell Maggie about the specifics of his dis-virginity since he said he had never told anyone about it.

"Bibi was just an incident in Richie's life, Tobi, it's not like you didn't know he had a baby and that the baby has a mother." She says maturely.

"The baby is not my problem. But, it seems like this Bibi girl may just decide to hang around him forever and to tell you the truth, fighting for love would never appeal to me, so she can have him for all I care."

"But, he doesn't want her. It's you he wants. It's unfortunate that Richard is a victim of what most of us get away with. This baby issue happened because he chose to be responsible and accept Bibi's baby as his. He could have walked away like a lot of boys do. I'm not sure my own brother would own up like that, especially with a notorious girl like Bibi."

"Serves him right anyway, he should have had a better sense of judgement than that kind of girl."

"My dear, life is not a bed of roses, you have to keep on weeding the thorns."

"Are you sure Richard hasn't paid you to make a pitch on his behalf. I'm beginning to suspect you, Maggie." I look at her quizzically.

"Tobi, Richie loves you to blazes and you know that. And you know he would do everything he can to protect you. Is it his fault that you didn't come into his life before Bibi? Next time, plan to arrive earlier, okay?" She pops three balls of the chocolate into her mouth one after the other, like that is her prize for solving my issue. Case closed.

"Thank you for your vote of confidence."

Biodun's door creaks and she comes into the common room with a packed overnight case. I had thought she was out.

"Tobi, you disappeared yesterday. Did Richard kidnap

you?" She pulls my left cheek and smiles. I smile back, weakly. She steps back from me and goes to stand beside Maggie's settee, still looking at me shiftily. "Hmmm, is there something different about her?" She asks Maggie.

I flush inside me, embarrassed. Can people actually smell sex or is it because they know I spent the night with him?

Maggie giggles. "Guess what she was up to last night."

"Tobi, Tobi, welcome to the club." Biodun chants. "We should pop champagne for you." She glances at her watch. "Maybe, when I come back."

"Where are you going?" I ask her, hoping to change the topic.

"Is someone picking you up?" Maggie asks her before she could answer me.

"Need you ask, doesn't someone always pick her up?" Biodun is in her final year now. Quiet, but gracefully calculative, she is one of those girls that say 'Yes' to any fella that has some cash to throw around, I have lost count of how many big men who come to see her, always with one gift or the other, like the collection of electronics in her room. At least she has her head screwed up right on that one. I wonder where she's going this time. She was full of tales about Ghana where she spent last Christmas with one of her boyfriends while her illiterate parents thought she was busy in school.

Maggie gets up from the settee, while I remain seated. She gives Biodun, who it seems, is trying to make up her mind what to say to me, a pat. "Don't mind that girl." She says cheerfully. "If no one is picking you up, Chuks would soon be here, so you can ride with us." The Biodun that I know would rather hitch hike to sample another catch.

I don't know what highfalutin tale Chuks sold to Maggie, but they are still together. Chuks rushed down to our hostel to see Maggie the following day after our encounter with his mother and they were locked up in her room for about three hours. Next thing I saw was a happy giggling couple, although behind the giggles were two pairs of reddish cloudy eyes — Maggie's. I hope she knows what she's letting herself into. Picking a suitor from the enemy's camp does not seem wise at all. The foolishness of the tragedy called Romeo and Juliet never left my mind since the day I played Juliet.

"Maggie, thanks, I'll be fine. I actually wanted to give you girls these." She gives one envelope to Maggie and brings the other one to me, pulling my hair before handing it over.

"Yeee, that hurts." Now, I am forced to give up the coverlet. Jolly good Biodun, though about four years older than us, is always thoughtful and never one to easily take offence. We call her big sis sometimes. Inside the envelope are a Christmas card and a beautifully crafted invitation to her Christmas-day engagement and birthday party. My jaw drops and I jump to my feet and give her a big hug. "What? When did this happen. Wow, this is wonderful." How do girls like Biodun get away with getting engaged and girls like Bibi only get away with a baby? I think it should be something called sensibleness.

Maggie's eyes are full of admiration. "Who is the lucky guy?" she asks. She meant which one of the guys got lucky? Biodun doesn't really discuss her affairs with us except when she wants to make fun of a suitor she doesn't fancy much, so trying to guess who she's engaged to would be a futile activity.

"You would have to come for the engagement to find out."

Biodun responds with a wink. "And come with your IV because it's going to be strictly gated." Out she goes.

Life! I am very happy for Biodun though. She has really done well for herself; coming from a poor and uneducated family, she had maintained very good grades in school despite the fact that she had to practically fend for herself and pay her tuition. Most likely, that had guided her choice of boyfriends. And getting married right after school is as sure as one's future can be, I think. She had told us from day one that she was going to marry rich. "If you want to marry rich, you must have a game plan." She had advised. But, that advice was a couple of months late, since I had started dating Richard. If she had told me earlier, I probably would have stuck it out with dunce arrogant Abubakar and marry into a rich family. Oh, that is if his Fulani parents would accept a Yoruba girl like me, at least there aren't so many tales of Hausas and Yorubas betraying each other. I look at the invitation again. Even the card feels and looks rich? I wonder if Biodun is marrying for love or security. Love, what is love anyway if it can't guarantee your emotional security?

"Really!" Maggie exclaims. "That caught me off guard." She brings me back to the present.

"You can say that again. I don't know if I can ever get over this, who would have thought?"

"At least we got one pleasant surprise today." Maggie remarks. "I don't know, I just have this feeling ..."

A car horn starts blaring in through the window. "I guess Chuks is here." Maggi glances at the wall clock. "That boy is something else with keeping to time. Are you coming?"

With no one else in the flat for company, I nod as I go to

my room to pack a bag and follow Maggie home.

TEN

Maggie has a problem with the concept of punctuality. She is kind of configured to start getting dressed on the dot of the time she is supposed to be keeping an appointment. So I always try to provide for thirty to sixty minutes extra in-between. Waiting for her gets me dis-oriented myself. To make matters worse, I'm home alone with Daddy and that is one of the most boring things that can happen to me. Daddy is not given to idle chatter; there always has to be a reason for saying anything, so before I talk, I have to think of why I want to say what I want to say, otherwise he gives me the lecture on how idle talk pushes people into trouble. If I hadn't met Maggie's father, I would have thought that is what being a lawyer does to people. Maggie's Daddy doesn't talk very much too and he travels a lot anyway. But when he is around, he deliberately comes around joking with the rest of us (since I adopted myself into their family). The day I saw him pat Maggie's Mummy on the bum in our presence, I was embarrassed to my bones. Maggie made fun of me and told me with a flirtatious grin. "She's his wife, what do you think they do behind closed doors?"

Typically on weekdays, once it's getting close to half past six, when Daddy usually comes home, Lami and I scamper out of the living room to our different rooms under one excuse or the other, leaving Mummy to wait up for him; after all she married him. If he meets us watching TV, we had to defend why we were watching TV at that time of the day; if we were reading we had to explain what we've learnt from the book and if we were in the middle of a discussion, he would eventually hijack the discussion as if we didn't have any opinion of our own. His regular response is "what do you know," when we try to disagree with what he has said.

Except in rare cases, Mummy has learnt to always agree with him the same way we've learnt to avoid him. When she does disagree with him on certain issues, it usually ends in a battle of silence and denial. Mummy wouldn't talk to him or cook for him; she would even go out without telling anyone of us so that Daddy would be left wondering and fuming since he wouldn't want to talk to her. It's at such times that Daddy softens with us and Lami and I are pushed in-between them to be the courier or the cook depending on what is required.

As ascetic and dominating as Daddy is, he doesn't know how to cope without his wife, so by the fourth or fifth day, he is looking for how to make amends and comes home with all kinds of foodstuff and unusual gifts. That is one good part of their cat and mouse game. Mummy's eyes would be aglow and her movement becomes slightly sprightly like she has won a battle. Then she would victoriously remind us of one of her many adages; "Inside every tough hard-boiled guinea fowl egg is a tasty protein meal waiting to be eaten, just crack the shell; or don't be deceived, silence is golden and there's much strength in humility; or men have only an illusion of power while women have the power of illusion."

When he is in a good mood, Daddy relaxes with a bottle of big stout while listening to Fela's music. It usually takes him over one hour to finish that one bottle. He also loves wrestling, and sometimes Mummy would tease, "I hope you are not learning how to wrestle me" to which he would respond, "God forbid I ever beat a woman." Maybe Mummy wants to find out how much she can get away with. He justifies his love of wrestling by proposing that it's a more practical game than twenty two boys chasing after an air-blown piece of leather called football.

With an allowance of forty minutes, Maggie should have come about thirty minutes ago before Daddy started watching his afternoon matinée and Mummy left charging me with the task of making lunch. Now, I have to shuttle between my room and the kitchen, while trying to avoid intruding Daddy's unwinding, that is if one can classify wrestling as unwinding with all the jumping, clapping and shouting that he does when he immerses himself in the game.

"Young lady." Daddy calls out to me in the kitchen. "Does it take forever to cook rice?" I became young lady when I entered university and Lami is young man.

I poke my head into the living room. "The rice is ready, but I need to make some stew."

"Come on, yes!" He doesn't look up from the TV, as he keeps on flailing his hands urging the wrestlers. "How long will that take?"

"Maybe another fifteen minutes."

"Maybe is not an answer." He admonishes.

"Between ten and fifteen minutes, sir." I cover the pot after tasting to check the seasoning is okay and come back to the living room. It wouldn't take long for the stew to get cooked and I am wondering if I should retreat to my room when Daddy invites me to sit with him.

"Sit." He says, tapping a space beside him on the settee. "You should be watching this sport once in a while, you know."

"Yes sir."

Fiam, the TV goes off! Including every other thing connected to electricity in the house.

"Not again!" Daddy exclaims. This is the second time it is happening today. "Are we ever going to find a solution to this *NEPA* problem in this country?"

I sigh and go to switch off the stabiliser, the TV, the AC and the fan. "Daddy, can I ask you something?" That is our usual opening when we want to talk to Daddy.

"Yes, what about?"

"What is the source of rancour between the tribes in Nigeria, particularly the Yorubas and the Ibos?" That question had been nagging my mind since Chuks' mother's unsolicited advice to Maggie, and even our Ibo friends in school had not been able to answer, saying they needed to defer to their parents. It would seem that only the parents know what the source of conflict was.

Daddy leans his head on his right hand, supporting it with the left hand across his chest and reflects. "That is a very long story. Didn't you read about it in one of Achebe's books?" Is there a conspiracy of silence not to discuss this plague with children? I wonder. I read Chinua Achebe's 'Things Fall Apart' in secondary school and that was talking about how the Ibos fought against embracing Christianity.

"We only read Things Fall Apart." I am sure I don't need to recount any portion of the book to him, because I know he would have read it as well. He is an avid reader and sincerely, it would be easier counting number of books he hasn't read rather than the ones he has. The room is beginning to get hot, so I go to open the windows and draw the curtains. We can only hope electricity is restored or wait till nine o'clock before switching on the generator, which we eventually have to switch off by midnight, just when one is beginning to translate to dreamland. What a life.

"Young lady, you have to sit down and concentrate if you know you want me to talk." He rebukes. He likes undivided attention when he is talking.

"Okay sir, please let me check the stew." I run to the kitchen and turn off the cooker. "Yes, I'm back. I'll serve your food when you are ready to eat." Knowing him, his hunger would disappear until he finishes his story.

"Did you know there was a civil war in nineteen sixty seven tagged the Biafran war?" I nod. "Do you know what caused it?"

"No sir."

"Haha, what did they teach you in history?" He asks again. Everything but the civil war, I guess. Maybe they taught us only for peripheral knowledge. "Anyway, there are so many ways to explain that war and nobody would be right or wrong, because it happened after a chain of related and contributory events which a lot of people conveniently forget. Although, as far as I'm concerned, the British laid the foundation for the war, the way they divided Nigeria as if it was a piece of meat, at the same time trying to govern it as if it was one entity without considering if we could or wanted to live together."

"How?" I prod him on, he has not said anything so far.

"In the beginning, Nigeria was divided into North, West and East regions plus a neutral Lagos. The war started as a reaction to a coup which was spearheaded by Major Nzeogwu, an Ibo soldier in nineteen sixty six."

"How can a Major spearhead a coup?" The current Head of state is a General and as ignorant as I am, I know an ordinary Major is way junior to that.

"The coup itself was a reaction to the breakdown of law and order due to the intensity of the malpractices and rigging in the nineteen sixty five general election. Well, Nzeogwu and others killed all the senior military men and politicians who were mostly from the North and the West, and Major General Ironsi became the ruler." Daddy has always refused to acknowledge military Heads of states as leaders or presidents, saying they were merely rulers by force and cohesion.

"Really? Then it's the Ibos that divided Nigeria." I interject.

"It's not exactly white or black, because a retaliatory coup was staged again in nineteen sixty six and Gowon, a Northerner and an ordinary unmarried Lieutenant Colonel at that time became ruler. Then he also killed Ironsi and other senior military men from the East."

"That's sad. But, what role did the Yorubas play in all of these?" There is a distracting knock on the door, just when I'm beginning to visualise the story. "Oooh, who is that?" I grunt and drag myself to open the door. It's Maggie. I quickly drag her into the living room. "Latecomer, come, Daddy is telling me an interesting story."

"Good afternoon sir." She curtsies and sits beside me on the two seater settee with an almost silent sigh.

"Young lady, how are you. And your parents?"

"They are fine sir, thank you sir."

"Daddy is telling me about the civil war." I respond to her curious look of what interesting thing can you possibly be discussing with your father.

"Oh."

"As I was saying." Daddy resumes. "Where was I?" He raises his brow to try and recollect his speech. I am sure he knows exactly where he was, it's just a test to confirm my concentration.

"Gowon became head of state." I remind him.

"Yes, okay. Then he reposted all military men back to their region of origin in order to stem the killing and violence which his own coup caused all over the country. That gave the Ibos the opportunity to converge and plot revenge under Ojukwu."

"Daddy, you haven't answered my question, where were the Yorubas in all of these?" Apart from labelling us traitors, the other noun the Ibos have for the Yorubas is coward. I'm beginning to see why.

"The Yorubas were minding their own business, getting educated and trying to develop their region. Apart from that, In the midst of all that chaos, it was actually the Yorubas, the Western region general election of nineteen sixty five that started the uprising preceding the Nzeogwu's coup, when Ahmadu Bello unjustifiably imposed an unwanted Akintola on the Yorubas. Then Awolowo joined the Gowon's cabinet and that gave much credence and power to the federal government"

"So every region had a part in it one way or the other." I conclude.

"Maybe the Yorubas would not have been so involved, but there was nothing else we could do since the Biafran soldiers attacked the West in their bid to get through to Lagos."

"And we became traitors because Awolowo joined the federal cabinet?" Maggie probes, in shock."

"Yes, Awo believed in the philosophy of one Nigeria which Gowon tried to sell to the whole world." Daddy sighs. "If Awo was alive now, he probably would be regretting that action because since the North latched on to power, they are still holding on to it believing that they have the prerogative of leadership. After Gowon, there has been Murtala, Shagari, Buhari and now Babaginda. How long has Babaginda ruled for now?" He looks at Maggie and me for an answer.

I recollect that Babaginda has been there since nineteen eighty five. "Six years." I respond.

"And does he look like he's going anywhere?" Daddy asks. We both shake our heads. Babaginda has discussed so many proposals about conducting elections and returning the country to a democracy, but all his proposals have remained empty promises.

"But if that is what happened, why do the Ibos think they are victims?" I probe further because I find it difficult to reconcile the myths and the fact as Daddy has presented them now.

"Because, young ladies." He stares hard at us. "The truth is sometimes relative and may have many sides depending on who is telling it. Although, to be fair, the war cost the Ibos a lot of deaths and impoverished them because the government only gave twenty pounds to each war returnee to start a new life irrespective of how much they had before the war. Even though they started the war, the world usually remembers who loses more as the victim."

"But sir, this war ended since nineteen seventy or so, and we've been living together as one Nigeria, why is there still a lot of acrimony?" Maggie asks.

"That is because the scars of war have not healed, especially because all the succeeding governments have been practising divide and rule rather than true democracy. All these federal character principles divide the nation more and make the Ibos more alienated. Maybe with your generation, the Ibos can let down their guards, but right now, I don't know how." Daddy shakes his head pensively. "They all start as good causes, but too many conflicting motives keep rocking the boat."

We all sigh in our different ways, a lot of information for us to process. Going by this story, everybody has a right to feel somewhat cheated about the war, not only the Ibos. Like Daddy said, maybe he has also told us the truth as he sees it. Based on that fact, an Ibo man may likely differ in his own account of the same story and try to pin it on the Yorubas, while the Hausa man would clearly say the Ibo man deserved what he got. No end to it.

Unfortunately, right now, with the way the country is being governed, no one is the wiser for it as the country continues to slip deeper into poverty and dictatorship. Is it about the Hausas or about the Military? It's difficult to tell one from the other because they have all either been Hausas or Military or both at the same time. Like Shagari who was democratically elected (but Hausa) and booted out by a coup. Oh, and Obasanjo who was Yoruba (but military too). But I can't even call that a reign because he quickly organised elections and handed over to Shagari. Was he trying to save his own skin? I wonder.

"But sir." Maggie is not done. "This war that ended since nineteen seventy, why should it hinder Ibo marrying Yoruba?"

"Hmm, if you are Ojukwu will you let your daughter marry Awolowo's son?" Daddy asks.

Maggie reflects on that briefly and shrugs. "Either way, it doesn't make any difference to me. We are not all an extension of Awolowo, why don't they keep the feud to themselves?"

"Young lady, a leader is a representative of his people, which means we all sent Awo since we appointed him our leader. And remember before the British came, we were all living as brothers and sisters. Every Ibo person is a brother or sister to the other, same for us Yorubas and even the Hausas, so one offence against one is against all. It's only when the brothers think the offence was deserved in the first place that they would scold their brother rather than seek redress for him."

"Now that we all still find ourselves in one Nigeria, won't it ever end?" I ask now, wondering how long it would take the scars to heal, if people are not willing to forgive and forget.

"Perhaps, one good thing that came out of the civil war is the NYSC, where graduates are posted to other parts of the country for the type of reconciliation and integration Nigeria needs. Unfortunately, that is also being politicised now." He flaps his hands helplessly. "You know if not for the NYSC, there's no how Lami will go to Port Harcourt. Now that he's there he would find it easier to appreciate the Ibos around him."

"So Lami can marry an Ibo girl." I declare with a hint of optimism.

"Maybe." Daddy shrugs and stays quiet thoughtfully. "But why would he want to do that, with all the good Yoruba girls around?"

Maggie and I exchange glances, confused. I discretely prod Maggie to probe further. "How will the scars heal if Yorubas continue to say their children can't marry Ibo?"

"The scars would definitely heal. How? I don't know." He responds as he starts rubbing his stomach. That seems like he has tactfully avoided answering Maggie's last question.

"Are you ready to eat now?" I still need to ask him lest he says I misinterpreted him.

He nods, but as I make to get up he stops me. "Wait!" His demeanour is suddenly curious. "Is anyone of you considering befriending an Ibo boy?" He asks. Maggie and I exchange glances again. The tone of that question does not require an honest answer right now. We both shake our heads.

Tough lesson in history!

"What are you going to do about Chuks now?" I ask Maggie. After that session with Daddy, their future together seems threatened to me.

"What do you mean by that?" She responds with a question, picking a stone and tossing it into the pot-hole pond of the once-tarred road leading into the estate. We had decided to come downstairs for fresh air, knowing that there would be electricity outage for a long time. In Maggie's house, the generator would have been switched on almost immediately. We had planned to go to the salon earlier, but since she came late and I had initiated that civil war discussion with Daddy, it had become rather impracticable to bother with the hairdresser's anymore. Tomorrow is another day. Seated by the playground directly opposite the entrance gate, it's easy for us to see everyone coming in or going out and pass comments on anything or anyone that catches our attention while enjoying the cool breeze that nature has to offer, not minding the generators' fumes trying to stifle the air. Daddy himself had decided to take a walk.

"If this tribal thing goes as deeply as Daddy explained, do you think you stand a chance?" I persist, bypassing her trying to play dumb with the issue.

"Chuks has told me he would handle it and that's enough for me. It's only his mother that has problems with him marrying me. He said his father is okay with whatever he decides, even though he won't say it outright to their mother's hearing. I think the man is afraid of his wife." Maggie chuckles. "Besides, it's Chuks I want, not his mother. She can go and hug cactus for all I care." It amazes me that she finds that amusing. If Chuks' father is afraid of his wife, does that not have an implication on Chuks too?

If there is ever a list compiled called Fools in Love, Maggie and I should top that list with our choice of men! I don't see how Chuks would survive his mother's domineering grip if anything he has told Maggie about her is to be believed, yet she believes he would handle her. Well, foolery must indeed have a place in love.

"I think next time he tells you he would handle it, you should ask him how he intends to do so, or what do you think?" I hope I'm not crying more than the bereaved here.

Maggie forcefully pulls out a strand of grass and tears through it with her teeth. "You know I've read somewhere that most of the things we worry about never happen." She's a bundle of contradictions; one time she's the sophisticated prim and proper polished lady, other times she's a down to earth, don't care, anything goes girl, like now. I am not sure I would put that dirty stem of grass in my mouth.

I wish I could agree totally with her "I just wouldn't want you to invest so much in this and then it doesn't go anywhere."

Suddenly, she gets up from the concrete bench we are sitting on and stands in front of me, forcing me to look up at her. "Look at me Tobi, do I look like I will kill myself if it doesn't work out?" She gives a wry confident snicker. "It would be Chuks' loss more than mine." She comes back to her seat, sobering up as quickly as she had flared up. "Honestly, I don't understand why someone would let the past blind them so much as to negatively meddle with their children's future."

"Probably because they don't see that their children's future should be different from the lives they've lived." I propound, wondering if that was responsible for my pursuing law simply because my father had nudged me towards that. And Maggie too; everybody in her house is a lawyer except their mother who owns and runs a school. But Lami is an engineer now and that gives me some consolation. Anytime I reflect on how Daddy relates with me concerning my career, the word manipulation usually crops into my head, although I try to push it as far back as possible.

I notice a girl coming into the estate, going towards the provision kiosk. She is holding a small boy with one hand, while trying to support the crate of empty bottles she has on her head with the other hand. "That's the new bride Hammed got himself." I quickly nudge Maggie.

Maggie screams. "This small girl?" I nod. The pretty, dark-skinned girl should be about twelve or thirteen years old. When the famous shoemaker who lives in one shanty room across the estate came to inform Mummy that he was marrying a second wife, we had thought he was joking until he returned a few days later with the poorly printed invitation card, asking Mummy to donate any amount she could afford. Mummy said she would give him half a bag of rice, but advised him to try and send his three children from his first wife to school. Three days after the wedding, grinning from ear to ear, he brought the girl to introduce to the estate residents he considered important. The way Mummy reacted, if she was his mother, she would probably have killed him on the spot, explaining that the girl was too young to be a wife and should actually be in school. When I told Maggie, she said I couldn't possibly be telling the truth.

"Yet as old as you are you can't even tell your father you have a boyfriend." Referring to me, Maggie puffs out and laughs.

"That's the irony of life. And come to think of it, do you think he could ever allow me marry an Ibo man?"

Maggie looks at me with a teasing glint in her eyes as I continue to shuffle the pebbles in my hands. "With all your Daddy's idiosyncrasies of a perfect man, I'm not sure he would allow you marry any man." She almost chokes on her own laughter. "But, you know I think Richie can talk his way through any parent if he sets his mind to it. That's your only consolation."

Hearing Richard's name brings a smile to my otherwise trying-to-act-annoyed face. Just like Maggie, I have my own issues to think about. My heart skips a bit as I remember that we have that visit to his father coming up next Saturday.

ELEVEN

The drive to Richard's father's house is gradually getting me distressed. The farthest I have ever travelled outside Lagos is Ekiti, when we observe the annual family visit to my grandmother and I usually dreaded it because of the notoriety of traffic jams on the road, since we often end up spending an average of one hour extra crawling to Ekiti. We had left his house as early as six o'clock, hoping to beat the traffic and get to Ibadan in less than two hours. But at eight o'clock, Sagamu is still a little bit ahead of us. It's a useless effort trying to persuade Richard to turn back since all the vehicles are driving bumper to bumper and everyone is stuck in the chaos.

If Richard wasn't driving, we probably would have joined the exodus of people who have opted to walk part of their journey. The stagnation, the scorching sun, the polluted air from exhaust pipes and the lack of a cooling system in Richard's car in addition to the fact that I wasn't even looking forward to meeting his family in the first place, are all conspiring to heighten my tenseness despite his attempt to make light of the situation. I can only pray inwardly that the Road Safety Corps officials that sped past on the other side of the road would untangle us from the traffic on time.

He has tried severally to distil my fears about meeting his family, but Chuks' mother keeps poking her face in my head. I love Richard so much I want his father to approve of me and as unexposed as I am, I know that if his father doesn't approve of me, our relationship may be going nowhere. Even though he hadn't exactly asked me to marry him, the only concept of dating a man I understand is that it tends to lead to marriage. And I know just as I know my name is Tobi, that I wouldn't mind becoming Mrs Aro. I like the sound of that – Mrs Oluwatobiloba Amanda Aro. How that will happen, I don't know yet, but it seems a very good possibility.

By a dash of miracle, the traffic begins to ease and we start moving again. Hopefully, we can make our trip back to Lagos in time for me to catch up with Maggie at Vintage Lodge, so I can fulfil my promise to spend some time with her. We've been seeing less of each other these days because I spend most of my free time with Richard now. I wish he didn't have to leave for UK so soon.

Richard's family lives in a suburban part of Ibadan in a small three bedroom bungalow with lots of undeveloped space, which has been turned into a mini-farm. He explained they were one of the first landlords to settle there, which made his father very popular. The plan had been for them to move in to the bungalow while his father developed the main house, but his mother had died shortly just as they were settling down and that had turned everything upside down. We are greeted by four boys – age ranging from about seven to thirteen - who were playing football in the compound.

Immediately Richard opened the gate, they all rush at him shouting his name and almost tripping him over. Then a girl of about five rushes out from inside and jumps at Richard, whom he catches in his hands, flinging into the air and looping her in two rounds. It takes about two minutes for the excitement to calm down and they start greeting me one after the other.

"This is Auntie Tobi." He says, moving to where I had been standing, watching the expression of affection between brothers and sister.

"Hello auntie."

"You are welcome."

"Good afternoon."

"How are you auntie?"

"Auntie Tobi." Only the girl drawls my name.

"Good afternoon, I'm very fine, thank you. How are you too?" I reply, not sure I need an answer to that.

"Is Daddy in?" Richard asks no one in particular.

"Yes." They all chorus, pointing to the unpainted house. The boys begin to disentangle themselves to return to their football, while the girl holds on to Richard. He gives one of them his car keys and directs him to bring the provisions we brought for the family. He had explained that he never visits without bringing stuffs.

"Taye and Kenny are twins." He explains, pointing to the two lookalike boys and this is Idowu their younger sister. And that is Yemi." He points to the oldest boy. "Femi is the one who went to the car. Ola and Ade are in one polytechnic somewhere" He whispers to me now. "From wife numbers two to four."

I wonder if he really expects me to remember all their names. The simple arithmetic I did in my head tells me they are ten children in all, including Richard's sister and brother. That is a complete football team if we count their father. I smile. The young girl is recounting her school's routs and bouts to Richard, while I try to picture my mother's reaction if I venture to bring her here. Nothing comes to mind. She may probably faint going by the fact that she keeps telling Lami and I that we've always been a handful and she could never imagine herself coping with more than the two of us.

If Maggie was here, this is the kind of living room she would call parlour; unpainted, barely plastered, and furnished with old settees clothed in faded fabrics. There is a wooden dining table covered in Formica which has started peeling and thankfully, the walls are free of decoration save for the wooden grandfather clock.

Richard is almost a replica of his father – tall, muscular, dark, and even the dimples. He doesn't look like the image of a drunk, frail man that I had in my head. He is clean shaven, with a deliberate tiny bush of moustache and looks very healthy. Only his pot belly and narrow blood-shot eyes give a hint of physical laxity. He is wearing a white singlet on a pair of khaki coloured shorts. The man seems to be in a peaceful daydream, humming quietly along with the fast-tempo Sunny Ade music with legs crossed over the plain wooden centre table on which sits a half filled glass beside an almost empty bottle of beer. He chortles loudly as we enter the living room.

Richard and I curtsy and chorus. "Good afternoon sir."

"You are welcome my children." His voice is reassuringly

warm. "How are you my daughter?"

"I'm fine sir, thank you sir." I curtsy again and move towards him when he stretches out his arm wide.

He gives me a half embrace. "No need to curtsy like that, you people said we are in the civilised age, and I don't want to be left behind." He smiles and when I withdraw from the embrace, he doesn't hide the fact that he is appraising me, my stomach churns. "Richard how have you been?" He asks his son.

"I've been fine sir. This is Tobi, the lady I told you about."

"Oh, sit down, Tobi." He points me to the settee across him, Richards sits beside me with Idowu still holding on to him. "Now I've confirmed that Richard's eyes are as good as mine to have fished you out from all the girls in Lagos." He concludes heartily. I try to hide my awkwardness, but Richard notices and squeezes my hand. I already like this man, with his free spirit, and there's so much fondness in his eyes, quite different from my father. I try to imagine what Daddy would say if he was meeting Lami's girlfriend for the first time. He may actually become tongue-tied in the first instance and then he would go on about her schooling and her career plans. "I can see you have been taking care of Richard. He talks highly of you."

Did I misinterpret the nuance in his statement? That 'taking care of Richard' sounds like it has some sexual connotation. How much does Richard tell his father? I hope not as much as our sex life which has been very active since the first time, I must say. My nipples tingle at that thought as usual.

"Idowu, go and tell your mother Richard is here." He instructs the young girl who it seems is besotted with Richard.

She reluctantly disentangles herself from him and disappears. "What will you eat, so she can prepare it for you?" He asks Richard, apparently referring to Idowu's mother. "Or will you join me?" He raises his cup of beer to us after which he takes a gulp from it.

Richard shakes his head. "We already stopped on the way to eat sir" He looks at me, asking if I want anything. I shake my head too. He leans towards his father a little. "There's something I came to tell you, Daddy."

"But you can't come to your house and not take anything. Did you come here to fight? Tobi, what will you take *jor*?" He turns to me.

"I will take coke sir." I reply in order not to rebuff his hospitality.

"Richard knows we don't drink coke in this house. It causes pile you know. But you can take some wine." I nod. He gestures to Richard and then to the mid-size fridge which is standing by one corner of the living room. Richard reluctantly gets up and goes to the fridge. "Don't mind him, anytime he comes here, he never wants to stay." He is referring to Richard.

"Thank you sir."

Richard returns with the bottle of wine and puts it on the table. He opens the curtain and calls out to one of the boys to get some glass cups. Passing through the back door, the boy appears with the glass cups from the kitchen; followed closely by a young woman who I guess should be Idowu's mother with Idowu right beside her hugging a doll. The boy disappears as soon as he puts the glass cups on the table. The woman should be in her late twenties or early thirties. What is she doing with a man as old as Richard's father? And she's pretty too even in her plain kaftan and scarf.

She greets Richard fondly. "Ha, good afternoon. It's been a long time, how have you been?"

I try to read the expression on Richard's face, but he reveals nothing, he gets up, smiling and gives her a short bow. "Good afternoon. I've been okay. And you? No need to tell me, you look very okay." He teases her.

She smiles. "Thank you, I can't complain. Sorry I came out late, I was busy in the kitchen. And Daddy didn't tell me you would be coming, I would have prepared your special dish." Richard's special dish is soft mashed beans with pepper stew. I am somewhat puzzled by the kind of warmth and love I feel amongst this people. This is supposed to be Richard's step mother, although going by her age and the way she mentioned Daddy, it's easy to think she's one of the siblings.

"This is Tobi, my girlfriend."

I get up to greet her, but she hops into a slow dance, in tune with the background juju music -*ma f'ijo yin oba ogoooo*.. leaving me bemused. "Good afternoon ma."

"Thank God, finally." She bypasses Richard to me and hugs me tightly, suddenly; I don't know how to respond. I glimpse at Richard, who only winks. She pulls back and looks at me and hugs me again. "You are welcome, I hope he has been taking care of you. Anytime he misbehaves just come and report him to me. I'm serious. What should I cook for you?" She asks as she lowers herself beside her husband. Is this real or she's just acting?

Richard rescues me. "We've actually had something to eat, because we stopped on our way. I thought we would get here earlier, but that traffic made us hungry. How is business?"

Idowu's mother is a seamstress or fashion designer as they are now called. She owns her own shop at the local Gbagi market and Richard said she's very successful. Richard had also told me that she takes care of all the children as if they were hers. I salute her grace.

Idowu comes to me now, I guess she has sensed that I must be somewhat important. "Auntie, do you like my doll?" She shoves the doll into my hand.

I collect the doll from her. "Yes, your doll is fine, just like you." She smiles and stays with me. Looking into her smiley face, I pick her up and sit her on my right lap, giving the doll back to her. She gets fixated on my braids and starts playing with it.

There's a quiet discussion between husband and wife and I used that opportunity to drink the wine, sharing the glass with Idowu. Thankfully it's non-alcoholic. I can't help wondering how this house is different from mine and it makes me feel more affectionate towards Richard. There are so many things money cannot buy. Yes, they are not as comfortable or even literate as us, but right now I feel I've missed out on a lot of family intimacy as sophisticated as my father thinks he is. How else can I explain that at nineteen I can't even tell my mother I have a boyfriend? Without uttering a word, Richard asks me if I'm okay and I nod. He takes my left hand and continues to squeeze it. Somewhat self-conscious, I try to pull away but he holds on to it. Can Lami hold a girl in my father's presence? This would have been termed as dis-respectful in my house.

"Please, excuse me, I've not finished in the kitchen." Idowu's mother opens the front door to call out to one of the children and retreats into the kitchen. Richard gently drops my hand and clears his throat.

"Daddy, I would be joining Benji next week." He says. He has exactly one more week before he travels.

His father doesn't react immediately until he finished the last drop of his beer. "Congratulations. But next week is sudden, why are you just coming to tell me?" He asks. I thought I would hear anger in that question, but there was none.

"I didn't know it would be early too. I got the visa three weeks ago and Benji said I should get there before Christmas."

"That's good, at least you too can be sending me pounds. So what about Tobi?"

What about me? There had been no concrete plan about us, except the assurances of love we've been declaring for each other. And I'm okay with that. It's difficult to plan when moving to an uncertain ground I figured. And I needed to face my studies as well.

"We'll sort it out one way or the other, once I get there. She's in school now and would definitely have to join me once she's through." Richard explains to his father.

"Tobi, are you okay with that?" His father asks me.

"Yes sir." I reply.

He nods repeatedly, and goes back to his music. Then suddenly he sits up and faces me. "My daughter, why don't you get pregnant before he leaves?"

"Sir!" I squeak in shock, almost pushing Idowu to the floor.

"Daaaaaddy!" Richard yells too. Get pregnant? It had never occurred to me. So I can tie him down or what? And what about school? And what will I tell my parents? God forbid. And that is acknowledging that he thinks we are having sex.

I'm flushed all over and wish I could disappear right now. "Tobi is still in school and I want to do it right with her." He declares almost admonishing his father.

The man only shrugs, unflinching. "Well, you two know what is best for you. Whatever you decide, I agree with you. Idowu go and call your mother. I want to pray for you." Idowu cheerfully glides from my lap and goes for her mother as Richard's father pushes the centre table to one side and gets up, for the first time since we entered the house. He is quite tall. Richard pulls me up, signalling me to kneel with him. His father clears his throat, just as Idowu's mother enters and he starts praying for us, fervently. I am shocked!

*

When Richard stopped the car in front of Vintage lodge, he kisses me passionately for a very long time, I am almost gasping. I wonder how long he had been restraining himself and contented himself with merely squeezing my hand all the way back, while telling me how proud he is of me. I tell him I am proud of him and his family too. In spite of their ups and downs, they've managed to keep some love and warmth in their hearts. I come out of the car, light-hearted and flushed, wishing that the kiss would last forever. He leaves immediately, apologising that he needed to look up a friend and promised to make it up to me.

Maggie had been waiting for me expectantly. I waltz into her room, where she is seated in front of the dressing table, tonging her short hair. "How did it go?" She asks.

"Splendid! His father is very jovial and you need to see his young wife. Very pretty thing and she's friendly too, she even hugged me. Ah, Maggie, there are ten children in that family. Would you believe that? I was shy initially, but they made me very comfortable. I think they've been praying for Richard not to marry Bibi, because they were very happy that he brought a girl home finally. And you won't believe what his father suggested when he told him he was travelling." I gush out excitedly.

"What did he say?"

"Can you just try to guess?" I tease, despite the fact that I am itching to tell her.

"That would be a waste of time, Tobi, tell me now or I will tickle the living daylights out of you."

"No, no need to do that." I plead, recalling the last time I dared her to tickle me; I almost peed on myself. "He said I should get pregnant before Richard leaves."

"What? He said that!" She gets up now. "Did you tell him you were banging the poor boy?" She mocks.

I roll my eyes at her, yet I feel the blood rushing to my head. "Banging which poor boy, is Richard the poor boy? Someone would think I lured him to sex." I hiss after a suppressed laugh.

"Oh, yes you did. One taste and you can't have enough. Just look at the lust in your eyes." She ogles and pokes a finger at my cheek fondly.

"Maggie!" I escape her finger and jump on her bed. I am joyfully embarrassed as I feel all my body tingle. I can't deny the fact that I lust after Richard's body, Maggie is right on target about that, but my feelings go deeper than sex. I venture into an idyllic reverie; I wish I could spend the rest of my life with him, caring for him, bathing him, cooking his food, driving about town with him, talking with him, soothing him when he is tired and ever basking in his love and affection. What else do husbands and wives do? I can almost feel his strong but big hands running over my body and his tongue probing my mouth, I wish…

"Mrs Tobi Aro, I hope you haven't rumpled my dress?" Maggie brings me back to life, pushing me aside. I hadn't realised I was lying on her clothes. That's the second time I would be hearing that today. Tobi Aro sounds just perfect. Yet Richard hasn't even proposed to me. He's travelling on Friday and we have not as much as discussed which way we were heading and I am here thinking about being Mrs Aro. Maybe I should top that Fools in Love list after all. "Chuks will be here soon, girl."

"Oh yes." I get up and Maggie takes her tee shirt, pulls it over her head and she's ready to go. "I already packed. I'm ready when you are." I leave to go to my room, all too conscious that Maggie's eyes are trailing Mrs Aro.

*

About an hour later, we are in Maggie's house. Since Lami moved to Port-Harcourt for his NYSC, going home had become unattractive and it's not likely he would even bother to come for Christmas. Moving to Port-Harcourt had changed Lami, no one could believe it. He had discovered girls or rather girls discovered him and from all his tales about his escapades, I think he has gone way overboard. Last week, my own Lami told me he can't spend a night without a girl beside him now.

"Tobi, after that first girl, it seemed like I just woke up, there are girls everywhere and even if you are just minding your own business, the way they throw themselves at you… and you know I'm not a proud person, so I just tag along." He had told me when he came home the last time. "It only costs you a bottle of stout and pepper soup." He had even started drinking.

"You are having a party again?" I exclaim in shock as we enter Maggie's house. "What's the occasion?"

Maggie looks at me as if she's as shocked as I am. Her mother is in her living room with three other women. If Maggie's mother wasn't running a school, she would have fared well as a diplomat's wife. It seems like they need to have people over at the house at the slightest excuse. Maybe that's one of the challenges of having a very big house.

Except for Maggie's room which is almost always in disarray, everything in the house is deliberately arranged. To be honest, being Maggie's friend has given me the opportunity to effortlessly expand my vocabulary about houses, people, events, art and some of the things I would ordinarily not have come across in my normal life. There is a bronze-tanned side table, which her mother calls console in the living room on which bits and pieces of family pictures and different colours and shapes of crystal (I used to call them glass) are arranged. The centre table is of the same stock with the TV shelf and the console, and carries a very big flower vas. That vase is the biggest I've ever seen on a table in real life and with real flowers picked daily from the garden instead of plastic. Maggie had told me at one time that their father got the design of the house from a US Architect while the mother imported the furniture including the tapestries -another uncommon word- from England. The dominant colour of the living room, based on the granite floor tiles is brown and the beige wall – which Maggie's mother emphatically calls taupe - is stylishly adorned with different artworks (canvass, pencil, even sand); the settees are clothed in mixed brown and beige damask fabric. Everything deliberately fits into a beautiful and cosy place I call simple splendour; hardly little, but not too much.

The sound of music from the living room downstairs confirms that Segun also has guests over. We all greet Maggie's Mummy and her friends and exchange some few words. Chuks excuses himself and goes on to join Segun while we stay behind for some chitchatting with Maggie's Mummy which she usually insists on anytime we come back from school. Sometimes, I wish I was Maggie's real sister. If I didn't come from such a repressive family, Richard would be welcome in my house just as Chuks is here.

"Congratulations, my dear." Maggie's mother says.

I look at Maggie in puzzlement. Congratulations for what?

"This is Tobi, Maggie's friend." She introduces me to her friends. I curtsy to them once again.

"Good afternoon ma."

"Her boyfriend is relocating to England next week."

I can see the spark and joviality in the women's eyes. "Congratulations!" They chorus.

"Are you getting engaged before he leaves?" Maggie's Mummy asks.

"Mummy!" Maggie yells, and drags me away from her mother.

I would never cease to be amazed at the difference between

Maggie's mother and mine. While I couldn't dare tell Mummy about Richard, Maggie's mother knew every bit about our relationship. Sometimes, she would chip in a word of advice, sometimes, she would remind us (Maggie and I) how lucky and smart we were to have found true love in school. "If a girl can't find a boy to marry in university, she's likely to end up on the shelf." She used to say. Seriously, sometimes, I wish she was my mother.

Maggie says something about joining the party. "Surprise for you, girl." She suddenly covers my eyes with her hands and leads me gently down the stairs to the general living room onto a settee. The music stops and there is a heavy cheer amidst the song, 'for she's a jolly good fellow'. What's the cheer about, I would know if today was my birthday, wouldn't I? After the song, the room goes quiet as Maggie guides me up from the settee and we take about three steps, she removes her hands and I have to rub my eyes which had been shut for the better part of three minutes. Whatever the surprise is had better be worth almost blinding me for. In a near- haze, I see Richard at the end of the room in a frozen position and then....

'My love, there's only you in my life...' He starts dance-walking slowly towards me, snapping his fingers. Since I started dating Richard, my life had been on a musical roulette, but this beats me to tears. He's doing a rendition of Diana Ross's Endless Love. I stand in the middle, too dazed to move. He is dancing round the room, taking his time in very slow motion and I continually turn around to meet every of his move. On the dot of endless love, he is at my feet, with his right hand outstretched, holding a tiny gold engagement ring.

Everyone is staring at us, Segun and his girlfriend, Chuks,

Maggie and two others guys that are Richard's friends, but their names escape me now. I am stupefied, almost too stiff to move. He takes my left hand and I raise my fourth finger above the others, it seems the most natural thing to do. He slips the ring on my finger. Everyone starts clapping. I lift my hand and look at the ring. It's beautiful! Right now, I can dance in the clouds.

TWELVE

The post card came one week after he left.

Days have been short
And nights too long
I miss your smile
That makes me glad
And your laughter
That lifts my spirit
I miss your eyes
Which see me through
And your body
Which gives me warmth
I miss you all the time!

I miss Richard very much. With each phase of life comes a different set of challenges. I find myself wandering into supermarkets, shopping for cards that convey how I feel. I never thought getting a suitable card could become such a task. Finally I found one:

> There's a thing called love
> I found it with you
> There's a person called love
> It's no one but you

Then the letter came also.

My baby,

How do I begin to tell you how much I miss you. I miss you from the deepest part of my heart. The cold here is killing and I wish you were here for me to just hold. Almost everyone here is also cold, people hardly smile at you. London is just like Lagos, traffic everywhere and everyone in a hurry to get somewhere and seriously the two cities are not so different except that it's more organised, there's twenty four hours electricity and water and the trains are still working, but you pay through your nose for everything. On Christmas day, it was like a ghost city, because the buses don't work. So if you don't have a car or food at home you are stranded. We couldn't go out anyway because the snow was just too much. How are you my love, Tobi, I miss you very much. How did you spend Christmas and New year. Did you attend Biodun's engagement. Please send me some pictures, the ones I took with me have expired. I'm still trying to settle down, but I got a job with McDonalds already. It's very tiring, I'm on my feet most of the time. There are so many lovely things I wish I could buy for you, but don't worry my baby, once I get on my feet. I'm staying with Benji, and he says I have to get my own place as soon as possible. His wife is nice, but he says I shouldn't be fooled that it won't last for long. We live in a city called Peckham and it's just like living in Festac Town, Nigerians everywhere and lots of multi storey buildings. With this cold, the temptation to drink is high, but I haven't done so, I'm trying to make do with coffee. Baby, I need to be able to speak with you on the phone. Please, maybe you can stay at Maggie's house on Sundays. You know I'm not very good at writing. This took me the whole day. But for your love, I would do anything, that's Stevie Wonder. I can't ever stop singing for you in my heart.

How else can I say I love you? I love you, Ma Cherie, je t'aime. Ich liebe dich. I asked my French and German friends at work. Please keep your heart for me. I'm keeping mine. I miss you so much.
Yours forever
Richard.

I hug the letter as if my life depends on it. It has been two months since Richard left and it has been two months of agonizing loneliness and wondering what was happening to him. The week before he left had been especially full of activities. I had felt very happy getting engaged to him, especially the way he had proposed – completely swept me off my feet. That's what Richard does to me; always sweeping me off my feet. That night, I couldn't be bothered to spend the night with Maggie anymore. Spending the night with him seemed like the right thing to do, besides it was what I wanted; to spend my soul and my body with him.

Things we do for love. I used to wonder why girls go to live with a guy when they weren't married, until I practically moved in with Richard for that one week till he travelled. I wished I could tell my mother about the engagement, but I knew she wasn't ready to admit that I was old enough to be dating at all, not to talk of getting engaged. When I told Lami, he was happy for me and advised that I couldn't afford to mess around with other guys now that I was engaged. As if any other guy could compare with Richard.

But getting engaged is not just about feeling good, it comes with some responsibilities. I had to help Richard dispose of most of his belongings because he had to work till the last day he left. He had some debts to settle and even after selling his car, he had not raised enough money for his trip, so I had to empty my savings account and also borrow some money from Maggie to add up to buy his ticket and some spare change. When he expressed concerns about not being responsible enough for Faith, I volunteered to get some clothes and provisions for her also. At the airport, it had been difficult to let go; I cried and he cried as we hugged and held on to each other, until eventually Segun prised him from me and he was gone, promising to get in touch as soon as possible. Thank God I had the ring for comfort. And when we attended Biodun's engagement ceremony, I flaunted my ring, teasing her that she was my junior, after all, I got engaged before her, even if it wasn't an elaborate ceremony.

Love of my life

Every time I look in the mirror, I see your face smiling at me. But I wish you were here with me physically. I miss you so much it hurts. You didn't tell me it would hurt this much otherwise I wouldn't have let you go. I am trying to be romantic here, although I mean every word that I've written. I miss you to my bones. How is your job, your brother, and every other thing around you? I hope to meet Benji one day and I hope that day is soon. A lot of my friends envy my ring. All thanks to you, you make me proud. You know sometimes I wish we could have eloped to get married. But I guess you wouldn't want to offend your future parents in law. My father would have killed you anyway. Mummy and I travelled to Ibadan last week and it was around your Daddy's house, and I was wondering what she would have said if I told her about you then. I hope she doesn't wake up one day to find out I've disappeared to London.

Maggie and Chuks are making progress, Chuks is sure his mother would back off very soon. I keep wishing them luck.

What have you done about school? Are you starting anything soon? Biodun's engagement was fine, come and see display of money. That her boyfriend's family is very rich I couldn't believe it. And she was very happy. She's moving out to start living with him and she has introduced Jemima to take up her room. So we are going to be three in the flat again.

Second semester exams start next month and I've switched to serious mode. I will do you proud definitely, I owe you that my love.
I love you once, twice and forever.
Tobi.

The week of valentine, I got three different cards and I was wondering if Richard contracted them to someone locally for delivery, but the stamps on the envelopes showed they were all posted from London.

In this card .....
I've enclosed my heart
Knowing it's safe with you
Happy Valentine's Day

We keep exchanging letters. With each letter I receive, my spirit soars and sometimes I would wish he was beside me, just talking to me and squeezing my hands.

Tobi Light of my life,

Since you are the light of my life, it means the world is very dark around me. I wish you were here right now to brighten me up. Not that I am depressed or anything like that, but that is my way of telling you how much I miss you. When are your exams starting? I wish I could be there to give you moral support although I trust you will give it your best. You are one of the most intelligent persons I've ever met. And I know you'll keep on doing us proud. How are your parents. Is Lami still rocking Port Harcourt. Poor guy, I hope he finds someone like you soon and settle down.

Richard

*

And despite the fact that Richard wasn't around anymore, all my friends knew I was engaged, except my parents of course.

"Oluwatobiloba." I quickly rush to answer my mother. Anytime she calls me by my full name, it's often a sign that I've done something wrong or right, rarely. "Monday, just brought the letters, this is for you." She gives me a letter. It's from Richard and I smile in relief, thankful that he didn't miss this week. "So, when do you intend to tell me about him?" She cuts into my thoughts.

"Who?" I ask nervously.

"The boy that sent you that letter in your hand."

"There's nothing to tell, Mummy, he's my friend." I suddenly become shy and uncomfortable. I knew this day would come, but how do I begin to discuss Richard with Mummy?

"Amaaaaanda!" She drawls my middle name from a low to a high pitch. "He's my friend." She mimics mockingly. "Do I look like a fool?" I shake my head, not daring to raise my eyes to meet hers. How does she expect me to answer this? "I'm your mother. Don't you think I should know about your affairs? This boy has been sending you letters from London for a while now, and he's just your friend. Humm, thank God I can read?"

"I'm sorry Mummy, I don't know what to tell you."

"Just tell me everything. Do you like him, does he want to marry you, where's he from? He must be really serious for him to be this persistent. I pick his mails every week. And I'm sure he's the one that has been sending all those clothes you've been flaunting up and down. Or do you have a sugar daddy now?"

"Why would you even think that, Mummy?"

"What do you want me to think since you won't tell me anything, or you think I am blind? For your information, there's no antic you can play that I won't catch up with you." I'm not really sure if she is cross or teasing, so I say nothing, although I can't help remembering this is the same way she brags that she would know if I tell a lie, I keep the mocking smile to myself recounting how many lies I've told that she has fallen for. "Is he a Christian, who are his parents, what's he doing in London?"

Does she really want to know? I'm not sure. Why is it this difficult to predict her? And sincerely I don't know what part of Richard's pedigree would impress her, except that he's a Christian. I need to exercise some caution here and be sure she's really ready to know. What if I tell her and she tells Daddy. They may decide that I should start going to school from home. But how long will this last, how long will they keep treating me like a child? I can imagine what Daddy would say. "Because you're in university now, you think you can be doing whatever you like; no, not under my roof." I recall a lecturer's advice one morning when he was teaching communication in the ethics class, 'minimize information so you can manage expectations; reveal only what is obligatory per time and save the best for the last and only when it is absolutely necessary.'

So I tell Mummy about Richard. He works as a sales person in McDonalds and he is trying to go back to school, his mother is dead, but his father lives in Ibadan, and I think he likes me because he asked me to marry him before he travelled.

Her ears must be twitching. She goes to switch off the TV and comes back to sit. "He asked you to marry him, so what did you tell him?" She asks suspiciously.

I shrug. "Nothing."

"He asked you to marry him and you said nothing, and he keeps sending you letters and gifts, is he Father Christmas?"

I start fiddling with the belt of my dress. Thank God I don't wear my ring at home, otherwise this conversation would be heading in another direction. This woman, my mother is highly erratic and I'm not sure which answer would be appropriate now. I remain quiet.

"Tobi, sit down." She gestures. Ah, this is getting worse. Anytime she says sit down, it's a prelude to a lesson in moral instruction or historical fable. "At what point did you intend to let me know all these, when did you meet him?"

"Last year." I reply. That came out without thinking, not that I intended to lie.

"Last year? You've been consorting with a man since last year? So what are your plans?"

Let me play the good daughter. "My plan is to finish school and start working before I start thinking of settling down. It's not like I want to marry tomorrow." That is the perfect answer; that is what she and Daddy always preach. Please don't ask me about sex, I pray silently, recalling that she had once boasted that she could tell a girl who had lost her virginity when she sees one. When I first had sex with Richard, I was afraid she would know and didn't come home for two weeks, hoping that I would be rid of the smell of a non-virgin. I keep wondering if she knows truly, but she has never brought it up.

"Hmm." She inhales. "I agree that's the best thing for you

and I hope you stay focused. You're a very smart girl and I'm sure you know we want the best for you. Men would only distract you from your studies." I nod, she shakes her head thoughtfully. "And if you come up with any surprises, you know your father would kick us both out." I nod again. Who is she fooling? Maybe Daddy can kick me out, but certainly he can't survive a week without her.

Richie boy,

I hope the weather is better now, since you are close to summer. You know this spring or autumn weather is still very confusing to me. So are you in spring or autumn now? I hope one day I will be able to tell the difference. How are you doing? And your brother, have you tried to reconcile with him since you moved out? Don't forget he is your blood, but he also needs to stand by his wife? Would you believe Bibi was actually nice to me when I went to drop those toys for Faith? I guess it's because she was trying to collect your address anyway. But she's looking better. She said she's gone back to re-write her GCE as I advised. I'm happy for her. Faith is bigger now and with chubby cheeks. I told mummy about you finally. She was asking me if I had a sugar daddy because she saw some of the stuff you sent. And then she advised me to face my studies and not get distracted. Can you believe that? I hope we won't be like that with our children? I want our children to be close to us and be able to tell us anything. At least you have a little bit of that with your own father. Have you written to tell him about your new place? Lami is still in Port-Harcourt so I'm usually home alone.

It's raining cats and dogs here, and would be like that until the August break and you know the annoying thing, people keep playing that Majek Fashek's song 'Send down the rain.' My first semester result was perfect. Even I was surprised but I think it's because of the practical exposure to real life cases now.

So, what have you been up to? I miss you stupidly. There's no one to nag or fight with and no one to sing to me. I miss that a lot. Sometimes I wish I could find a song for how I feel, but that's your area. The best thing I can do is Shakespeare or Milton. Is there a song that says I miss you? I know the one that says 'I love you, you, you, no one else will ever do'. Don't ask me who sang it. But I really do love you. Oh, and there's that one that says, 'Nothing compares to you.' I'm not doing badly, am I? I hope you like these pictures? I went to the studio just for you. Maybe I can get Bibi to also send Faith's pictures now that she's my friend, hahaha. Are you smiling?

Take care of yourself my sugar pie.

Your baby,

One and only Tobi

*

Once we were able to agree on Richard calling Maggie's house to speak with me, his letters became fewer but not the cards and gifts and money. Sometimes, he would send things to Maggie too. I also discovered a place I could make international calls cheaply somewhere close to Vintage Lodge. Hence, there was hardly any need to write and besides he didn't like writing, but we kept exchanging cards which conveyed more feelings than we could ever have written or verbalised. Whoever invented those Hallmark cards is God-sent. Sometimes, it seemed like we were competing on who could send the most creative and romantic card. I must say it's difficult to beat Richard at that. And once in a while, just out of the blues, he would write a letter.

Barrister Tobi Aro,

You should be getting used to that title by now. And I would walk proudly behind you and say, that's my wife. I'm so proud of you. I wish I could just summon the courage and go back to school. But, there's really no push here because you don't need to be a graduate to make it big in London, once you get a good job, and you are good at your job, you can rise to whatever level you want. I think one graduate is enough for our family anyway. You will be shocked that all those people called managers here are not graduates. It's getting cold again and people are going on holiday, so I can get an extra job. I hope you like the clothes? I bought them from Camden Market. It's just like our market back home, you can haggle and get a good bargain. Remember Boy George that sang Ain't nobody's business how I live my life' I learnt he got some of his identity from there. It's a bubbly place. I think that is where people learn body piercing and tattoo from. Have they started tattooing in Lagos, some of them look horrible. Please let me know what you need for Christmas. There's usually a lot of sales around that time. Everything is going on fine. The only problem is just about my immigration status. I need to do something more permanent. Benji said he would arrange it, but it would cost a lot of money, so I may be hard up a little. People get deported everyday Tobi, its not even funny. That is not an option for me at all. Please pray that everything works out fine. I started going to church now. It's amazing that churches are getting empty in London. Forget that they brought Christianity to us, the average Oyinbo would go and play ball on Sunday morning. Have you ever seen the picture of Aso Rock? I passed in front of the Prime minister's street yesterday and no one harassed me. I wish Nigeria would break away from military rule and people can be free to live their lives. Apart from that Britain has its own problems too. There's too much liberty for children you will wonder who is in control.

And the way they treat dogs and cats, even a human being does not command that respect in Nigeria. It's a wonderfulment, like Fela said.

You can see that I have tried by writing this long epistle. How are Maggie and Chuks? Who is Segun's girlfriend now? I miss that bunch you know. But I miss you most.

Your husband to be - That's my new title.

THIRTEEN

It's nineteen minutes after my four o'clock telephone appointment with Richard and he hasn't called. I continue to glimpse at the crystal clock adorning the wall in Maggie's middle floor living room intermittently, removing my gaze only to stare at the phone. I wish I could will that phone to ring now. My mind begins to wander as I continue to mindlessly flip through the Cosmo magazine in my hands while struggling to follow what Maggie is saying.

"Chuks said the company has offered to retain him."

"Hmm, what did you say?"

"I said Chuks' company has offered to retain him in their legal team." She tosses a ball of chocolate into her mouth.

"Oh, that would be nice." That means Chuks wouldn't need to start looking for work after his Youth Service. Lucky guy!

"You want some?" Maggie offers me the chocolate. I shake my head. "Better relax yourself girl. And if you've finished with that mag, you can have this." She extends a newspaper to me.

"It's about time you started reading important stuff."

I shake my head again and she shrugs. "You know, one of these days, I think we should swap places, so you know how it feels." I say sulkily.

Her face lights up. "I would gladly swap places with you Tobi Bolade. It can't be as bad as having a xenophobic mother-in-law."

"Ha, Margaret Abiola, that grammar is too much for one woman." I manage to laugh. Xenophobia is one of the big words our history lecturer introduced to us last week when we were discussing South Africa and I guess Maggie had been looking for an excuse to use the word. She's right though, I would rather be an across-the-ocean girlfriend than having to deal with Chuks' mother. "Maybe you should get pregnant too." I tease, referring to Richard's father's advice.

Maggie had eventually succeeded at deflowering Chuks in her room at Vintage Lodge one of those days every other person was out. The wile of it usually makes me laugh. Chuks' house curfew is ten o'clock, Maggie said at about eight o'clock she had locked the door and kept the key in her pant and started removing her clothes one after the other, until Chuks couldn't stand it anymore. If Maggie wanted something enough, no one could stand in her way. Except Chuks' mother, perhaps.

"Hey, you want to kill me." She startles, laughing. "That's when you'll know that my father is not a very nice person. Ha. And mummy will pretend she has never laid eyes on Chuks." She swallows more chocolate. "Anyway, as I was saying, Chuks said he would soon start looking for an apartment to rent. That way, I can have him all to myself." She boasts.

I continue flipping through the magazine now. "So the only reason you are…" My attention is drawn to a page. "Maggie, come, come." I beckon. "I think you should read this." She gets up and comes behind my settee, peeping. The page reads, 'Seduce Your Mother-in-law - Ten Ways to make your mother-in-law eat from your palms.'

"I think you have your head in the clouds, Tobi. Do you think the writer of that article knows the kind of prejudice troubling Chuks' mother?" She goes back to her seat. "What you should be reading is ten ways to retain your man. That's what I need right now."

The phone rings and I almost jump to grab the receiver, but Maggie picks it up since she's closer to it. "Hello." Pause. "Yes, how have you been?" Pause. "She's been expecting your call." Pause. "But she stepped out just now…"

I grab the phone from her, my body pulsating. "Hello, Richard, I'm here, she was only pulling your legs." I roll my eyes at Maggie. She goes to where I was seated before and starts reading, flipping through the magazine.

"Tobi, darling, I'm sorry I'm calling late. I worked late last night and I overslept. Are you okay?"

"Yes, I'm okay, I was just wondering if something happened to you." My insides start tingling; that is how I usually feel when I'm talking to Richard. "I miss you very much." Without any notice, he starts singing Lionel Richie's Hello. My sudden quiet and the pleasing smile on my face must have told Maggie something, as she gestures to me that she's going to her room and leaves. "…*I love you.*" He rounds off.

"I love you too Richard and I miss you. So, what's been happening to you?"

"I'm good, very good. I got promoted and I just got my own car, it's with the mechanics now, but I will send you the pictures when it's fixed. I wish you were here. What are you wearing?"

I quickly look at what I'm wearing. I had quite forgotten that. "I'm wearing a purple dress, yes. Remember, it's one of the dresses you sent the last time, the one that has chains. And I've done million braids." I run my hands through my long silky braids. "Have you received the pictures I sent to you? Do you like the braids?"

"I love the braids, I only wish you were here so I can admire it and touch it life. Can I tell you something, are you there alone?"

I nod only to remember he can't see me. "Yes, I'm here alone. Maggie has gone to her room."

"Tobi, I feel like making love to you right now. I've missed you so much, you can't begin to imagine how much."

I can tell I'm blushing inside out. I like it when Richard talks to me like this, it makes me feel beautiful all over. "I feel like that too Richard."

"Maybe you should start thinking of getting a visa, so you can come for a visit. If I could leave, I would have come just to hold your curvy body in my hands and kiss you silly, but I can't come until the immigration issue is sorted out, otherwise, getting a visa to return to UK would be difficult. Why don't you talk to your folks and see if they would allow you come after your exams. Just try, for my sake, please."

"Okay, I'll try." I promise, not quite sure how I can swing that. "Guess what, Biodun is getting married in December."

"Oh, that's cool. To the same guy I suppose."

"Of course, remember she got engaged." And then I remember we had actually gotten engaged before Biodun.

"Yes, yes." And as if reading my mind, Richard assures me. "Don't' worry, once I legalise my status, I'm coming to whisk you away, whether your daddy likes it or not."

"What about school?" I ask.

"You will finish your school one way or the other, Barrister." I can hear the humour in his voice.

"Whatever you say sir."

"I've sent you some things for Easter and for Faith too, I hope you don't mind."

"Of course I don't mind. I'll take them to Bibi once I get them."

"Thanks my baby. You don't know how much I appreciate you for your selflessness."

I go flushing all over again. "Please don't make my head swell. I'll do anything for you."

"I will remind you about that one day." He teases. "Should I call you next week?"

"Oh no, I have a test on Saturday, let's make it the week after."

"Okay darling. Say hello to the whole clan for me. I love you."

"I love you too, and I miss you."

As the phone goes dead, I reluctantly drop the receiver and stay a minute to compose myself. It's never easy hanging up when I am talking to Richard. I go to Maggie's room and she sits up on the bed when I enter.

"Lover girl, I hope you are filled now" She teases. Lying on one side of the bed, she's still reading the magazine. I yawn, realising only now that I'm tired. I want to bury myself in her bed and relax, so I push her inwards and drop on the bed. "You know I've been thinking, maybe Chuks is not the right guy for me, I will do myself a favour by stopping this nonsense now."

"Is that what you've been reading in that mag?" I ask her. This is about the first time I will hear her express any real doubt about Chuks.

She shrugs. "No, it's just a feeling really. Come, let's go and see what big brother is up to downstairs." She says suddenly. This girl is impossible, one minute she's hot, another minute she's cold.

"Oooh Maggie." I sulk as she jumps out of the bed, pulling me. I follow her reluctantly.

"That can't ever be true." Segun screams. "I'm not in the least interested in the arts or any stuff like that." He is in the middle of a discussion with one of his friends. Apparently, the guy had said something Segun is reacting to.

"What untruth are you yelling about?" Maggie asks.

"This joker said I will get into music."

Maggie and I burst into a loud laugh as we take our seats. "No way man, if you had said that about me or Daddy, maybe I would agree. But Segun can't even compete with a frog, not to talk of becoming a big star?" Maggie chips in, shaking her head profusely.

"Why should you compare me with a frog, chicken legs, I thought your vocabulary was richer than that?" Segun yelps. Whistling, he picks his cup and goes behind the bookshelf for a refill of brandy.

"Call me whatever you like, it won't change the fact that

you can't sing." Maggie insists.

The joker - Tai Coker is Segun's friend, mixed race Jamaican/Nigerian twin who claims he can now read palms. He returned from Jamaica after a two-week break and said he learnt palm reading from his grandmother over there. After examining Segun's right palm, he had surmised that he would get into music. Becoming a big star is Maggie's interpretation of getting into music. Segun works in their father's law practice, and besides, as Maggie said, when Segun sings, we all wonder if he had just had a quarrel with someone. It's either Tai knows next to nothing about him or he's just trying to clown. If palm reading took only two weeks to study, then everyone in Jamaica should be a palm reader.

"That's what I see and I can tell you it's definitely going to happen." Tai insists. He sips some water from his glass.

I pat Segun teasingly. "Maybe that is where your midlife crisis would lead."

We all laugh, except Tai. Segun shrugs and shakes his head, unconvinced, but stretches his palm to Tai, again. I wonder why, after the first gaffe. Tai begins to trace his palm lines and goes into a quiet incomprehensive chant under his breath.

"Something is going to break your heart before this year comes to an end." Segun smiles and tries to pull his palm away. We all know that is impossible, Segun is the serial heart-breaker and he doesn't have his heart with anyone. Although, he has been going steady with one girl for about three months, we know it won't last and we know that the girl won't be the one to call it off. But Tai holds on to the palm and goes on. "Something drastic is going to happen to you that would change the course of your life forever."

"Can you tell me something more specific, so I can come and kick you if it doesn't happen?" Segun says with an askance posture. Tai should have known better than going near Segun's love life. He seizes Segun' palm again and pronounces. "You are moving away."

I can't say if Segun is amused or angry, but he bursts out laughing anyway and we all join in.

"Although that would be good riddance." Maggie teases. "I can't say I will miss you."

"If you believe that, you will believe anything, Maggie. Are you that gullible?" Segun responds.

"I hope you don't intend to make a living out of this?" I inquire. "Because, I'm sorry, I don't see you going too far."

"Tai is a doctor, Tobi." Segun reassures me. "Maybe, fortune telling would help his practice in treating heartaches."

"Do you want me to read your palm too?" He asks, looking my direction. Did someone ask him to make us guinea pigs? With all the mocking comments, he's still bent on making a fool of himself.

"No." I shake my head. "Not going by Segun's reading, count me out."

"Why not, it won't do you any harm. Just for the fun of it." Maggie says. "Okay, my turn now." She stretches her hand to Tai.

"No, your left palm." Tai says.

"Why?"

"Because your left hand is where all your life experiences are recorded." Tai explains.

Maggie's eyes widen in amazement. "But you read Segun's right palm."

Tai nods. "It's different for men and women." He must be taking himself seriously.

"Okay." She says, giving him the left hand.

"You have a relationship with a good man, but that relationship is threatened and you're confused about going ahead. The man is yours."

Maggie and I exchange glances as she nods her head along with Tai, who is encouraged and goes on talking. "You will make better grades in school this session." Well, he may be right on that also, because the first semester result was actually better than we had expected, even though we couldn't attribute it to any extra effort on our parts. "You are going to get a gift you didn't bargain for." Is that not why it's called a gift, silly? Maggie nods and smiles at that, who wouldn't want an extraordinary gift? She pulls away her palm, maybe afraid that Tai may see something that would contradict what he had previously said. She thanks him and unconsciously wriggles into an unintended dance.

"How come you have all the good stuff for Maggie?" Segun asks.

"Because I'm special, dude." She responds, definitely in high spirits. "But being a musician is not entirely a bad idea, maybe I can meet Sunny Ade through you when you start. I might consider trading places with you on that one." She nods at me. "Tobi, your turn."

I shake my head, although I know there's no how I'm going to escape this since Maggie has already done hers. Segun grabs my hand and places it in Tai's. I shut my eyes. Why does the touch of his fingers feel cold? He begins to trace the lines on my palm, pressing in. "You are very lonely now." He is right about that, maybe there is some truth in his reading. "You will meet your husband this year." I'm not in the market, dummy. Why did I stop wearing that engagement ring? Tai is definitely a farce or a joke, whichever one is appropriate. I just finished speaking to my husband. Duh!

FOURTEEN

"No, Maggi, you can't wear that to a wedding, what's wrong with you?" I got into Maggie's room only to find her dressed in a black sequined mini dress which clings to her body like a body suit.

"I'm tired, I can't find something cute to wear and you know I can't afford to get lost in the crowd." She says in exasperation.

"Yes, this would definitely make you stand out like a sore thumb." It's Christmas Eve and Biodun's wedding. Maggie has been raving on as if it's her event. The dress she brought out was fit for nothing but a night club. Biodun had told us to dress classy, so I can understand Maggie's frustration. The wedding reception is going to hold at Sheraton Hotels, exclusive for only forty guests. We were lucky to be on that list, but not Chuks, thank God, because it means I could have Maggie to chat with. I dig into Maggie's wardrobe and bring out a purple satin dress suit. It's the one Richard asked me to give her the last time he sent me a suitcase of clothes. The suit has some shimmering effects, at least to make up for the sequins she would miss in the black dress.

"Here, if you wear this to church, you can remove the jacket right after the service, for the reception since you always have to show off your shoulders."

"Well, you have to look for the shoes to match this then." She accepts the suit grudgingly. "This is so formal, why can't I just wear a dress without a jacket like yours?"

I am wearing a burnt orange flared dress I had intended to wear on Christmas day. "Maggie, remember you always forget to buy dresses that have sleeves. And this purple is just beautiful, with the gold sandals. Please dress like a lady to church." I add. "Let me check if Jemima is ready."

"This is the exact same sandals I wore to her engagement." She shouts after me. Only Maggie keeps record of what she wore to where, so she can avoid repeats. She says it would make people think she doesn't have enough clothes or shoes and I would tell her (like my father would), that people who even notice such must be jobless and shallow-minded. Jemima is the one that took over Biodun's room. She had been devastated when Biodun told her she already had a Chief Bride's Maid and we should all simply come as guests.

Jemima had thought she could attract the Best Man. She had been very active at the engagement and she had hinted us that she was hoping one of the groom's friends would make a pass at her. Unfortunately, none of the pompous looking breed even did as much as say hello to any one of us, maybe because they all wore dark sunglasses and couldn't see us. I must say they were a handsome bunch, richly dressed in white kaftan *Aso-ebi*, black leather sandals, black wrist watches and black scarves tied around their necks. Maggie whispered to me that she was sure they were wearing black or white underpants too, since they all wore *Aso-ebis*. I had thought it was only girls that were allowed such level of vanity. Lanre, Biodun's groom comes from a lineage of rich high-society family and apparently, his friends also. Birds of the same feather, they say flock together. Why Jemima thought anyone of these guys would notice her beats me; but on second thought, if Biodun could get away with Lanre, why not Jemima?

"You look very gorgeous." I tell her. She is wearing a mint green A-line dress and it suits her very much.

"Thank you." She says. "I hope Maggie is ready, she's the one that spends all day doing make-up."

"I got her to do her make-up since yesterday, so we won't be late."

Jemima smiles and glances at the clock. "The guy should be here within the next ten minutes. Biodun says he keeps to time and we shouldn't keep him waiting."

Biodun had arranged for one of the groom's friends to pick us up. Maybe there was hope for Jemima after all.

The ride to the church was one of the most boring and slowest I've ever had in my entire life, taking a bus might have gotten us there faster and more interestingly; at least on buses, you meet clowns who hawk drugs that cure every ailment. After the exchange of hellos, our chauffeur kept to himself, apparently preferring the music from the radio to anything we might have to say. He didn't even tell us his name. I pity Jemima as she must have felt so dreadfully uncomfortable sitting beside him. I have never seen a more careful driver as he crawls along on the road, slowing down at every bump and waiting for cars to pass across him at every intersection, even when he had the right of way.

"Are we ever going to make the church service?" Maggie whispers to me. I shake my head in total disbelief and before I knew it, Maggie dozes off. I follow suit. That bad! The only consolation is that we arrived in style; in the latest three series BMW, black.

"So we meet again, my name is Obaniyi, but people call me Oba." He offers his hand for a handshake.

Hmmm, Obaniyi, no wonder he was feeling kingly cool. "So you have a name." I retort, ignoring the outstretched hand. I had the misfortune of being seated next to our mute chauffer. "I thought you lost your voice in the car, where did you find it?" I wish I could be more caustic, what right does he have to think he could switch on and off with people as he wished?

He looks taken aback. "I'm sorry. I didn't know you ladies would want to talk, I didn't want to intrude and I didn't know what to say to you since I only met you."

Intrude? Is that not what men always do? "Excuse me, you picked us up and ignored us as if we were mere articles in your car, and you say you didn't know what to say. You could have turned off the radio for starters."

"But you didn't ask me to turn off the radio. I would have done that if you had requested."

This guy must be a joker. "Did you ever read James Hardly Chase?" I ask. He shakes his head, no. No wonder! "He wrote 'Joker in the Park' and you remind me of that. So we come into your car and ask you to turn off your radio. Then you can label us rude girls."

"Okay, I said I'm sorry. Sincerely, I'm a rather quiet person and since none of your talked to me, I thought you didn't want to talk, so I let the music play. Truly I didn't feel I could engage three beautiful ladies in a long discussion."

For the first time, I decide to deliberately look at this joker. He looks painstakingly together, dressed in a navy blue suit and sky blue shirt, with matching sky and navy blue flowery tie, and a neatly polished pair of black brogues. If truth be told, he's not a bad looking guy – baby-faced, a beautiful set of teeth with a tiny gap, clean shaven with a bit of Afro hair. Disappointingly, debonair is the word that comes to my mind. He seems to be serious about being sorry and he has just a hint of smile on. What kind of guy is quiet these days?

"I hope I'm forgiven." He pauses. "You haven't told me your name."

"Tobi."

"Lovely name."

"Thank you." I scan around the room to look for Jemima and Maggie. I wish Jemima was sitting beside him, not me, but it seems she's having a better time than me, sitting between two pretty looking gentlemen and chatting away. She's laughing now, and patting the guy on her right side. Already? Maggie is seated close to the couples' table, beside the Chief Bride's Maid. They are already talking too. She is showing Maggie something on the wedding programme.

"Lanre and I go way back to secondary school and university days. We used to be best of pals then, still is though, only that we are both busy and don't get to see each other often. You know, Lagos life and all that, and he travels a lot too. When I got the invitation for the engagement, I thought it was a joke until I got there that day. They make a very perfect match, don't they?"

If he's referring to the newly married couple, he's definitely right, but I shrug and give him a second look. "I thought you said you were quiet."

He goes quiet for about two minutes. I can't be bothered. "Yes, I was just trying to make conversation to make up for my previous error." We both go quiet. "Can I tell you the truth?" He asks after some time. Thank goodness he found his voice again. The silence was beginning to get awkward for me and I was just thinking about how to redeem the conversation. What could he have lied about in this brief period? I nod.

He goes on, "You know, when I saw you at the engagement, I thought you were really beautiful and elegant. You stood out amongst your friends, but I couldn't talk to you because you were always in that cluster and when I asked Biodun afterwards, she said you were engaged."

Biodun's engagement was exactly a year ago. "I would have said I'm flattered, except that I'm sure it wasn't me you noticed?" I'm pleasantly surprised. This is a colossal loss for Jemima who had spent so much time dressing up to attract attention. Sometimes, you just never know what men are looking for.

He nods. "You wore a cream flowery dress with peach belt and shoes and your braids were longer than this one." This guy is incredible, even I have forgotten what I wore. He goes on. "Then two weeks ago Biodun called to assign me to bring you here. I was happy and really looking forward to seeing you. But I got to your place and there were three of you and then you took the back seat."

This is getting really interesting. "So did you ask Biodun to seat me next to you now or what?" I ask.

He shakes his head. "I think sometimes, providence plays a role in the things that happen to us. You can't imagine how happy I was when I saw you take that seat. And you still have that grace of elegance about you even when you are pretending to be annoyed."

"I am not pretending, I thought you were just arrogant. Thank you for setting the record straight, and I would like to set the record straight too. One; you are not quiet, you've done most of the talking since, two; Biodun told you the truth, I'm engaged and not available, even though you haven't made a proposal. Three; can we not talk about me? Thank you."

He nods and goes quiet again. I bet he wasn't expecting that. But what could he have been expecting; that I embrace him and tell him how cool he looks and thank him for being attracted to me? Men! The MC is making a toast to the couple and he reminds us that it's Biodun's birthday, so we sing the usual happy birthday song. After which he asks us to move around and clink glasses. I clink with Oba and move away to other tables.

"How did you get that guy to talk Tobi?" Maggie asks me when I reached her.

"So, you noticed. He says he likes me."

"Tobi baby, that's a catch." Maggie hails.

"A stupid catch, I'm not in the market."

"Yeah, I know, what a waste."

"You can have him." I tease, and head back to my seat. Maggie frowns at me, no messing around. Oba is already seated when I got back.

"You don't mix much do you?" I ask him. I want to avoid another round of awkward silence.

"I like minding my own business. If that's what you mean by not mixing much, you are probably right."

"That's interesting, and what's your business?"

"My business, as in what I do?" Can't this guy even take a joke, why should I be interested in what he does? But I nod out of being polite, so the conversation can go on. "I'm a stockbroker. I just started my firm two years ago."

"Oh, that is one business I don't understand." My father's explanation of investing in stock had never been embraced by anyone in my family. How can I put down my money in exchange for just a piece of paper? And then he said the prices fluctuate and sometimes people get unlucky and lose good money.

Oba's face lights up and he goes on. "I read actuarial science in school, but my first job was with a stock broking firm, so I thought rather than just calculating risks, let me take the risks and make more money. I worked with them for a few years before venturing out on my own. Stockbroking is a risk management business, where you are entrusted with people's money and you try your possible best to ensure that the money is well invested with the right company to give good returns. We invest in stocks and some other financial instruments on behalf of individuals and companies. We buy and sell on a platform called the stock exchange. You know the Nigerian Stock Exchange?" I nod, why did I ask about his business?

"That is where we conduct our trade. You can come around and see our trading session one day, I can arrange it.

We make money by making money for other people. That's as simple as I can put it. What about you, what would you like to do? Biodun told me you were reading law."

"I want to specialize in commercial law, so maybe you can retain my services when I'm through."

He smiles, "That would be really nice."

The background music stops playing. "All the single ladies in the house please march forward." The MC makes a call for the bouquet throwing. As usual, ladies are reluctant to come out. Oba nudges me to go, but I shake my head. As far as I am concerned, this bouquet exercise is designed for guys to fish on available girls at weddings, whereas nobody deems it fit to ask guys to file out to be screened. But the Chief Bride's Maid pulls Maggie up, Jemima is on her feet, and then the ladies start trooping out.

Oba nudges me again. "Won't you go? It's just a sport."

I get on my feet to go to the aisle. I become somewhat self-conscious knowing that he's feasting his eyes on my body. There are about twelve of us ladies and I am one of the tallest, so I stay at the back, right beside Jemima who is almost as tall as me. Biodun, beaming with smiles, turns her back to us and the MC counts, one, two, throw. There is a little bit of struggle, especially between the Chief Bride's Maid and Jemima, but Jemima triumphs eventually and lifts the bouquet up for all to cheer her. Good for her. I hope that helps her attract a man of her dreams; maybe one of the men on both her sides.

"How do you girls cope with these high heels?" Oba asks. "I have two sisters and it's just the same with them."

"A girl's got to do what she's got to do. It's called gait bro." He shakes his head and smiles.

After the groom's vote of thanks, the dance floor is declared open. Oba looks at me and asks, "Do you dance?"

"Of course, I do. What kind of question is that, do you know anyone that doesn't dance?"

"I know a guy called Oba, who doesn't know how to dance, so he sits and watches others hoping that one day he would learn."

He must be more boring than I initially imagined. I keep that thought to myself and shake my head. "What a pity. We have to teach Oba some dance steps, come let me show you." I offer my hand.

He takes my hand but refuses to get up. "I will only trip over you, I'm serious. I'm so clumsy at dancing and that's putting it mildly."

How does a guy get to be successful in business and clumsy at dancing? I wonder. Now, I don't know if I should just sit with him or join the dance. I sit. Then he tells me it's okay to go and dance with my friends even though I can't remember asking for his permission. I remain seated as my legs become heavy in anticipation of Oba's screening stare. Jemima is dancing with that guy at her right side and Maggie beckons to me. I shake my head, I don't want to provide free entertainment for Oba.

"Can I ask you a question?" He nods. It had been on my mind since he got the car on the road after picking us up. I never knew I would have the opportunity to ask him. "Seriously, no offence meant. Did you just learn to drive?"

He shakes his head and laughs, for the first time. "There's no one that rides in my car that doesn't ask me that question and it always amuses me especially in view of the fact that I always drop them off safely. I was trained to calculate risks, Tobi. And if you remember that it only takes a millisecond for an accident to happen and that you can never accurately imagine the impact of one if it does happen, then you will pay that extra attention. Do you know what an accident is?" That sounds like, did I go to school, but he doesn't even wait for me to respond. "An accident is an undesirable event resulting in a negative outcome, often caused by an unintentional action. What that omits is that somebody somewhere had committed an act of omission or commission. So, my dear, I try to avoid accidents as much as is humanly possible." He must feel rather accomplished for that short lecture.

The ride back to school was better. Nothing to do with the speed, but at least there was conversation. Maggie and Jemima had decided I deserved the front seat and I got the singular privilege of introducing Oba to them officially. He would have relapsed into his tongue-tied self, but I was sensible enough to mention he was a stock broker. That changed the atmosphere immediately and he began to discuss the nature and intricacies of his business with us and how if we had been saving part of our pocket money from year one, we would have been quite rich by now, in our own rights. My conclusion; Oba has his own definition of quiet different from what we all know.

He comes out of his car as if he was coming inside with us, but he stays by the door instead. "Good night ladies. I hope you will be buying stocks in the nearest future."

"Good night." We all chorus.

"Thank you for the ride." Maggie says.

"I'm sure we'll see you soon." Jemima adds.

"Can I talk to you for a minute, Tobi?" He asks so quietly I think I may have been the only one that heard.

"Me? Oh, okay." Does this guy not know a red flag when he sees one?

"Do you mind if we sit in the car?" No response. "Please, it's a windy night and I don't want you exposing yourself to cold."

One of the problems of trying to be an enlightened courteous lady is that it's difficult to tell a guy off if he hasn't made a proper pass. One is expected to be friendly and unassuming until he properly asks before one can say 'No'. Otherwise, one could be labelled a snob because the guy could turn around and say, 'but I never intended asking you out'. So I sit in the sleek car.

"I just want to know if I can come over and see you some time."

Of course, that is where it usually starts from. "Oba, do you know this adage that says you shouldn't smell what you don't intend to eat? I'm engaged, I don't two-time and I don't keep male friends." I reply.

"But we can just hang out." He presses on.

"I don't hang out with guys." I open the door and pat his hand. "You seem like a good guy and there's one girl out there for you, that girl is not me. Good night."

FIFTEEN

Richie boy,

We are going to be rushing our first semester exams by this month. It seems Babaginda is serious after all, maybe the election would hold, but the school is not taking any chances. They want to end the whole session before June. So we'll be quite busy. I would find a way to call you in school, because definitely we would be having intensive classes and won't be going home at all. Biodun's wedding was yesterday and it was simply splendid. I wore that orange dress and I was happy with myself. First time I would be attending an exclusive wedding reception, and at Sheraton for that matter. Boy, there's a lot of money in this country. We made friends with a stock broker, and I think he's trying to toast me. Too bad for him. Something terrible happened to Segun, his girlfriend died in an accident along that notorious Warri/Patani Road. It shook him quite a bit; apparently he was in love with the girl. For the first time, can you imagine, Segun in love and then only to lose her to death; he's been inconsolable, he shocked us all. Perhaps you should give him a call. Every other person is fine. That incident has made Segun simmer down a lot. But Lami is another matter entirely, the last time he was telling me how a girl liked him so much she brought her friend for him too. Can you beat that? I think Daddy is improving, although he won't subscribe for Satellite TV, but he plays ludo with Mummy most evenings and every Sunday now.

Maggie says I should enter for the Balanced Girl competition in March once we resume for second semester. The criteria are cool, calm and collected. What do you think? I may become popular if I win, but I can handle that. And the prize is one week all-expense-paid trip to London, change of wardrobe and lots of cosmetics. So you know why I'm even considering it now. We won't be wearing swim suits, I bet you were scared people will see me almost naked. Not me! Maggie's only fear is that I may abscond with you when I get to London. And that's my fear too, but I know you won't let me. I have just one more year to go after this to become your Barrister Lady. I can always work my way around avoiding the national youth service. But I still have to come back for Law school. Anyway we'll see how it goes. How do you find your new job? And your friends. Maggie said you bought that big car because you've suffered so much and you are on the rebound. Please take things easy dear. The man who runs the phone kiosk here has packed up, that's why I haven't been able to call you.

Richie boy, I miss you pretty much. Now I know why they say absence makes the heart grow fonder. I really wish you were here. Are you making progress with your papers, at least you can come home once that is done. I miss you, really, really.

Please take care of yourself, won't you start going to church again. Please.

I love you.

Your baby girl.

Things we do in the name of love! How did I allow myself to be talked into this stupid competition bid? They said it was the first time a year three student would be competing in the history of all the campus pageants. And I guess it's likely to be the last time too. Definitely, the organising committee never thought people like us would be idle enough to participate, otherwise they would have made it an exception. By the time we submitted the form, it was too late for them to change the rules. I wonder why it hadn't occurred to us one year earlier. Maggie was ever so determined to ensure I win and she turned it into a big time project. She told her mother about it and sincerely I can't say who got more energised between mother and daughter. Maggie's mother took us to two famous designers to kit me for the competition, one at Ikeja and another one at Surulere. Knowing Maggie's mother, I wouldn't put it beyond her to throw a party if I really do win.

"No way are you going without winning." She had said. We were to appear in four sets of clothing; Casuals, Traditional, Evening and English formal. Except for the traditional attire, I had actually thought I had enough good clothes of my own; Richard had done wonders to my wardrobe, but Maggie only made fun of me, saying my clothes were good enough for a common girl, not a Balanced Girl. Her mother also got me an appointment with a top class hairdresser who was paid to be on standby throughout the show. Next, she took me to a modelling agency in Surulere to learn poise and cat-walking for one week.

When I mentioned to Mummy that we were considering sponsoring one of our friends for the competition, her response was expectedly negative. "Is that why her parents sent her to school? That's how she would get carried away and think she has achieved something. And you that you are sponsoring someone, don't you have work? You people had better face your studies." When will this woman leave the group that thinks school is all about books and nothing more? So how will I tell her about travelling to London if I do win the prize?

"We'll cross the bridge when we get there, let's just focus on winning." Maggie had said.

Biodun, who has changed her NYSC posting to Lagos because she just got married, followed Maggie and me to the designers' for fitting, and afterwards volunteered to send me three pairs of shoes that would complement the clothes. Talk about friends in high places. Would the other girls take the competition this seriously? Maggie had asked us to invite a lot of our friends for cheering support. She put Jemima and her squatting roommate in charge of that task. Our friends on campus promised to invite their friends, who promised to invite their friends. Are we not taking this too far?

"What if I don't win?" I ask. I was beginning to see the folly in entering the competition. Headline news, 'Year three student fumbles at pageant', 'Balanced Grandma not balanced at all', 'Year three student beaten by budding beauties', 'From grace to grass'. These are the likely captions the school gossip paper would feature for the next four episodes, and that is putting it mildly.

"And what if you do win? Anyhow it turns out, you would have had your fun and don't tell me you are not enjoying this buzz." Maggi replies.

Truthfully, I crave to win and I relish the attention being lavished on me, I'm just not sure I'm prepared enough and being the oldest of the participants is actually something that calls for concern. In order to create some level of curiosity, thankfully the names of the contestants are usually not published before the competition, otherwise I would have caved in under all the side remarks I might have evoked amongst friends and foes alike.

*

Backstage is a hub of activities. There are eight contestants and we had blind-picked numbers to take turns. I got number four; I know two of the other contestants who are in my faculty, of course junior. It appears I am the only one with a professional dresser; the others just have friends over who continue to refresh their makeup and fan the sweat off them. Do people suffer this much backstage at the real beauty pageants? It's steaming hot, thank God it's an all-night event, it would have been unbearable in the ever hot afternoon.

The outgoing Balanced Girl gives a short speech about how she had enjoyed her reign and hopes whoever wins this night represents the school even better than she did. She bows out amidst cheers. Then the competition starts.

The first feature is casual wear. We all cheer the first contestant to go upstage as she is heralded in by fast-paced music. She is wearing a black silky top on silver-studded ripped jeans, patterned bandana with matching jeans bag and sandals. After parading the stage, the MC asks the contestant for the title of the track being played and the name of the artist. A few of us exchange glances as we heard the loud boos and whistling from the crowd when she couldn't tell who the artist was. Yet she returns backstage, still wearing the forced smile on her face. Wow!

The same ritual is repeated for number two and number three. One thing should stand me out in this first round, I hope; I'm the only one not wearing jeans. Then it's my turn as I hear contestant number four. I catwalk in with my casuals – sleeveless cropped top, designed with patches of multi-coloured Ankara and discretely revealing a flesh of belly button, under a short black lacy jacket on white linen trousers matched with medium heel black sandals and a colourfully patched face cap worn backward.

It is now I know that talking about stage fright and actually going through one are two different things. I've never had to face a crowd of ten, and here I am facing a crowd of over a thousand, it's totally intimidating and frightening. I had underestimated this until I walked into that charged hall and that is when I fully appreciated the import of all the professional help Maggie's mother got for me. I calm my nerves, one deep breath, stomach in, chest out, head high and a permanent smile. The applause is reverberating, whistling, clapping and what else I don't know. I see mills of heads, but I can't make out anyone's face except Maggie and Jemima, and that would be partly because they are right in front, jumping and shouting ahead of themselves and others.

It's a moment I would never forget in my life. The music played for me is 'Trapped' released in nineteen eighty five by Colonel Abrams. Going out with Richard has to count for something.

"The second runner up is number three – Tosan Akpabio." She runs on stage, and stays there.

Reality check, so what if I don't win? It had seemed like an unfair competition in my favour really, but what if the judges are biased or something? Throughout the competition, all the girls had maintained the same hairstyle, except me and every time I walked on stage, I looked like an entirely different person.

On the final round, I was dressed in a green, clingy, sleeveless satin evening gown with a fishtail, beaded at the bust line and with lots of shimmer all over, my curly long hair was delicately draped over my shoulders, giving me the image of a beautiful mermaid. The same way he asked the other contestants, the MC asked me to recite a poem. It's amazing how my mind fails me on resources when I need it the most.

In spite of my mental reservoir of poems, the only one that came to mind without faltering is *Pussy Cat, Pussy Cat, Where have you been?* So when the MC asked me what I would do in London if I won, I said, I would like to visit the Queen's palace to see if I could indeed catch a mouse under her throne, the whole crowd went wild with laughter. I wasn't sure if that was a minus or plus, until someone started clapping and everyone in the auditorium caught the bug.

All of us remaining backstage look at one another shiftily, yet trying to avoid eye contact. Each girl must be praying to be the next one called. And that includes me. I would be glad even if I get the first runner up position.

"The first runner up is number seven – Bisi Noah." She manages to hug the girl standing next to her before running on stage and she stays there. Is there a pattern, the first two are odd numbers, mine is an even number, God! I am almost going breathless. And the winner of the Balanced Girl year nineteen ninety three is number four – Tobi Bolade.

For a moment, I am frozen until the girl beside me taps me gently and the other girls start clapping. I walk to the stage as graciously as possible. Now nothing can stop me from seeing Richard.

Congratulations, congratulations. It's all over; I am tired, very tired, but happy, extremely happy. The following evening, the flat starts buzzing with people. Unknown to me, Maggie and the others had organised a surprise party. What if I had lost? Some of the people I know, some I don't, some are from school, and some are friends of friends and the girls from the other three flats. Chuks had been with us since yesterday, Segun is also here, and Biodun with her husband, even Oba. I am so happy. I wish Richard and Lami were here. And Mummy too and maybe Daddy. I socialise with everyone in a haze. The competition is over, but my life is just taking a new beginning, on the way to London.

*

There's an adage that says, `when a road is too smooth, you need to be careful, because somewhere along the line, there would be a death trap'. Yes, I won the prize of an all-expense paid trip to London, but I couldn't get the visa to London. At the British Embassy, I was asked to submit my parents' statement of account, which of course could not be done. And that put paid my visit to London, to Richard and to the Queen. I was heart-broken to say the least. I had to content myself with going to Ghana with the first runner up. Maggi's Mummy bought her a ticket to follow me to Ghana and I told my parents we were going for an excursion. It's amazing what parents never get to know about their children, no matter how protective they are. This is one of those times I wish I was Maggie's blood sister. We would definitely be heading for London and not Ghana.

My Baby,

So sorry you couldn't get the visa. At least now you understand the pressure I'm going through here about the immigration stuff. Its getting tougher and I may have to do something drastic I don't know what. I am very proud of you, anyway. I showed the pictures to my friends and they were all asking me why I left such a beautiful girl in Nigeria. Balanced girl, I hope you enjoyed your stay in Ghana. Is Ghana really getting it better, because a lot of people brag here that they will soon overtake Nigeria. Please send the pictures. How are you managing your new found popularity, Miss cool, calm and collected. You must have a lot of guys flocking around you now. Hmmm, I'm getting jealous already, but I do trust you anyway. And remember that juju I placed on you is very potent. How are you getting ready for your final exams, my Barrister. We are getting close to summer and girls would soon start walking naked again. Sometimes I think they just like taunting us and the sun is an excuse. Men dey suffer o. I heard election has been slated for June 12. I hope Babaginda will get it right this time. Nigeria has a lot of potentials, but wasting away because of those people. I don't see how that country will change if that dictator doesn't leave. Tobi, you need to start considering coming to live here, and you have to promise to bring Faith with you. The difference is too much. Do you know everybody has a mobile phone here, and its such luxury for Nigerians according to your minister for communication. Its terrible.

I'm not in a very good mood today, there was theft at work and everybody pointed at me because I'm the only black. Thank God there was CCTV, that's the secret camera that records things life. I was exonerated after all. The manager apologised but its so sad. Anyway, that's what you get for living in oyinbo land. It's not their fault. I have to go. I love you dear, and I am so proud of you.

Richard.

But, despite all efforts by the academic office in school, the second semester exams couldn't hold before the election. Since Babaginda had cancelled several elections before then, everyone had thought this one was another bluff; hence little effort was made to meet the deadline. By the time the school realised that the election may indeed hold, it was already May and rather late. Lecturers complained they couldn't rush the syllabus. Even students protested to the academic office that the time was too short. So we went on in school as usual until one week to June twelve, when we got a break to resume one week after the presidential election. It was a break we all needed. The anticipation of whether or not our exams would hold had made everyone serious for that short period.

Richie Love

Mon Mari aimant, You have to get your French friends to decode this one for you.

The past few months have been quite hectic. The uncertainty about the election has been so much even the school got confused, that the exams had to be postponed. Other schools didn't hold their exams too and we've been put under so much stress to study. If only we can study like this without waiting for exams, then our grades would be better. But then, all work and no play would make Tobi a dull girl. I'm going home over the weekend, so we'll have to work out when you should call me at Maggie's house.

And by the way, Maggie's daddy bought her a 'Tokunbo' car after all, so we have our own ride now and we're gonna be painting the town red. Haha.

But the town can never be red enough without you, my dear. I miss you sorely. I'm not sure that English is correct, all I know is that I miss you very much.

Love, Tobi.

SIXTEEN

The events of the past months have brought a mixture of emotions and activities all over the land; anxiety, anticipation, excitement, jubilation and then disappointment, disillusionment, anger and then thirst for justice, protests and resistance. So many talks, gossips, fictions going round that no one knows what is true or false. They are not all new to Nigerians, except that this time around, it seemed to have reached a climax.

To everyone's surprise, the presidential election did hold, which means Babaginda was on his way out of office; finally, after eight years. Even I was happy, for the first time in my adult life, I witnessed and voted in an election that produced a president in my country without any form of violence. I was awed when I was told that Tofa congratulated Abiola after he was declared winner of the election. And we joked that Maggie may soon start introducing herself as the President's adopted daughter.

But all that was short-lived when different parties started

going to court to challenge the election results and before anyone got wiser, Babaginda had annulled the election two weeks later. Lots of people concluded that was his original game-plan; based on the antecedents of past elections, he never expected that this one would be successful and without any form of violence at that.

The feeling of despair and desperation and anger started gaining momentum until it culminated into a violent protest which left the country ungovernable. Even Babaginda's 'stepping aside' and appointing Shonekan as interim Head of State did little to stop the breakdown of law and order. Lagos in particular was very tense and people went out only when it was highly necessary.

Fuel was scarce, vehicular movement was controlled and most people had to walk from one district to the other to see friends and families, and to do petty trading which kept the economy moving somehow. Many events such as weddings were either postponed or happened without the anticipated fanfare, since only few would venture out for a social event. Schools remained closed and a lot of businesses were only able to run minimally. Parents tried to keep their children at home as much as possible in reaction to several reports of maiming and killing caused by the violent protests.

Neither Maggie nor I attempted to walk the length of my house to hers and vice versa, so I had to make do with writing letters to Richard, and even at that, delivery and dispatch of mails had slowed down greatly. That was how I spent over four months at home, instead of a two-week break from school.

Yet, every family had to find a semblance of normalcy

somehow.

"Tobi, how do we get to talk sense into your brother's head? There has to be something we can do."

"Mummy, I think Lami is old enough to decide who he wants to marry. He didn't ask you for help, so why are you stressing?" I reply. The political impasse means I spend most of my time with Mummy alone while Daddy continues to find his way to work.

My mother had been going on about getting a good wife for Lami since he moved to Port-Harcourt. I wonder if all parents are particular about whom their only son would marry. Maybe that is what Chuks' mother wanted to do also. Mummy's recipe was to appraise her friends' daughters and she settled for Sade Badmus. To be honest, Sade is very pretty, cool-headed and career-minded. She got her ICAN certification even before finishing her diploma at Yabatech. How she would agree to this matchmaking venture beats my imagination.

When Lami came home one of those rare times, Mummy took him to Sade's house and left him with her. He told Mummy they would give it a trial, but he told me Sade was too serious and he couldn't give her the kind of commitment she wanted right now. "She's the kind of girl that would say 'let's pray before we have sex,' she didn't even let me kiss her." How did Lami become so brazen? Apparently, Mummy had not noticed that he was in the wild-oats sowing stage. Of course, by the time he went back to Port-Harcourt, Sade was no longer on his radar.

"You know the problem with you children." She goes on. "You always think you know more than your parents. Lami is my son and I won't open my eyes and let him marry one girl that would make him turn his back on his family."

"Ah, is that your fear, Mummy? So it's not even about whether they love each other or not."

"What do you know about love?" She sneers. "You think it is only love that makes a good marriage. My dear, it is much more than that. That is why you need someone from a good home, who appreciates the meaning of commitment and responsibility, someone that would be with you through thick and thin. Like Sade, such a sweet homely girl."

I shake my head, no need arguing with Mummy. She's supposed to be on her way out anyway, what's she waiting for?

"I'm asking you what we can do to make him see reason. Haven't you been talking to him?"

"Lami is not looking for a wife now, he's just twenty four and you told him he shouldn't think about marriage until he is twenty eight, or have you forgotten?"

"Times are changing." She says reflectively. "Once a boy has finished school and starts working, he has to start thinking of settling down, otherwise he would become a chronic bachelor and I don't want that to happen to my son. If he was here, I would know how to direct him."

I muse. You woke up too late, mother, I think you've lost your son. "Mummy, you can't direct him forever." And suddenly, I feel like pulling her legs. "When are you going to start shopping for a husband for me?"

"You are still a small girl." She hisses. "You need to face your studies."

"I'm going to be twenty in November," I remind her.

Ignoring my question, she rolls her eyes and continues. "If

only your father would fix this phone, at least we would be able to talk to Lami as often as possible. I don't particularly like talking to him only once a year."

The mention of fixing the phone got my attention. "Mummy, why don't you pay for the thing?" Getting that phone fixed is one of the best things that could happen to my relationship with Richard. Going to Maggie's house to use the phone every Sunday had not been as easy as we thought, it's either I get there too late or too early, and this unexpected political curfew has done its best to try my resolve to keep communicating.

"I think I have to do that now, even though your father would tell me I'm just as corrupt as those technicians. I can't believe this house has been without a phone for six years." She pauses. "I have an idea." Her face lights up. "Maybe, I should take Sade with me and pay Lami a visit."

"Mummy!" I scream, that idea doesn't sound good at all. "That would be taking it too far."

"You wait and see, if it is love, he will come to love her. It's just because he hasn't taken time to know her."

"Well, I wish you luck." I leave for the room, hoping to continue with Othello, there is not pretty much one can do under the circumstances. That Sade had better go and look for her own husband. A few minutes later, Mummy calls out to me.

"Here, Monday brought this. It seems you are the only one getting letters in this house now." She hands me a letter from Richard. My face brightens up. I haven't received a card from him for over a month, no thanks to this clampdown. I hope Mummy fulfils her promise and gets the phone fixed.

There's a knock on the door, Mummy winks at me before opening the door to let in Sade's mother. No wonder she has been waiting.

"Good afternoon ma." I curtsy.

"My dear, how are you." Mrs Badmus responds to me and turns to Mummy. "My in-law, sorry I'm late, there was a little accident at the roundabout, even with few cars on the road, people can't organise themselves."

Are these people for real, when did they become in-laws? They both leave for where I know not.

"Bye bye ma." I shut the door after them and head straight to the room to consume the sweet words from my darling Richard.

Hello Tobi,

Definitely you should know by now that something is not right. I got married last month and my wife is not pleased that you have been writing me all those love letters. Because of you, we have relocated and I have changed my phones. Please, don't try to contact me again and move on with your life.

Richard.

No! It's not possible, this can't be Richard. Someone must be playing a prank. Richard would never do this. I bring out one of his old letters to look at the handwriting. It looks the same. No! My mind is in a crazy frenzy. But I still spoke with him; when? I can't even remember. Married to whom? Richard can't do this to me. Maybe there's a mistake. I look inside the envelope again, there's probably another letter. None! No postcard. How can this be? Did we quarrel? No. What went wrong, what did I do wrong? No, this can't be the end of three, no, almost four years just like that. I bring out the last letter he had written. Yes, he had told me how much he loved me and he even mentioned that we might get married sooner than later. That was just two months ago. Oh, my God, I need fresh air. My whole body is shaking. I walk out of the house, not knowing what to do, my mind goes blank.

"No, Richard won't do this to you, I'm so sure of that." Maggie reads the letter a third time. "Something must be wrong somewhere."

I had walked the length of over one hour from my house to Maggie's house. I just sit there as she continues pacing from one end of the room to the other, with the letter still in her hand.

"Tobi, I'm so sorry, this must be very hard for you." Only then did the tears start flowing as she takes my hand in hers. And she starts crying too.

*

What does it feel to be heart-broken? Hopelessness, sadness, despair, emptiness, pain? How do you describe pain when all you feel is numb? Maggie tried calling Richard, Lami tried and Segun tried, but there was no response. His phone had been disconnected. Segun promised to track him down. He said he felt responsible that he allowed me to trust Richard. But I know it wasn't anybody's fault. Whatever it is, Richard must have a reason for doing this. I know he would never deliberately hurt me. There was no use writing him since he said he had changed address. I was ready to beg, plead, cajole, cry and cling to him not to leave me, if only I knew how to reach him. People say a girl has to have some pride, that's a girl that has never been in love. Richard is the only guy I ever loved with all my heart, I knew no other love. I wanted no other love.

*

A month later, Segun calls the house. Mummy had fixed the phone as she promised. He says Richard had called him and pleaded with him to explain things to me. He was sorry for the pain he caused me, he was indeed married, but it was a marriage of convenience because he had to get married to be able to live in the UK legally. When the wife found out he had a girlfriend all along, she had forced him to write that letter in her presence, and she had continued to threaten to walk out on him if he was found playing any hanky-panky. Which means he would be deported, Segun says Richard said he still loved me and he hopes I find it in my heart to forgive him. But he didn't say he was coming back.

How do you forgive someone when you don't think he has offended you? I don't feel offended; just empty. I don't even have the strength to cry again.

SEVENTEEN

When you lose a loved one, it would seem like your life should stop; you cry, you grieve, you query, you rue, sometimes you blame yourself, you wish you had done or not done something, you hate yourself, you hate life, you withdraw from family and friends, and you lose control of almost every other thing that is important to you. I see Richard in everything I do. When I pick a dress or shoe to wear, he shows his face; when I pick a book to read, I see his writing; when I talk to Maggie, I remember I met him at her house; when I see a child, I see Faith reaching out to him; I see his face, his smile, his dimples; I see him dancing, humming, singing, I see him driving carelessly, I see him holding me and whispering to me that everything will be all right.

When you love someone as deeply as I love Richard, you would wonder if you could ever stop loving them simply because they were mean to you. People say when something stops growing, it dies; I don't think it's the same with love. Even when love stops growing because there's nothing to nurture it, it doesn't die; it just stays somewhere in a limbo. There's that place Richard occupies in my heart and I don't know if he would ever get dislodged.

You try to ignore the pathetic stares, the pitiful remarks, the shifty eyes and the sometimes derisive 'I knew it would happen' looks. You get shut out of conversations, because no one knows what to say that would get you offended. Then one day, you wake up and you realise that no one is bothering about you again; they moved on to something more alive. You realise that the world would not stand still for you and you begin to find reason to live again.

Gradually he begins to fade, but slowly. I look for little things that can make me smile, little gestures that stimulate response, and little acts that I can appreciate. I look for motivation to eat, to sleep, to read, to go out and to pick up the threads of normalcy.

*

"Let's go to the library. The case revision is for five." Maggi reminds me. Suddenly, it's December and three weeks to second semester exams. There's less tension in the country now since Abacha took over and brought the full force of a repressive military might with him. As the whole nation began to pick back the pieces of their lives, students had to go back to school and write their exams whether they were prepared or not.

"We still have thirty minutes, what's the rush?" I ask. I get up to start doing my make up anyway.

"We need to get a good position to sit. I don't want to be

standing and leaning on people's shoulders like the last time." She replies.

"You know I don't mind standing, so I can excuse myself easily. That library gets really choky and I'm sure they won't have repaired the AC. I don't want to die because I want to pass."

The library's air conditioners had been getting less effective in recent times. Maybe it was the air conditioner or the fact that more students were using the library, we couldn't tell for sure. The last time we were there, a girl almost fainted as there had been about twenty of us huddled around one table for the group discussion, and the air had been very stiff and tepid.

"We got a table by the window this time." Maggie insists.

"Same difference, just give me five minutes to pack my hair, you should have nudged me earlier."

It takes me twelve minutes to get myself together.

"Hey, I'm sorry I startled you."

"What, what are you doing here?" I almost scream. It's Oba and he almost fell in when I opened the door.

Maggie sees him and smiles. "Are you okay?"

"I'm okay, thanks. I'm so sorry, I was just going to knock. Really, really sorry."

"What are you doing here?" I ask again.

"Actually, I was in the neighbourhood and decided to drop by. Tobi, what happened to you, you've lost weight?" He looks really alarmed. Is it that bad?

"Oh, I'm okay, thank you for dropping by, we are ..."

"Please come in." Maggie cuts me short and she makes room for him to come into the common room.

"Maggie, we'll be late for the library." I give her that what-are-you-up-to look.

Oba doesn't bother to come in. "In that case, let me not keep you. Can I drop you in school then?"

"Actually, we had planned to walk. It's good exercise for us." I respond, getting restless.

"Did someone tell you you are fat, what are you exercising for, after losing so much weight? Is everything okay?" Now, he's really concerned. He looks at me as if examining me and then he looks at Maggie, expecting one of us to answer him.

"I'm okay, Maggie can drive us to school, but we just wanted the walk because sometimes its' faster and less stressful. And I'm okay really."

"Please come in for a while, at least let's give you something to drink, since you came to see us." Maggie cuts in again. He looks undecided but she pulls him in and leads him to a settee. "Please sit, Tobi, don't worry, I will have to stand this time. Oba, we baked a cake yesterday, let me get you some. And a coke?" She hurries into the kitchen, not waiting for him to answer.

"Are you sure you are okay. I'm sorry, but you don't look so good?" He asks me again.

"I'm okay, really. I just had some rough time these past months. But I'm okay. What about you?" I'm sure he would have heard about my being jilted from Biodun. Who is he fooling?

"I'm okay too. Business is good, thank God. When are you ladies coming to my office? I thought we would have started building your shares portfolio. When do you want to start?"

"Maybe, we'll start when we start working and making

money." Did he really think he convinced us?

Maggi comes in with the cake and coke and excuses herself again. "I'll be with you shortly." She says.

Oba nods and thanks her. Silence.

I thought this guy would have left my case. What kind of guy chases you for almost two years and keeps going? Even though the last time I saw him was at the Balanced Girl after-party, he had been to Vintage Lodge at least four times since then and he would usually drop his business card, scribbled 'Tobi, I was here. Take care.' Always the same line. He appears to be a nice guy, always looking smart and careful and he doesn't have to stress to impress anyone that he is successful. But boring all the same, an *Effiko*, even Chuks with all his gentility makes fun happen in his own way. What would I do with a guy like Oba? Nothing. And many others like him. Maggie has to be more creative with this matchmaking assignment she has saddled herself with.

After this, there's just one more session to go in school and based on my discussion with her, I think she holds her mother's belief - that if I can't get a potential husband in school, I will end up on the shelf - very sacred, so over our forced holiday, she'd been plotting how we would get me a husband when we got back to school. And since we resumed, she has tried to push me one way or the other, as long as it seemed a guy was there.

Just a week after we resumed, she talked me into taking a walk so she could say hello to one of her friends. I was surprised she had a friend I didn't know already, but I followed all the same, only for her to introduce me to a year four Physics student, who wasn't exactly unknown to me too. He had won the Mr Cool competition at the first ever school gala night we attended. Then he was in year two. Except for the library or amongst mutual friends, Science and Law students don't have any meeting platform.

I know it's not beyond Maggie to tell him I needed a boyfriend and perhaps, he also wanted a potential wife before leaving school, because I simply couldn't comprehend why he would be keen to start a relationship in his final year. He came to Vintage Lodge every day after our meeting until I told him I wasn't in the least keen on being his friend. He seemed like a nice guy too – tall, dark and handsome, and he didn't have dimples like Richard. But his name is Ade, same as Richard's middle name. How can I ever trust a guy whose name is Ade?

"Er." Oba clears his throat to speak after the spell of silence. "What are your plans for Christmas?"

I shrug. "There's a Law students' dinner two days before Christmas. And of course church on Christmas day, but after these exams, the only thing I want to do is relax, with myself."

"A lot of people were bored staying at home all this while. I'm surprised you still want to spend time with yourself."

"My name is Tobi Bolade and I'm different from those people." I say dryly.

"Yes, I know, I'm sorry, but can I take you out on Christmas day?" He asks.

How can you say no to a guy like Oba and not sound rude? I shake my head, slowly so it can register well with him. "Why would you want to do that? But no, thank you." Where is Maggie now? She had better come and finish what she started.

"Tobi, can I ask you a question?" I nod. "Could you just consider being my friend?"

That sounds like a harmless enough question, but somehow it seems I've heard that line before and it turned out not to be harmless after all.

"Oba I'm sorry, maybe things could have been different if we had met another time at another place. But to answer your question, I already told you I don't keep male friends." Maggie saunters in then and he rises to his feet.

"Are you leaving already?" She asks him.

"Yes, thanks for the cake." He says, even though he hadn't touched it a bit. He heads for the door and we follow him, but he stops just short of reaching the door, turning back to face us. "There's a beauty pageant at Eko Hotel in January, would you ladies want to go?"

Maggie doesn't bother to ask me before answering, excitedly. "Ha, yes, of course, we would like to go. Wouldn't we, Tobi?" She nudges me then and I manage to smile. Maggie is not about to give up soon.

*

"Can you see him Tobi, over there?" Maggie elbows me. "Just ahead of us, on your right. I don't want to point."

"Who?" I try to follow the direction to my right. I can't see anyone other than the waiters. "Are you talking about the waiters?" I ask her.

"No." She hisses. "Can't you see your boyfriend Rudimentary, that silly boy that played Romeo in school? He's sitting beside the waiters."

I look again. And right beside where the waiters are converged is Jibola indeed. "Yes, I can see him now. What's he doing here?"

"It should be the same thing you are doing here, dummy. What kind of question is that?" Maggie replies, eyeing me.

We are at the interschool Law Students' dinner at Durbar Hotel. For some administrative reasons, the dinner is starting late and people are milling around in small chatter groups. Maggie and I secured a free table for six so we could sit together before the hall fills to the brim. Even with the little time the organisers had to plan, I must say they've done a good job, rallying people to come.

I can never forget Rudimentary, my Romeo. The last time I saw him was at the school café after our GCE exams, that was some five or is it six years ago and we didn't know what happened to him after that. How time flies. Maggie and I nicknamed him Rudimentary, when, after the first kiss, he said I needed to learn the rudiments of kissing. He went on to appoint himself my teacher and started teaching me at every stolen opportunity. It had been continually electrifying until that incident with Maggie. What if…?

"Should I invite him over?" Maggie asks, interrupting my thoughts.

"Why do you want to do that?" I respond surprised, but she has already started waving frantically at him. It was a known fact that Maggie couldn't stand Jibola in school, why she would want to talk to him now beats me.

She shrugs. "We are here, he is here. We might as well catch up on old times." Because he is a little bit far from us, two other people wave back at Maggie, but she points them towards Jibola until she got his attention. He waves back, absentmindedly at first. Maggie keeps waving and nodding prompting him to look closer. He stares hard at us before opening his mouth wildly, and then he pushes his chair back and heads towards us, beaming all the way. Wearing a heavily starched white cotton shirt, he moves with his old pompous gait, hanging his arms and shoulders as if his body is about to take flight.

"Hello damsels." He quips. "Surprise, surprise." We both get up to greet him; Maggie extends her hand for a handshake which he grabs jovially. "Ha, today should be my lucky day, Maggie, how are you? No need to answer, you look good as usual. Girlfriend, I always imagined you'd be stunning in a black dress, you look ravishing." He hugs me from the waist, drawing me close to himself after shaking hands with Maggie. Oh yes, he hasn't changed at all.

"You look good yourself, what have you been up to?" I ask him, gently recoiling from his subtle grip.

Before he answers, Maggie interjects. "Would you like to sit with us or are you with someone, Tobi?" Maggie nudges me to ask me what I think which doesn't make sense since she has already invited him. I shrug. Jibola catches my eyes and winks. As the hall continues to fill up, the sound of music in the background confirms that the programme is about to start. He looks back at his previous table where there are only two chairs remaining and nods.

"Okay, although I don't know how I can handle two beautiful ladies on my own." He smiles with a hint of flattery. Expectedly, Maggie points him to sit beside me, which places him across her since I'm sitting at the head of the table.

"So what's been happening to you? Tobi was wondering why you were here. Are you a law student too or here by courtesy?" Maggie asks.

"I bet you guys would think I wouldn't go to university, right?" He asks. Maggie raises her brows quizzically and then nods. I recall she had mentioned something like that about him in the past when she was trying to dissuade me from lusting after him. "I got admission into College of Education and later moved to Unilag. Although I passed JAMB the first time, but GCE Maths wasn't good, no thanks to Tobi." He grouches, I look at him curiously. "You were supposed to be my Maths' teacher, remember?" He finishes off. Oh, I do remember, except he turned around to imply that I was a dullard, silly boy. But I only smile. "You know I'm going to be the first graduate ever in my family and that feels very good, much better than being a layabout like I was trying to be back then."

"Good for you." Maggie commends. "I'm sure your parents would be proud of you."

"What about you? I'm surprised you two are still together. Tobi, you've been quiet, or did I cast a spell on you?" He tries to hold my hand which is on the table, but I recoil.

"You have a false sense of importance." I retort calmly with a smile. "That spell was broken even before it started working."

"…. Please, welcome with me current Balanced Girl, Tobi Bolade for an opening speech." Somewhere in the background, I hear the MC's modulated voice announcing my name. Just like that? How did that happen? Why me, of all people? Maggie and Jibola start clapping. I can tell Jibola is extremely surprised, but he smiles all the same, gesturing for me to get up. I'm too shocked to react, and I sit there but people continue clapping and the MC announces again. "Please give her a standing ovation …Tobi Bolade."

The applause becomes louder and everybody stands except me, Maggie pulls me up and I begin to walk slowly to the podium. What will I say, especially at a place like this, where you have students from two different schools and different levels? I gather myself together; stomach in, chest out, head high, take deep breaths before you get to the mic. Apart from the usual presentations in class, the last time I faced an opinionated crowd was at the Balanced Girl competition and that had been for a good purpose. Oh, except that the purpose turned out to be a farce after all. Richard's smiley dimpled face looms in my head for a split second before I got to the MC and that disconcerts me somehow. I shouldn't allow him have the best of me at a place like this, I talk to myself while trying to focus on the principles of speaking I was taught in school.

The best line of defence in a speech when you are least prepared is to open with an adaptation of a famous speech people can identify with. Collecting the mic from the MC, I take a short bow and start talking, starting with my favourite Mark Anthony's line; "Friends, fellow students and countrymen, lend me your ears. I am here to talk and not to praise anyone." Make it sound important but short. "But at overwhelming times like this, words fail me. Since we are all students and aspire to succeed in our studies so that we can become successful lawyers…" Insert a famous quote. "I will leave you with Winston Churchill's words, 'Never give in. Never give in. Never, never, never, never—in nothing, great or small, large or petty—never give in, except to convictions of honour and good sense'." And take a bow. "Thank you all." I take a bow and hurriedly return the mic to the MC as the audience applaud with a standing ovation. Why do I feel like crying? Is it the mention of me as Balanced Girl or Richard's encroachment in my head, whichever one it is, they are both related.

"That is the most fantastic unprepared speech I've ever heard." Maggie hugs me as I got back to the table. I can feel my eyes begin to blur when Jibola hugs me too, but he can't see my face, only Maggie can and she's beginning to stare at me. The other two gentlemen and lady sitting at our table extend their hands for a handshake too before I sink into my chair.

"I didn't know you were a beauty queen." Jibola says, unable to hide the surprise in his words. "I knew you always had it in you my girl."

Who is his girl? I shrug with a faint smile.

"Tobi, are you okay?" Maggie asks. I nod, but a string of tears is already on my face and I pick a hanky from my bag to dab my eyes. If I hadn't met Richard, quiet, docile Tobi would not have become Balanced Girl.

Jibola turns aside to look at me now. "What's the problem?" He looks from me to Maggie, who only shrugs, raising her brows. "Do you want us to leave, if you are not okay?" He asks again, this time cradling me from his side.

"I'll be fine, I'm okay, thanks, I was just overwhelmed back there." I mutter.

"But you did quite well and Maggie said it was impromptu, I'm proud of you." He says, jabbing my shoulders.

"Thank you." I mumble, dabbing the last bit of tear away, hopefully. The last time Richard said he was proud of me was after I won the Balance Girl competition. Not again! I should stop thinking about him. For good. You wish. The voices in my head are at each other. Well, what's to be gained if I don't? Nothing. So move on girl. Okay, it's just painful.

Thankfully, the rest of the night is uneventful, except for the occasional Balanced Girl wink and chatter and our few schoolmates who come to our table to compliment me on the opening speech. And soon it's time to go.

"Can I drop you ladies off?" Jibola asks as we walk towards the exit via the lobby. He's beside me, since Maggie decided to strategically walk behind.

I almost ask him who gave him a car. Instead I shake my head and respond with a surface smile. "No thank you, Maggie drives her own car."

"Oh, okay then." He turns to Maggie, and I make room for her to close up the gap between us, yet she continues her pace. "Thank you very much Maggie, for inviting me over. It was nice meeting you as a sweet lady after all that childish rancour between us. You are very graceful." He says and Maggie's face glows with a smile.

"The pleasure is mine." She responds. "At least, now I know you can't deceive my friend anymore." I roll my eyes at her and Jibola laughs.

"Your friend has grown to become a lady to be cherished." He declares. "If she would allow me, but I'm afraid she may find me unworthy of a beauty queen." He takes my hand, expecting an answer, but I don't' respond, so he starts swinging it as we walk along. When we got under the entrance canopy, Maggie asks Jibola to wait with me while she gets the car, giving him the opportunity to make his last minute pitch. "Can I drop by and see you some time? It would really be nice for us to get together again." He says.

For whom will it be nice? I wonder. "There's no need for that, we'll keep in touch somehow, if it's necessary."

"But I would like to see you, I don't want you to slip through my fingers again. You know we were quite young back then, if that's what you're thinking. I'm a more mature person now and so are you."

"No doubt you are more mature. But right now, I can't think of any reason why I should want to see you." I pat his hand, consoling him.

"Do you have a boyfriend? If you do, I will respect that. But you don't look like you have one."

"Do people write boyfriends on their foreheads now?" I snap. "And if you must know, no I don't have a boyfriend and I'm not looking for one. Thank you." I start walking towards where Maggie's car is parked, I'm sure she's deliberately wasting time. Jibola comes after me.

"Tobi, we are friends, surely we can have a conversation without annoying each other. I'm sorry if that sounded intrusive."

Surely, Jibola has matured. He would never apologise back then in secondary school. "It's okay, I just don't feel it's right that you must try to date all your old friends you come across. It shouldn't be that difficult to be friends without any string attached?" I soften my tone.

"I don't try to date all my old friends. I only wanted an opportunity to be your friend again and who knows?" He says flippantly.

"I know and I know that nothing is going to come out of it, so beat it." Maggie drives up to me and I enter the car, waving at him. He returns my wave and smiles back yet looking bemused.

And Maggie does the most unexpected. She beckons to him to come to her side of the car and pokes her head out. "Anytime you feel like popping in to see us, you can look for Vintage Lodge at PPL, it's not very far from school." With that she smiles and speeds off to her house at Ikeja, so we can catch up with her brother, Segun who is travelling to the US tonight. He had gotten admission for a Masters programme and he said he wanted to spend Christmas without his family for once.

EIGHTEEN

"What happened to you, why are your eyes red, have you been crying?" I ask Maggie. She is crouched on the bed and hadn't answered when I knocked. The pillow in which she had buried her face is all wet. She bursts into tears. Maggie never cries, she's the stronger of the two of us and usually laughs away any mishap, no matter how big. Whatever happened must really be serious.

Today is Jemima's graduation and we can't afford Maggie to be sad at this moment. The resultant chaos of the cancelled last June twelve elections has disrupted a lot of things in the country, including the school calendar. Nowhere in the short history of the school has a graduation ceremony held in March, but that is the case now since final exams was only written in January. "Maggie, please talk to me, what is it, hope nothing bad happened to Chuks?"

She shakes her head. We had parted ways yesterday when she said she was going to see Chuks and I went to spend the night in another hostel, since Jemima had also gone home so

243

she could come with her parents for the graduation ceremony. Between yesterday and now, what could have happened to upset Maggie? She wipes her eyes and starts talking.

"It's that woman again."

That woman, I guess must be Chuks' mother. I don't know what magic Chuks performed but gradually, his mother had started talking to Maggie civilly. Although, only for a while, because she soon started complaining about Maggie – she comes to the house too much, isn't she supposed to be in school; why does she wear too much make up; her nails were too long and always painted, does she do any domestic work at home; why does she allow Chuks to stay out till dark? Chuks settled his mother's issue by renting his own apartment just two months ago which was long overdue anyway.

"We went to tell her about the wedding plans yesterday." Maggie goes on amidst tiny sobs. "And she said over her dead body." Last week, on Valentine's Day, Chuks had formally proposed to Maggie and she said yes and they agreed a date, August sixteen, Maggie's next birthday.

"That's sad, I'm sure she would come around over time. Isn't that the same way she barked at us the first time we went there? There's no need to cry over that. What did Chuks say?"

"He said I should ignore her. And he actually told her off and stormed out of the house. That's another part of it I don't like. I don't want him to fight with his mother because of me."

"Well, if you ask me, I would say she deserves it, somebody needs to have the nerves to stand up to her. Did you tell your mother?"

"Not yet." She reverts to the sobs. "The last time I talked to her about it, she said she doesn't want any problems for me and if Chuks' mother doesn't want me, we should let her go and marry her son. So I've told Chuks to give me a break."

"No Maggie, you didn't do that. You know that's going to hurt him the more. That's not fair on him."

"Is it fair on me, that I have to put up with his mother since and then this?" Maggie hisses.

"But you can't come this far only to give up. You already knew it would not be easy with that woman so you have to stand up for your love, my dear."

"She doesn't even give me a chance, what else should I do?" She queries.

"As long as he says he wants you, I think that is what matters. If she says over her dead body, maybe she wants to die before you two get married, really." Maggie smiles at that.

What is wrong with parents, or mothers, to be specific? Even my own mother is worse. She had actually gone ahead with her plans to take Sade to see Lami in Port-Harcourt, only for them to meet a girl living in with Lami. Extremely shocked at her son's lifestyle, she had ordered the girl out and sat Lami down to give him the story of his life. When she finished, Lami had walked to Sade and apologised for everything. Then he asked if he could take her out for a drink. Mummy said she was really overjoyed that he had reasoned with her. But Sade came back crying; Lami had taken her out for lunch and then to a supermarket to buy her some stuff, and brought her back to the house, but with a warning. "If you let Mummy deceive you, you have yourself to blame. You are a beautiful girl, please get yourself a nice guy that would take care of you, I am in love with someone else." And then he drove off, leaving Sade and Mummy to spend the night alone in the house.

Mummy said she had never been more embarrassed and on top of it all, she couldn't sleep; both out of anger and worry for not knowing where Lami went to spend the night. Serves her right I thought in my head, I warned her. And of course that put a strain on her relationship with Mrs Badmus. In-law my foot! The next time Lami called the house, he told Daddy to warn his wife to stop meddling in his affairs. That is my Lami, the one that used to be reticent.

*

As usual, the graduating students sit through the ceremony in a haze. Whoever listens to the routine speeches by the VC and his guests? From the pamphlet, we could see that of all the graduating students, only six made first class and they were the ones worthy of mention. In two hours it was finished and they all troop out for pictures and merriment. It's another one of those jamborees and really a sight to behold. Some people came with a whole clan, with drums and minstrels; some had brought food and drinks and spread out on the grounds as if they were at a picnic, the one that caught our attention is the guy who came with a masquerade. The same guy we call Community Effort, because he was on scholarship by his local government.

We greet and congratulate Jemima's lovely parents and her two sisters, hanging around them and rendering narratives of the people and activities on the school grounds. About an hour later, we excuse ourselves and Maggie and I continue to move about snapping pictures with other friends who were graduating as well; it would be a long time before we come across some of them, or maybe even never. Once again, I am assaulted by a nostalgic feeling as I remember memorable moments I had shared with some of them. It's never easy saying goodbye, yet we have to keep on moving in this journey of life. Will it ever end?

Apart from my family, Maggie's family had been the only constant thing in my life and now that Maggie would soon be getting married. I shudder at the thought as my mind wanders. Even Richard failed to remain constant. Ah, Richie boy. But he's somewhere in my past now, and it would be best he stays there. If only... but I cut short that line of thought, no need crying over spilt milk.

Maggie nudges me. "Is that not Oba? She discreetly points at him, about five feet away from us, amidst a small group of people, but particularly holding a girl in a near-embrace. He is impeccably dressed as usual and spotting dark sunglasses. He sees us now and starts walking towards us after whispering to the girl in his grip, probably excusing himself. Thank God he's found himself a girlfriend. Men are impossible! He still came to Vintage Lodge two months ago when he said he was just passing by. Quite typical, he didn't as much as mention that he knew any girl in school.

"Hello ladies. Did you come to rehearse for your graduation?" He removes his sunglasses and makes to shake hands with Maggie, but she ignores his hand and gives him a bear hug as if he came to save her day. That means he would expect me to hug him too. Goodness me, Maggie and her pranks. But instead, he holds out his hand to me with a big grin on his face. I hug him half-heartedly, while he clings on a bit.

"I've looked forward to this day since the first day I set eyes on you." He whispers to me.

I disentangle myself. "I'm not the one graduating, so you still have another year to look forward to." I respond, trying to feign ignorance of his implied meaning. And what about the lady he was with a while ago?

"I wasn't talking about graduation, I've been looking forward to holding you that close ever since I met you."

"Dreams do come true sometimes, maybe your fairy godmother was up all night." I smile at him, trying to loosen up myself to tease him. "Although, I wouldn't think anything of it if I were you."

"Let me worry about that. Those brief seconds felt like a hundred years." He pauses. I look about and realise that Maggie had conveniently disappeared. How timely. "Why don't you like me, Tobi?"

What kind of question is that? If I went about rationalising why I didn't smile at every guy who says hello to me, I should have written a book by now. But seriously, why don't I like Oba? Truth is I don't know myself. Except that he is not anywhere close to Richard. Ah yes, he's too serious. That's one reason. If I told my mother I didn't like a guy because he was too serious, she would ask me if I was in my right senses; every sensible girl should look for a serious guy to marry, she would have said. He is too reserved. Isn't that almost like saying he is too serious all over again?

"It has nothing to do with you. It's not that I don't like you. I just want to face my studies and not get entangled in any relationship entrapment. Sincerely, I think you are a great guy. I'm simply not the girl for you."

"Love is not an entrapment." He says as if giving a lecture. If only you knew, I muse. "If it's about school, I don't mind waiting, at the most, you will be done next year, right?"

Actually, we should have been done this year, if not for the school closure. I look at him intently. "Oba, are you sure there isn't more to this? Seriously, must it be me? Did they ask you to bring a pretty lady for sacrifice at Ijebu?" He had mentioned to me that he was from Ijebu. Fable has it that the Ijebus have the highest number of witches in the entire Yoruba tribe, so people easily joke about them offering sacrifice to all forms of deity. Hubert Ogunde, the theatre legend, who is from a branch of Ijebu, seemed to have reinforced this myth with his mystical films and operas on the world of witches and wizards. Sometimes, you couldn't tell between fact and fiction.

He looks away now. I'm not quite sure what he might be thinking; his eyes look distant. I hope he's not taking me serious. Then he turns back to me and smiles. "They asked me to bring a pretty Yoruba lady, who can talk so that my life would be a little bit more interesting; who can cook, so I can be well fed; who is well read, so someone can try to challenge me; who is extremely beautiful, so that she can engage me; who is intelligent, so she can manage the home; who is affable, so she can be nice to my friends and family." He pauses to look at me for effect. "Should I go on?"

"Now, I am blushing. Thank you for all the compliments. Anyway, I think you can still get a prettier Yoruba lady for that sacrifice, so she can be more acceptable to the gods."

"I've confirmed from the oracles, you fit the description well, Tobi."

"Won't you ever give up?" I think we are both beginning to

enjoy this conversation. Where is Maggie for goodness sake? I start walking slowly towards the faculty, greeting people along the way, perhaps I would see Maggie or some of my friends to get him off my back. Maybe he would return to his girlfriend, but he walks beside me carefully. "By the way, what happened to your girlfriend?" I ask. I want to hear what he would say about that girl now. I ought to have asked him a long time ago, except for the fact that I wasn't interested and I didn't know he would persist for this long. A successful man like him doesn't go about without a girlfriend. Yet, I wonder.

He slows down his pace and his voice goes a pitch lower. "Do you really want to know?"

"Yes." I nod, why else did I ask? It would be interesting to listen to a guy's tale for once.

"It's a long story." He pauses. What can be long about a girlfriend's story? I stop to look at him, urging him on, I'm not about to let him off that easily. "Can we sit there then?" He points at the concrete garden bench. I nod. After sitting, he exhales and stares emptily ahead. "She passed on five years ago, they said she had leukaemia or something stupid like that. We had been dating from university and we were supposed to get married three years ago." He shrugs sadly. "But I guess life happens anyway it wants. It's not a good thing to lose anyone Tobi, it was devastating for me."

Tell me about it! Even though Richard is not physically dead, I hope, I don't know how else to describe losing him. And it seems something in me, which I've not been able to define, died with him too. "I'm so sorry, I didn't know, I wouldn't have asked." I suddenly feel sorry for Oba, he usually looks very composed, yet underneath that is this grave loss. I look away from him, staring emptily into the celebrating crowd. "You must have loved her."

His voice is even quieter now. "Her name was Titi, but I used to call her Baby, she was very sweet and selfless and ..." He shakes his head unable to complete the sentence. I remain silent, not sure of what to say, maybe he's remembering fond memories of her and I don't think I should interrupt that. After a while, he lifts up his face and looks at me. "It's okay, the living has to find reasons and means to embrace life. It's painful, but what can I do. Some things are never meant to be, no matter how good they are?" He says philosophically.

"I agree with you." If I agree with him, then maybe Richard and I weren't meant to be, even though I felt he was the best thing to happen to me in my adult life. But, somehow, I feel Oba's loss is more bearable than my loss of Richard, since his girlfriend is dead, it's easier to consider that chapter closed, but Richard is still living and sometimes, in fact most times, I can't help wondering what's happening to him and how he can bear to make love to another girl, knowing the feelings we had for each other. Am I being naïve as Segun had said? Men don't make love, they have sex.

"After she died, I had to start learning not to take life too seriously"

"Really?" I stifle a laugh. "You are learning not to take life too seriously?" He looks at me quizzically. "I'm sorry, I don't mean to be insensitive, but if you say you are learning not to take life too seriously, I'm wondering what your life was like before. You say you don't talk much, you don't party, you don't drink, you don't smoke, and you always look like a dotted I and a crossed T. Is there pretty much anything you do that is interesting apart from your work?"

He doesn't seem to mind my silliness as he nods. "I don't need to do all those things, but I'm happy all the same and I take each day as it comes. But if you are ready to teach me, I'm yours."

I ignore his last line. "Surely, there has to be a girl you fancy. Five years is a long time ago." I prod, expecting some more information.

"Well, there's this girl. Her name is …" He smiles but I notice his attention shift ahead of us. The girl, the one whose name he is about to tell me has surfaced from the crowd, he waves at her and she heads in our direction.

"Here you are. I've been waiting for you." She says to Oba, then she looks at me with her sparkling eyes nods. "Hello, Balanced Girl."

I nod back. We, famous people don't need introductions.

"Tobi, this is my cousin, she's graduating today." The fact that she's graduating is pretty obvious, with the scroll in her hand and the academic cap. She has gotten rid of the gown. Smart girl.

"Hello, congratulations." I say with a smile.

Her smile is all over her pretty face as she jabs me jovially. "You are the one giving my big cousin sleepless nights. I forgive you, because you are beautiful. But I would advise you not to miss him, he totally adores you and men like him are hard to come by. I have a girl for him but he wouldn't even talk to her. If you let..."

"Chris!" Oba interrupts fearing she might do more damage than good, I guess. I am utterly speechless and somewhat amused. If he had earlier introduced her to me as his advocate, maybe we would have long concluded. She's absolutely delightful.

"I'm sorry, Tobi, don't mind me, but that's the truth." She turns to Oba. "I'm leaving now, you can stay with her, I'll leave with my friends." And she turns back to me. "Will you come to my party this evening? You can come with him."

"Tobi, will you come?" He asks me.

I shake my head. "No, it's kind of impromptu."

"Don't take life too seriously girl. Impromptu has its own place. Just come and let loose." She prods, patting me on the shoulder jovially.

Is not attending a party on impromptu notice taking life too seriously? I wonder.

"Thank you for inviting me, but my flatmate is also graduating today and she's having a party." I had said it before I thought about it. I hope Maggie or Jemima don't show up now to burst my bubble.

"I can excuse you from mine then, if you are going with Tobi." She nudges him mischievously. "I will just tell Daddy one girl kidnapped you."

"There would be no need for that." I protest. "I'm sure he would attend your party."

But she whispers to me as if she didn't hear what I said. "They'll be so happy if you truly kidnap him." We both smile. What else can you make of a girl like this? She sounds like the female version of Richard – no cares in the world. I envy her. "I should be on my way now. Very nice to meet you finally, Tobi. I hope to see you again." And to Oba. "If I see you fine, if you go with her, I will understand." With that, she saunters off, greeting people along the way and soon disappears into the crowd.

"I'm sorry, I hope you're not offended." He asks.

I still have a smile lingering on my face. I like that girl, so self-confident and full of life. "She said we shouldn't take life too seriously. So, I am taking it lightly. No offence."

"Ironic that you accused me a short while ago that I'm too serious. Now it's time to take your own advice and loosen up." He smiles too. "She has been trying to marry me off for some time now, she said she's afraid for me, can you believe that?"

Hmm, that makes the two of us dude. I nod. "People like her always need a project to keep them alive, she has a lot of energy. Besides five years is enough time to get people around you concerned." If by loosening up, he means I should allow him into my life, then he had better think again.

"Won't you invite me for the party?" He asks.

"Hmm, it's not my party. It's Jemima's." Why did I tell that stupid lie, if he presses on I have to cook up another story to cover the first. That's the problem with lying and I'm not very good at it.

"Well, you can ask her, I'm sure she won't mind me coming if you don't mind. And you can tell her I won't take any drink or food, so I don't shorten the ration of the authentic invitees." He laughs, looking at me for an answer. "I just want to be with you."

As if on cue, I notice Maggie and Jemima making their way towards us through the flurry of human traffic. God help me, this is a disaster looking for how to happen. I shouldn't be caught lying simply because I'm trying to avoid a guy. I wave to them and turn back to Oba.

"I change my mind, I'll go with you to your cousin's party, I think I need the change."

NINETEEN

"I think you are over-reacting, Tobi. Didn't you kiss Richard the same day you met him?" Maggie exclaims.

That seemed so long ago. "Well then, exactly why I shouldn't do the same with another one of them." I replied, not willing to admit whatever Maggie is trying to insinuate.

She shakes her head. "You know what? You are just a bouquet of dilemma. It's either they are too much like Richard or too little like him. Why don't you move on? Really move on."

"It's easy for you to say, why don't you just leave me alone and stop trying to throw me at every guy you can find." I storm out of the room, fuming and slamming the door behind me.

I lay on my bed replaying in my mind the events of yesterday evening. Chuks had taken us out to dinner for his birthday and to celebrate their engagement. It was a ten-some and there were just two of us unattached – deliberately, I suppose. The way the single guy latched on to me suggests he must have heard I was affection-deprived; I couldn't wait for the dinner to end. When we were parting he actually made to kiss me. Thankfully, he got only my cheek. When I told Maggie, she simply laughed it away and said I was over-reacting. Am I over-reacting not to want to kiss a guy I just met?

It's been just about eight months since I got ditched by Richard and since then Maggie had tried to fix me up with as many eligible bachelors as she knows. It had even gotten worse after Chuks proposed to her and there was an agreement that they would get married on her twenty first birthday. Despite several attempts to reason with her that I didn't need a boyfriend, she keeps on insisting that I move on with my life like I was some sulking stranded girl that a school bus left behind. On a regular turf, maybe I may have considered Chuks' friend, but he was too short and rather brash for my liking, with a pucker brow that made him look more like an old man. And that attempt to kiss me had totally turned me off. I thought I would get Maggie's sympathy, but once again, she had asked me if I was waiting for Richard to come back to me.

I can't even remember how the conversation got to Richard. That question jolted me because it had a ring of truth in it. Somewhere on the inside of me is this faint glimmer of hope that he would one day turn up on my door step and ask for forgiveness and life can go on as if we never parted. Yet, I knew that was impossible, he was married and for the life of me, I don't wish his wife dead, but he rightly belonged to me. Life is not fair indeed.

Someone had said it's only people you love that can hurt you. Richard had hurt me to the depth I didn't know existed and I don't know if I could ever love or trust anyone as much as I loved him. Yet, I couldn't find it within me to blame him or hate him; after all, he did what he had to do. Isn't that what is called survival instinct? If I were in his position, would I have done differently? I don't know, and I may probably never know since I'm never going to be in that position. Sometimes I get annoyed with myself when I remember I had been warned about him before I threw myself into that relationship, although he had captivated us all, eventually.

No one could have anticipated what happened and it definitely wouldn't have happened if he hadn't gone to that stupid London in the first place. Perhaps if he had sincerely mentioned what he was going through at the time, it would have been easier for me to understand, maybe, maybe not. At least I would have been warned. That letter he wrote seemed like he wasn't considering my feelings in the least when he wrote it. Sometimes, I don't know which one hurts the more, the fact that he got married or the fact that I hadn't seen it coming and he hadn't bothered to talk to me. It's all so confusing and distressing.

There's a knock on my door, definitely it's Maggie. She pokes her body in without waiting for a response and sits on the chair by the reading table.

"Tobi I'm sorry." She says quietly.

"It's okay." I respond tersely.

"To set the record straight, I'm only sorry that you feel this way, not for what I said."

Maggie is mad; why bother say sorry at all. I smile all the same. "Or maybe because you won't have anyone to talk to."

"*Moi*, if you don't talk to me, I will look for a well and dip my head inside, you know the well is a good listener and it would respond to me through its echoes."

It's difficult to stay angry with Maggie. "I've been thinking really, maybe I need help." I say, getting up from the bed and sitting in my favourite crouched position.

"Help with what?"

What were we talking about dummy? "About my love life."

"Oh, you have a love life?" She mocks. "Where have I been?"

I ignore her sarcasm. "You brought this up and you had better get serious. What should I do about guys?"

She comes to sit beside me by the bed tenderly roughening my hair in the process. "It's up to you really, I just need you to move on with life and stop comparing everyone with Richard, he's come and gone and he's living his life, it's time you lived yours and live it well, for yourself." She advises.

"That hurts." I almost feel like cringing.

"I know and that's why what I'm going to tell you would sound eccentric, but I can bet you it's going to work and help you get over a Richard you may never see again till you die."

"Maggie, you don't have to be that graphic, you can say it in a nicer way, you know." I uncoil and beat her with my heart-shaped pillow - the one Richard had given me. That makes me feel like it's him beating her. I smile. There are too many memories of him around me; maybe I should start getting rid of them. She is looking at me, waiting for me to ask her for the magic solution. "Okay, shoot!"

She looks me straight in the eyes without wavering. "I think you should find yourself a good looking guy to have sex with."

"What? Are you out of your senses?" I yell at her as she

ducks off the bed and returns to the chair while she continues to stare at me.

"I'm serious Tobi, once you have sex with a guy, your mind stays with him. It's probably the reason you're still fixated on Richard. You need to break the jinx." She taps my breast teasingly and I slap her hand off. "And I think you can do with some tender loving care too, try to loosen those nuts and bolts that have gone stiff in your body." Her face is extremely aglow and my mouth is wide agape.

"How can you even think of that?"

"What do you have to lose, no one except you requires your faithfulness now, so why not?"

"You are simply impossible." I scowl at her. I need some breather. I get up and pick the almost empty bottle of water on the table, gulping everything down, while the thought of having sex with another man fills my mind. Suddenly and surprisingly, I feel my nipples tingle and I walk to the window to look at nothing in particular, but mainly to avoid Maggie's discomforting stare. I know she's waiting for an answer. Do I have it in me? My voices begin their dialogue: Who can I have sex with? Are you even considering that? Why not, like Maggie said, what do I have to lose? Your dignity, girl! Do I still have that, I don't think so? You don't have to take every advice, you know. Well, this one sounds good and the thought itself is liberating. What if you get hurt again? (I shrug). It won't be the first time, will it, besides it's just for the sex? And what if the sex is disappointing? Hmm, there's only one way to find out and I'm not in it for the thrill, remember? Okay, who are you going to sleep with then? (Pause) Oba of course! Why him? Why not him?

I exhale loudly.

Maggie's stare is almost boring into my soul. "Are you thinking about it?"

I turn my back to the window, facing her. "Thinking about what? You only just mentioned it, besides even if I wanted to, who would want to have sex with me?"

"Tobi, you underrate yourself." She starts counting on her fingers one after the other. "There's Oba, Jibola, Ade, even Abubakar, and that silly boy in class that has been chasing you since year two." She lifts up her hand and spreads her fingers wide, almost shoving them in my face. "You've got five solid options girl, I wish I were you. But I'd pick Oba over all of them. At least if you are going to eat a frog, eat the one that has frogspawns, that's what our elders say."

Hmm, Oba seems to be scoring high this evening. And if truth be told, if anybody has earned having sex with me, it's him. He had been persistent for the almost two years I've known him, he's well settled, mature, polished, handsome and rich. Yes rich, I always dreamt of marrying rich, yet when presented with the choice, I turned my back. Should I have said yes to him earlier? Who knows what would have happened. At least if I'm taking him on now, it's with my head screwed in the right direction. As stupid as Maggie's suggestion sounded at first, I'm getting excited; the thought of having sex again is surprisingly exhilarating. But how do I lay my hands on Oba?

*

True to Maggie's words, she came up with a formidable

plot, which included not making it obvious that I was throwing myself at Oba. She called to tell him we (Maggie, Chuks and I) would be hanging out around his neighbourhood on Saturday evening and he could join us if he didn't mind. Of course, he didn't mind. "I'm sure he's going to ask to show you his place." That was Maggie's joker. "And you can take it up from there, baby." I wish. My only reservation about this arrangement is that it would probably remind me of Richard since he also used to live in Surulere. I had sincerely hoped his house would be far enough not to evoke the ghost I hid in my mind.

We spent the evening eating and drinking and sometimes singing along to the background music. It did remind me of my days out with Richard, but I kept in line with the conversation, smiling, chipping in and laughing when required. Oba and Chuks had met before, so no introduction was needed and they kicked off an engaging discussion about the economy, politics and sports, while Maggie and I focused on the happenings around us, gossiping about everything and nothing in particular. Talk about being reserved, Oba is not, he just needs a stimulating topic. He was very relaxed talking with us and I realised he was quite knowledgeable about a lot of things and down to earth too. When Chuks signalled for the bill, Oba offered sharing it with him, but Maggie and Chuks protested, insisting the outing was on them. He reluctantly pocketed his purse.

Shortly after the bill was settled, Maggie starts the drama. "Hmm, what are we going to do about you now, Tobi?" She asks me, pretending to be reflecting.

"What do you mean by that? Is there any problem with

Tobi?" Chuks asks her. Not knowing if Chuks is on to our
plan or he is sincerely puzzled causes me same embarrassing
moments as I stand there looking from one to the other.

"It's a long way dropping Tobi off at Ogba before we head
back for Festac, Chuks."

"So?" Chuks doesn't think that's a problem at all, good for
Maggie. "Do you want her to take a bus home at this time?"

"But, I can take her home, if it's okay with you, my lady."
Oba volunteers, trying to catch my eyes. He had started calling
me my lady this evening as if something had changed me from
plain Tobi.

I shrug indifferently facing Maggie. "The next time we go
out together and you plan to elope with your boyfriend, please
let me know ahead." I storm on with some facade of
annoyance and they all follow me. We shouldn't make it too
easy.

"Please why don't you let Oba drop you off? Really, I didn't
think of going with Chuks until a few minutes back. And I
forgot you weren't going back to school. You know I'm not a
very good planner." She looks at me with eyes that could melt
the most hardened heart.

"It seems I'm the cause of all these, Maggie...." Chuks
interjects uncomfortably, unsure of what to do next. That
confirms to me he wasn't aware of our plan, thank goodness.
And I need to stop the gentleman from insisting on taking me
home now out of guilt.

"Oba, are you sure it's okay? Traffic heading to Ogba may
be terrible now." I turn to him

"It's not a problem at all. At your service, my lady." He
takes a bow, smiling.

Maggie switches on her winning smile. "Oh, thank you so much. Tobi, don't worry, I owe you one."

"Okay, see you on Monday then." I smile at Maggie and Chuks while Oba shakes hands and leads me to his car. I'm dancing inside.

Oba lives in one of those look-alike planned but dilapidating estates in Surulere just behind the national stadium. Richard's house – my former love nest is just about twenty minutes' drive from there. Most of the buildings on his street have been converted to shops, turning the once quiet estate into an active commercial centre. It was difficult to drive through the streets as cars were carelessly parked on both sides of the road without consideration for most of the fading signposts reading 'No Parking'. Someone had even parked in front of his gate. After driving through the street twice without getting a space to park, he parked on an outer street explaining that it was a regular occurrence and it was okay since we would be going out later. The house, a two bedroom bungalow obnoxiously stands out from the others because it is fenced and gated with a beautifully crafted wrought iron.

As we start walking towards the house, he pauses intermittently to greet people along the way, – the dry cleaner, the chemist, the cobbler, the barber, the provision vendor, and a few kids who call him uncle and some young Hausas loitering about his gate – smiling cheerfully. One of the Hausas helps him open the gate, hailing him continuously while slotting in an account of the events of the day. Oba continues to nod and smile until we got into the house and the gate was locked behind us.

"I think you'd probably win if you contested for election

here, you seem to get on with everybody."

"I've lived here for about six years and I've known all those people since then. It's a kind of close community, where we have to look out for one another irrespective of status." He responds while opening the door.

"That's good, so you feel safe here." He nods. I almost tripped as I stepped into the depressed floor of the dark living room.

"Easy, easy, sorry, I should have warned you." He catches me midway and our bodies touch for a split second before he draws back. I feel the stirring in my body and my mind begins to race. Not a bad way to start the evening, considering my mission here today. I'm sure if I had drawn him closer and assaulted him with my lips, like they do in the movies, he wouldn't have been able to resist. Sadly, I've lost that moment.

The living room is small but very beautifully and brightly decorated; I fall in love with it immediately he switched on the light. The floor is rugged dark brown, with brown leather settees positioned L-shaped and a complementary square centre table covered in the same leather. The walls are painted cream on which hang two opposite paintings. Only the TV shelf is domineering, but everything inside it is deliberately arranged.

"You have such good taste!" Except that it looks too tight it doesn't feel lived in.

"I shouldn't take the credit for it, I'm sorry, but Titi did every bit of it. You remember the lady I told you about?" He goes to draw the curtains aside and I feel my body tense a bit, it feels like a twinge of jealousy. Why should that bother me? Although I hope we won't spend half the time talking about her. "Can I show you round?" He stretches his hand to take mine and leads me first into the equally neatly-arranged kitchen, the guest room which has a small sized bed and a computer table, and his room which is typically painted blue, with two beautiful wall paintings and a neatly-made king size bed. My mind dwells on the bed for a while, imagining Oba pushing me onto it and making love to me passionately. Stop that, you came here for sex not love making, Oh, I'm sorry.

Thankfully, there's no picture of any lady in the house, I wouldn't want to feel like someone was watching me with funny eyes from above. At the bathroom, which is so cosy I could easily fall asleep and have sweet dreams, he washes his hands with soap and asks me to do the same, reminding me that we had been at a public bar.

We are back in the living room and I'm seated on the soft leather settee.

"My lady, how can I entertain you? I'm sorry, I may have lost touch. I've not done this in a long time."

"Neither have I, so you are in control."

He looks lost and heaves. "Okay, would you like to watch a film, why don't you pick a CD while I get you a drink?"

"You can slot in any film you want, I don't watch TV that much, let me get water, I think I've had too much to drink already, although we have to be conscious of time." Without waiting for him, I disappear into the kitchen. Phew! I was beginning to feel awkward. Why did I ever think getting into bed with him would be easy? He's not the kind of guy that would hassle a girl and I've not learnt how to hassle a guy either. I have to give kudos to guys like Segun and even Richard. I've never even kissed Oba. God help me. Maybe I should have tried Jibola. I open the fridge and I'm amazed at how well stocked it is, assorted range of fruits, wine, juices and carbonated drinks. I pick a bottle of red wine which reads 5% alcohol - at least that should calm my nerves and make me lose my senses partly.

I grab a tray from the stack and two glass cups, clear my throat quietly and go back to the living room. He has already switched on the TV, but it's muted as he is also playing blues in the background. The song is familiar, but I don't know who the artist is and that takes my mind to Richard. I hiss inwardly, Richard has no place here today.

He opens the wine and fills the two cups. "Can we make a toast, my lady?" He pulls me up. "To what?"

"To friendship." That sounds non-committal enough, before he starts getting any ideas about my intentions. He drowns his wine and I follow suit, self-consciously.

"Can I have the pleasure of our very first dance?" He pleads quietly. "I know I'm a terrible dancer, but I'll try not to step on your toes." My throat is dry, very dry and I can only nod as he draws me to the front of the TV, holding me gently. Is he going to sing for me like Richard too? I pray not, that would be too much for me. But, he doesn't sing, he just continues to move slowly to the rhythm of the music, moving me with him, my head resting comfortably on his shoulder. I don't feel any bulge, but I feel my own body rioting in different directions, not wanting him, yet wanting him. I raise my head, to look at him, his eyes are shut. Impulsively, I reach out and kiss him and he kisses me back, gently, but he hugs me tightly after pulling away. Suddenly, I am stricken by a flood of emotions and I begin to cry, silently at first until it rises to louder sobs. He leads me back to the settee and kneels in front of me.

"Are you okay?" He whispers in a hoarse voice. I nod as he wipes some tears from my eyes with the sleeve of his blue kaftan, only then did I notice that he had also shed some tears. What a coincidence! "I'm sorry, I didn't mean to upset you."

I shake my head. "No, it's okay."

"Then why are you crying?" He sounds genuinely concerned.

"I'm sorry, it's just a whole lot of emotions. I haven't done this in a long time."

"Neither have I, I don't know how else to court you Tobi, but I want to love you and care for you as if you are mine." I can only nod to his affectionate voice. "But I need you to be sure." I nod again. I don't know what he needs me to be sure about, but feeling the stirring in my loins and wetness in between my legs, I'm sure I want to be made love to. As the music whirrs on, I stoop and kiss him again, for longer and as I continue to feel the fire in my body intensify, I kneel beside him and begin to unbutton my shirt, he pulls back and looks straight at me. "Are you sure?"

Did I ever think this guy doesn't talk enough? I place a finger on his lips teasingly. "Shoooooo." I drawl. He starts kissing me all over, removing his clothes and the remainder of mine. We don't bother to go to the bedroom, we are both too hungry to bother about finesse or protection, we keep on exploring, touching, kissing and rolling over each other and eventually I guide him inside me. I don't feel any pain, only pleasure, pleasure of satisfaction and liberation. I burst into tears again.

I lay in his arms with a sheepish smile on my face, tracing the contours of his face and body. He had been good and very considerate, but passionately so. I wonder why I hadn't done this earlier, even if only for this unrivalled euphoric feeling of bliss.

He turns towards me with a satisfied grin on his face. "Thank you, my lady." He leans forward to kiss me, draws himself up and reaches for the wine. "Here." He presses the glass to my lips, before drinking some himself.

"Thank you." I sit up properly and start gathering my clothes suddenly becoming self-conscious.

"Let me get you something to cover yourself with." He leaves for the room and my eyes follow him, a wave of emotions sweeping all over me and at that instant I know I want to have sex with him again. I keep on wearing my clothes and by the time he got back I am fully dressed. "Why are you dressed, won't you take a shower?" He drops the coverlet limply, and then decides to cover himself with it.

"I'm going back to school."

"What?" He is shocked. "Why?" He glances at his watch which he had left on the floor beside his clothes. "I'm sorry, I didn't intend to keep you, but surely you can spend the night here. I will sleep in the guest room if it bothers you that much."

I shake my head. "It's not my habit to sleep in a guy's house, Oba, I have to go." I need to keep to the plot.

"But I'm not any guy, Tobi. We just had sex and I count that as special." Some men are simply naïve, and this one tops them. I start rubbing my hand on my face, but I remain quiet. "And it's not my habit to have sex with girls, if you must know. I love you my lady, I hope you understand that." He cuddles me in his arms.

I sigh deeply, now is when I need the right words to say. How do I begin to explain that I don't much fancy a guy I just had sex with without sounding like a tart? *Ashewo*! That is the word my mother would have for me if she ever hears of such a thing. I hold his hands. "It was special for me too, but I need to sort out my head about someone in my past, because I still feel him in my present and it's confusing and honestly, you are a good man Oba, I like you a lot. I'm just not sure yet."

"But I asked you if you were sure and …" He leaves the sentence hanging, pausing gloomily, probably recalling that I hadn't particularly said I was sure. "Do you want to tell me about this man in your past?" I shake my head. No! He runs his hand through his Afro, in confusion. "Okay, you know what, it's rather late and heading to your school now would be suicidal. I promised to take you home, and I can still do that. I don't know why you want to go back to school."

"It's too late to go home now. My parents don't like me commuting at night."

"Then why don't you spend the night, please? I'll do whatever you want me to do."

"Like kill a ram for sacrifice." I tease in order to redeem the situation.

He smiles. "Even that, don't dare me. This is the heart of Lagos, you can get anything at any time." No doubt about that. The sound of the music blaring in from the streets confirms that there's still a lot of activities going on, even though it's pretty late. I'm not surprised though. Rumour has it that the estates in Surulere were built to resettle the former residents of

271

Isale-Eko, the Island that never sleeps. They apparently came with their merry lifestyle.

"Can we go for a walk then?"

"Now!" He shakes his head in disbelief. I nod. And then I remember this is not Richard, but Oba that sees the likelihood of accidents in every movement on the road. "I've never done that in the night before, but if you want to…" He pauses. "You'll make a promise if we go for that walk?" He asks eagerly. Sure, as long as it's to have sex with you, I wouldn't want to miss the final opportunity, just in case it never happens again. I nod. "You'd let me bathe you when we come back."

Is this guy for real?

TWENTY

"Can I take you out today, my lady?"

"Are you serious, why?"

"What do you mean by why?"

"Don't you think you should tell your lady what she did right to deserve such a treat, milord?"

"Hmm. Let me think." Pause. "You are Tobi, right?" Pause, I nod. "That's what you did right. Being simple Tobi. How about that?" He comes around and holds me from the back. "And we should celebrate that simplicity."

"You flatter me so, milord, very flattered. But if you keep rubbing thyself against me as you are doing now, you may end up with a burnt offering of stew and there goes your breakfast."

He turns me to face him, kissing my face all over. "As long as I have you, breakfast can burn to blazes."

"So you can tell me I can't cook. I know thy pranks by now, milord, you can't catch me." I turn back to stir the stew.

We spend most weekends together now, mostly indoors,

273

because Oba is an indoor person as I've always known which I don't mind. I'm also introverted in a way, but he doesn't believe that. "Tobi, don't try to change for my sake, I love you just the way you are. An introvert wouldn't put herself up for a beauty competition, and win like you did." How many people can I convince that I did Balanced Girl for love? Until I met Richard, I was simply plain Tobi, conveniently following in Maggie's shadow.

Did I forget Richard? Yes, in a manner of speaking, particularly regarding sex. Did I continue to see Oba? Yes, in a manner of speaking, particularly regarding sex. But only Maggie and I know these. Oba is in love and I wish I was too. Maggie thinks I am, and sometimes I believe I am, truly, until I start comparing him with Richard, yet again. Why do people always lust for what they can't have? And by people, I mean Oluwatobiloba Amanda Bolade. Maggie said there's no reason for you to lust after what is yours, that's why. Phew! Why can't I just accept Oba's love and move on with life? No, I have to look for a way to punish myself. Maggie said, sometimes, we get so used to pain we begin to enjoy it, then we do all we can to prolong it. Sage Maggie!

But somehow, it didn't seem possible that we could separate having regular sex from having a steady relationship, so I'm in a relationship with Oba, yet not exactly in a relationship. A real bouquet of dilemma! It suits me just fine though, I don't know about him and neither do I care much for that matter. Like he said, I only want to take each day as it comes and enjoy it to the fullest.

Believing that he needs to make my life more interesting, Oba makes an extra effort to go out on my behalf which is fine by me too.

"So where would you like to go, my lady, while the offer lasts?"

Unfortunately, my mind is blank. I've never really scored high on socials, because I've always flowed with whatever was available or presented by friends. "I'll leave that to you, let me see how creative you can be."

"Ah, well, I can drive you to Ghana and lock you up for a whole week."

"Oh, yes. I would love that very much. But, pray, I beseech thee milord, wouldst thou allow me come with my mother?" We both laugh at that. When we first started dating and I told Oba about my family, he had been amused about my parents' austere outlook to life, especially my mother's. "I think women should be close to their daughters." He had said. According to him, his family runs informally and his mother knows all there is to know about his two sisters. As if Mummy had been part of that discussion, when I got home that same day, I realised she had developed a new interest in my love life. I think it suddenly dawned on her that I would be leaving school this year and she hasn't particularly seen me with any man.

Of course she had noticed that the letters and all the other spoils of love across the ocean had stopped coming and I explained to her that Richard had married someone else since I hadn't particularly given him the green light. A few weeks after I told her about losing Richard, she went into an amazing frenzy out of the blues. "Why should you lose a man that loves you that much? You shouldn't have scared him off like that. You could have told him to wait for you. But Tobi, you should have managed him better, do I have to teach you everything?"

Then one day, she told me that the church was organising a mid-year programme for Singles and I should try to attend since I would likely meet eligible men there. Sometimes later, when I told her that Maggie was planning to get married immediately after exams and that I was the Chief Bride's Maid, she asked me if Maggie wasn't my best friend and what was I doing when Maggie was getting herself a husband? Have you ever heard of volte face?

"If we take your mother to Ghana, you'd lose me forever, 'cos, I can bet you she's going to fall in love with me."

"Milord, has anyone told thee that thou possess a false sense of importance?" The food is done. I cover the pot and start rinsing my hand, intending to go take a shower.

"Won't you add soap to that water?"

Sometimes, Oba can be insufferable about cleanliness. "I'm going to take a bath now, and that bath would include soap if you are good at your job." He takes delight in bathing for me and I never deprive him of that one chore, though I had been uncomfortable with it initially. I suspect he thinks the whole world is a risky place to live in.

"Still." He tries to insist. I shake my head and push him out of the way to escape from the kitchen.

*

He had refused to tell me where we are going, so I'm just wearing my regular shirt and jeans. He drives to one of the commercial streets and asks me to wait in the car while he enters a boutique and comes out with a half-filled bag about ten minutes later, smiling mischievously and tossing the bag to the back seat. We continue to make small talk as we hit the expressway facing Ikeja while maintaining Oba's typical speed. It used to be very annoying, but I'm gradually getting used to it.

He seems to be confident that he would thrill me with this impromptu treat, I choose to play along hoping that he won't go and dump me at home now. I usually want to get home as late as possible so I don't have to endure much of Mummy's old wives' tales. Apart from the fact that he rarely eats out, we had just eaten before leaving his house, so I'm quite surprised when he drove into Airport Hotel, wondering what we would be doing here that he thinks would delight me and frantically hoping that he hadn't set up a business meeting of some sort.

He comes to open the door for me, taking a bow with a boyish grin on his face. "My lady, please step out." I enjoy this role play with Oba a lot, because it evokes the Shakespearean spirit in me. The way aspiring lawyers were harassed to read Shakespeare's in secondary school, one would have thought that is the courtroom language. I give him my hand and he leads me out of the car with the shopping bag in his hand.

My whole body jerks to life as I realise what the treat is. "Oh milord, thou art such a genius." Airport Hotel has one of the biggest and deepest swimming pools in Lagos and because it's a non-membership pool unlike most others, it's also about the busiest. I had learnt and absolutely enjoyed swimming in primary school and even used to win competitions. I haven't been to a pool in a long time, except for the occasional swimming in Maggie's house since form three.

After paying at the counter, he takes out his gear from the shopping bag and gives me the bag where my swimming kit is.

I'm so happy. "Please rinse the suit before you wear it, it's on the instruction." He had to say that.

"Yes milord." I curtsy and disappear quickly before he starts reading the riot act.

But we don't go to swim immediately. Oba delves into the cautious narrative of how it is unwise to engage in an energetic activity like swimming less than two hours after eating. So we look for a comfortable spot to sprawl, talking about nothing in particular, mostly about the history of Airport Hotel, his work and general family relationships until my attention is drawn to a couple who just entered the swimming court.

"What are you staring at?" Oba asks trying to follow my line of view.

"There's something about that girl that is striking, but I can't place it. I feel I know her familiarly." He follows my gaze. The fair-toned pretty girl in question is sporting a pair of dark glasses and wearing a daring low-back swimming suit.

"Maybe someone from uni or someone from your secondary school. Do you want to go and say hello to her?"

I shake my head dismissively. "No, it's not necessary. I just had that gnawing feeling. I'd remember before we leave if she's that important." The girl and her partner walk towards our direction, looking for a place to settle in and they stop short just a few yards from us. She looks about before dropping her bag and I think she noticed me, because she's pointing at me while talking to her companion. She smiles and waves and I wave back. Oh no!

Now I remember her and I wish I had just tugged my face away from sight. But why would you want to avoid her? One voice asks me. Beats me, the other one responds. I remember her definitely. When was the last time I saw her, two years ago? No wonder I couldn't recognise her. Bibi, Richard's ex used to wear very flamboyant clothes and crazy hairstyles. She looks like another person entirely, except for her low-back suit anyway, the short weave she's wearing suits her just fine. And the gentleman with her looks mature too. That's my imagination I chide myself, very few men look immature in swimming trunks, particularly if they have flat stomachs and six packs. There has to be some explanation for this transformation.

"I know who she is now." I mutter to him gently and before I can offer any additional information, she's right in front of me. Maybe you can be friends now since there's no Richard to fight over anymore, that stupid voice seems to be mocking me now. Very funny indeed, the other one replies. She's not looking bad anyway. You are right on that. I put on my winning smile as I get up to greet her. "Hello, Bibi, you look good. How is it going?"

"I'm very fine thank you." Her smile is expressly confident.

"How is Faith, she must be a big girl now?"

Her face communicates a lot of excitement. "Yes, she's becoming a handful. But I've left her with my mother finally, so she can get some stability."

"Please meet my friend, Oba, Oba, this is Bibi." He gets up and shakes her hand, smiling.

"Very pleased to meet you."

"Me too." She responds and turns back to me. "I told you I was going to try and get back to studying. I did." Unexpectedly, she hugs me tightly, I almost choke. "Thank you Tobi, you may not know it, but you are one of the people that challenged me." How in the name of God did I do that? "I'm in Yabatech now, for accounting."

"It's good to hear that, congratulations. I'm in final year now and will be going to Law school next year." I'm truly happy for her. At least she grabbed the opportunity not to allow one lousy mistake ruin her life on time. And all for what? I hope we can continue this chitchat without alluding to our mutual friend and could she please leave. "Remember Maggie?" She nods. "She's getting married in November, would you like to come?" Now why did I say that? What else could I have said under the circumstance?

"I would love to, is it a Saturday? Will you send the card then, do you still remember the house?" I nod. "Okay then, I will expect the card. I have to go back to my friend, thanks a million." She turns to go and I quickly move to walk with her so she doesn't change her mind. "Tobi, I'm sorry it didn't work out between you and Richard." Finally, she said it.

I nod and smile. "Thanks." I wave to her friend and return to Oba. And for the first time, I tell him everything about Richard.

As Oba drives into my compound to drop me off, we had the misfortune of meeting Mummy there. She had just finished parking her car, apparently coming from a party and about to enter the doorway when she sees his car pull up. It takes her a second look to realise I was the passenger while I wished I could simply dissolve into thin air. She nods and stays there, so I come out of the car and greet her.

"Won't you invite your friend up?" She hurries ahead of us, not waiting for an answer, just in case I want to argue with her.

When Oba said okay, I wait for him to lock the car and he follows me up the stairs.

"Honestly, you don't have to come in." I try to dissuade him. "She's never met any of my boyfriends, so I don't know what she has up her sleeves." Not like I've had many boyfriends, anyway.

"It's okay, I'm sure she won't bite me." He settles into the living room, while I go in to drop my bag and go to the kitchen to get some drinks, if I can find any. I'm not disappointed; as usual the only drink in the fridge is water. Daddy has become a health freak and has stopped supporting stocking the fridge with 'all those sugar-filled, acidic, coloured water'. I take the jug of water to Oba and starts chatting edgily with him, just making small talk as we wait for Mummy.

Oba gets up immediately she enters and curtsies. "Good afternoon ma." He doesn't look uncomfortable in the least. Has he done this before? Oh, yes, he had been engaged to be married.

Mummy gestures him to sit. "You are welcome, and what is your name?"

"Obaniyi Odusote."

"Oh, you are from Ijebu." Most parents can tell the tribe of origin from the surnames as if they had special training in decoding names. She waits for him to nod before asking the next question. "And what do you do for a living?"

"I'm a stock broker ma. I run a small company called Real Crown Securities."

"Oh, I see, you are one of the people who collect money from us and give us paper in return."

Oba only smiles. "I can explain how it works, if you want

me to ma, it's quite simple." I eye him discreetly. Does he want to sleep here today?

Mummy shakes her head, but smiles. "That won't be necessary, I don't think I can ever learn what my husband has failed to teach me for over a decade." She looks at me. "Tobi, why don't you prepare some food for him?"

What? I look at him and thankfully, he shakes his head. "No ma, thank you ma, I won't be staying that long ma."

"Are you sure?"

"Yes ma, thank you ma."

"Mummy, where were you coming from?" I ask intending to shift her focus off Oba.

"Ah!" She replies excitedly. "I thought I told you today was Sade's wedding, remember Mrs Badmus' daughter? It's a pity your brother let her go." She concludes ruefully.

"I'm so happy for her." And indeed I am. Sade Badmus is the lady Mummy tried to match-make with Lami unsuccessfully. "Do you know her husband?"

"Of course, that girl is such an angel, Anu is lucky to have won her hand in marriage and it was such a beautiful wedding."

Anu is the son of another one of Mummy's friends. That's interesting. There must be something about Sade Badmus that only our mothers know. I wonder if Mummy would also try to marry me off when I finish school, although I'm sure Daddy would put his feet down on that one. He's a staunch believer that people should be the architects of their own lives, especially where marriage is concerned. All her plans to foist Sade on Lami had been without Daddy's knowledge until Lami reported her and all hell had broken loose. I wonder if Lami has had his fill in the ladies' department now. The last time we talked, he was still gallivanting with girls in different shapes and shades, according to him. What kind of system would corrupt a boy like Lami? On the other hand Segun had said he always knew Lami had it in him, but had only been suppressed by Daddy.

"That's good, which means Mrs Badmus won't hold any grudge against you anymore."

"I would like to leave now ma." Oba pulls himself to the edge of the settee, ready to stand.

"Oh, yes, Oba, do feel free to come around anytime. Are your parents in Lagos?" He nods. As innocent as that question may sound, I have an idea of what Mummy may be thinking, if his parents are back in the village, she would likely conclude that they still belong to the fetish past.

"I will, thank you very much ma." He takes his leave and I excuse myself to walk him out.

And my mother fell in love with Oba. Phew!

TWENTY ONE

"Maggie, please don't pick this dress, the neck is too low, do you want to assault the pastor with your tiny breasts? Only people who have something to flaunt should wear a dress like this." I tap her breast teasingly as I pull her away from the dress she has tried twice now. It's obvious she likes the dress and it's equally obvious the church ushers would have to give her a scarf to cover her cleavage if what we know about that church is anything to go by, except they've changed from being Anglican. She has tried three other dresses already, yet she came back for this one.

"You know what, Mrs Busty Body, I'm just going to sit down there while you look for another one. I'm tired and I promise any other one you bring now, I will go with it." She goes to the lobby. I am not fooled that she would go with any dress I pick, but I don't have a choice now.

I'm tired too, we've spent over two hours here just to pick Maggie's wedding dress and possibly one for me too, as the Chief Bride's maid. Yet, it doesn't seem like we are anywhere close. I beckon to one of the attendants. "Please, help me pick out two dresses; it has to be cream, long, organza or satin, ball gown like Cinderella's type, lots of trimmings on the top and the neck must not be too low." Not too much to ask, is it? I join Maggie at the lobby and suggest that we could go across the road to the ice cream shop while the attendant does her job. Maggie can never say no to ice cream.

Apart from the fact that a friend of Maggie's mother owns the boutique on Allen Avenue, it is reputed to stock the best and the most in wedding dresses, so if we can't get one here, we may have to go to Balogun Market and neither of us is willing to consider that option. Suddenly all the dresses we used to admire every time we pass in front of the boutique don't seem as beautiful as we had envisioned.

Maggie's wedding is in two months and despite her mother's warning that we should try and get the wedding dress sorted early, we had kept on postponing it under the guise of being busy at school. And that was a good reason too because we just finished writing our final exams. Nobody would have ever thought that universities would be writing second semester exams in September, but the political disturbance surrounding the June twelve election and the mysterious assumption of office of General Sanni Abacha as the new military President of Nigeria had changed the course of events forever affecting the lives of millions of people including my best friend's wedding. Maggie's father had insisted that she finished school before the wedding, so he gave her the option to move the date from her birthday to November or wait till next year August if she still wanted her birthday as her anniversary date. Maggie chose the former.

Until now, I hadn't realised that it could cost such a fuss and a fortune to organise a wedding – a one day ceremony running into millions of naira, the marriage had better last forever. And to think that picking out this wedding dress and a pair of shoes is the only assignment we were saddled with out of the whole wedding plan. Oh, Maggie and Chuks also had a say in choosing the reception venue. But every other thing had been contracted out by her mother; the beautician, the photographer, decorations, catering, the traditional clothes, the souvenirs, and up to the wedding invitation.

Segun would be coming home for the wedding and Maggie had mentioned that he would stop over in London to buy the grooms' men's suits. Out of curiosity, when I spoke with him on the phone, I had casually asked if he would be seeing Richard in London and I felt very stupid when he ignored my question and asked me if I had any message for him. After I said no, there was a short silence on his part before he answered me. "Little sis, why do you want to stop walking away from the troubles in your life? Remember Lot's wife?" I felt even more stupid. Lot's wife had turned into a pillar of salt for looking back at the city of Sodom and Gomorrah.

Maggie and I used to imagine how Chuks' mother would be seething with rage over the fact that she didn't have so much a say in her precious son's wedding because as Maggie's mother pointed out to her, the bride's family is responsible for the wedding ceremony in Yoruba land. Especially that the bride's family has more money, she was gracious enough not to add.

It was almost chaos at the formal introduction of the two families. Traditionally, the bride's family usually hosts the groom's family and it had seemed like Chuks' mother was forced to attend, considering the permanent frown she wore on her face even when an activity called for a jovial response or action. When she had time to talk, she had made a speech about how Chukwugozie was her only son and a traditional red-cap chief and how he shouldn't allow anything to hinder him from performing his traditional obligations as and when required. She even refused to eat when food was served. It was obvious that she was on her own in this battle against the wedding because all the other family members, including Chuks' father were visibly agreeable.

After the official ceremony and everyone dispersed in different directions, some of the guests were admiring the magnificent compound and congratulating Chuks on his good judgement of marrying into a good family. Maggie's father and his counterpart in-law got engaged in an animated discussion about politics and how it affects the lives of everybody. Unaware that there was a meeting of sort in the kitchen, Maggie and I stumbled on the two mothers' discussion on our way to Maggie's room. And it was in the subtlest of tones.

Maggie's mother: So it is because of tradition that you are threatening my daughter.

Chuks' mother: Did she report me to you. How did she say I threatened her? I simply advised her not to marry my son. Couldn't you find a good husband for her?

Maggie's mother: The same way you couldn't find a good wife for your son. Why didn't you warn your son to leave my daughter alone?

Chuks' mother: Do I know what she gave my son to eat.

Maggie's mother: Then you should have warned your son to watch where he eats. A good woman makes sure that her son doesn't go hungry, especially her first and only son. Anyway, I just want to warn you, if my daughter ever complains about you to me, you will be shocked at what hit you. I hold my daughter precious and that's why I respect her judgement and would allow her to marry your son, if you are sure you brought your son up properly, you would respect him and stop meddling in his affairs. Whether you like it or not, this wedding would hold. I only think it is fair to warn you.

Chuks' mother: What can you do?

Maggie's mother: You don't want to find out my sister. Do you have any other thing to say?

Chuks' mother: Are you threatening me?

Maggie's mother: Call it whatever you like, it's your problem. We can be friends if you like and if you don't want us to be friends, fine. But don't think you can do anything to my daughter and get away with it. And for your information, you can still tell your son to leave my daughter alone, we are not afraid to cancel the wedding as long as it is their decision, not yours.

We moved away then, extremely shocked that Maggie's mother had actually said all that to Chuks' mother. Serves her right anyway, someone should have given it to her a long time ago. We went back downstairs to position ourselves to see how the two women would behave when they come out. Maggie said she wished she could have recorded the conversation, so she would have something to show her children about their grandmothers when they grow up. She was still looking at the funny side of things.

Not long after, we saw them come downstairs, one after the other. Maggie's mother had her smile back, hugging and thanking everyone for attending - she would have been a good actress. Chuks' mother's face was actually difficult to read, definitely not smiling, we just couldn't figure out if her face was up in defiance or down in defeat. Maggie got up and I followed her, unsure of what she wanted to do, only for her to go to Chuks' mother, curtsied and then embraced her, thanking her for everything. The woman was taken aback, but managed to smile faintly, without bothering to return Maggie's embrace. Poor woman, she had gotten more than she bargained for on this one occasion. It's incredible how powerless people can become when they are on someone else's turf.

"Do you know what I'm going to do if that girl can't find me a dress I like today?" Maggie asks, after munching some popcorn. For a Saturday afternoon, the ice cream shop is rather active today, as people usually flock here at night. It's the sudden shout of "goal!" that makes us realise that the unusual crowd is attributable to the football match on TV. And there were a lot of hisses, abuses and blames followed by total quiet upon realising that it wasn't a goal after all.

"You will go naked." I respond mockingly. I can't exactly put it beyond her.

"*You dey craze*. I will go to the market and buy Ibo traditional wrapper and blouse, so I can destabilise Chuks' mother the more."

"Maybe you look for another Chief Bride's Maid, because I won't tie any wrapper with you to church. On the other hand, it would be nice to see her expression, which might put you in her good books." Once we finish our popcorn and ice cream we would have to get out of here as fast as possible as the shop continues to fill up even with the little space remaining. What exactly is this obsession with football?

There's something vaguely familiar about a rough looking guy that just walked in through the door. I had absent-mindedly watched him snuff his cigarette out before opening the door and only now realised that I probably know him as he got closer. He's with a girl who is dressed like someone my mother would call *Ashewo* and she's holding on to him like he's the most precious object in her life. I try unsuccessfully to remember where I could have met him. Am I developing a pattern? Maybe I should consider the optician's advice about getting a pair of glasses. That's how I ran into Bibi last month too and I didn't recognise her until she got too close. "Maggie, do you know that guy with the lady wearing tattered jeans, by the counter? He looks kind of familiar?"

Maggie turns her head discretely to avoid being obvious and waits to see the guy's face clearly. Her face lights up. "Is it old age that is worrying you? That is your former boyfriend."

My former boyfriend? How many have I had even if I counted from secondary school? Jibola, Abubakar, Furo … "Yes, it's Furo." I almost shout as the realisation hit me. It's true, now I recall everything about him. But this shouldn't be Furo Cookey, he looks very pale, gaunt and dishevelled and he has dreadlocks now. He simply reminds me of James Hardley Chase's *Hippie on the Highway*. Not someone I would like to be seen with at this time in my life. What could have happened to him? This is a guy I wanted to trade Richard with. I hope to God Richard doesn't look like this now.

Life! If only we could all know the outcome of our decisions before we take them, things would be far less complicated. He could have easily been the first one I had sex with. What a shame? Furo had been asked to withdraw from school in Year two, after being on probation thrice. I recall he used to miss classes and just lay about aimlessly. When he left, I had thought he would try for another university, but from what I can see, that didn't happen. Maybe I'm jumping to conclusions; I shouldn't judge a book by its cover. But, it's at times like these that I appreciate the kind of parents I have; call them old school, I don't care!

Remembering how Jibola had started calling me girlfriend at the Law students' dinner, I pull Maggie to her feet, lest such nostalgic feelings beset Furo if he sees us. "Please, let's get out of here." I'm surprised she agreed instantly.

The attendant had ingeniously laid out two bridal dresses, and one for the bride's maid. "This is me, Tobi, this is so beautiful." Maggie exclaims, picking the cream dress with some sparkles of peach and orange.

I pick up the orange chiffon dress brought out for me. Except for the crossed neck, it's an uncomplicated, yet delicately beautiful dress. "I love this too, where did you keep these dresses before?" Jovially, I jab the attendant who only smiles in response. I can already picture myself draping my eternally long false hair on my shoulders. "Are you sure people won't mistake me for the bride?" I ask Maggie, as I place the dress against my body, starring at the elegant girl in the mirror.

"Unfortunately for you, it is only the bride that has the tail, which you will be struggling with by the way." She pokes her tongue at me. "And I think you should go and try it on before you start getting all excited." She suggests, heading for the changing room, followed by another attendant.

TWENTY TWO

"Auntie Tobi, Auntie Tobi." That's Monday's voice calling from downstairs. I walk back to meet him to find out what is amiss. Monday is the young houseboy in flat one and he is very hardworking and intelligent. His guardians had decided to send him back to school with their own children when they realised he had a hunger and zeal to get educated, which was highly commended by some of the estate residents. He was ten years old when he first came and I used to pity him, wondering how he could effectively combine running errands, doing house chores and attending school until Mummy pointed out to me that he would be luckier than most of his peers back in Cotonou and she gave me a brief lesson on child-trafficking which I couldn't make sense of except to conclude that it should be a crime for people to bring children into this world when they don't intend to take care of them.

"Auntie Tobi, one uncle has come here to look for you three times. He said he would come back again."

One uncle? "What's his name?" Who could that be? It's

definitely not Oba, because I had been with him since yesterday and he only just dropped me off some minutes ago to get fuel and would soon be back to pick me up to Maggie's house. He has become an acceptable feature in our house since he met Mummy. He has equally met Daddy and they found a mutual ground in discussing the history of the world, but neither of my parents has asked me anything further than if I'm sure he is serious, like they knew that was his middle name.

"He didn't tell me his name, he didn't come down from his car and he said he would come again."

And he expects to meet me at home when he comes again I guess. He would be disappointed since I'm leaving shortly for Maggie's house. The wedding is next week and we have an appointment in church today at five o'clock for the dress rehearsal. Maybe it's someone from school or even from my secondary school. We've lived in this house for as long as I can remember and anyone who knew my house then would find it easy to find me now. "Did he ask for anyone else?"

Monday nods. "He asked for Uncle Lami the first time and I said he doesn't live here anymore."

Well then, maybe he's one of Lami's friends and the last time I checked Lami had just four friends that had ever been to the house except for Segun, Maggie's brother. Perhaps, Monday can give me a description to match. "Can you describe him?"

"No auntie, he didn't get out of the car. And his car is very fine o."

Not of much help. Who do I know that has a very fine car? Likely to be a rascal from secondary school, who may want to come and impress me. Maybe. "Okay Monday, I'm going out soon, if he comes again tell him to drop a note for me because I won't come back until tomorrow. "I turn to go back upstairs, but on second thought, I leave another instruction. "Or tell him to come to Auntie Maggie's house, you remember Auntie Maggie?" He nods. If he's truly my friend, he's likely to be Maggie's friend as well. "Thank you, Monday, how is school?"

"Very fine, auntie, thank you." He remains on the spot even when I turned to leave.

"Is there any other thing?"

"Yes auntie." His face takes on a more cheerful look and he dips his hand in his pocket and brings out a hundred naira note. "He gave me money, auntie."

"Oh, I see." By the time Monday is ready to go back to his parents, he would have become rich. I know that a lot of people in the estate give him money because of his cheerfulness and helpfulness. "You can keep it, but tell your Mummy, okay?" He nods.

"Thank you, auntie."

Not long after that Oba returns with his car fully loaded with fuel and we head for Maggie's house. I tell him about the strange visitor who unfortunately had not come back before he arrived.

"Maybe one of your secret admirers suddenly found your house on the map of Lagos. If he's come three times, it's either you have something of his or he has something of yours."

"It's just unusual."

"Chill out and stop thinking about it, okay."

"Yes."

"Better."

Even on a cool Saturday evening when traffic is light, it

takes us thirty minutes to get to Maggie's house because of Oba's speed limit. I've never stopped wondering why he bothered to buy a BMW rather than a Volkswagen so he doesn't have to struggle not to be a tortoise, a bad waste of potential, I'd say.

"I'll see you tomorrow then." I run my hand through his hair, knowing that before he leaves he would check his mirror to press every curly strand back into place. Isn't there any competition for Mr Immaculate?

Inside the house, Chuks and his best man were already waiting. Maggie had been considerate enough to tell me that the guy who tried to kiss me on Chuks' birthday was the best man, so I wasn't shocked to see him. I give him a wry smile which hopefully, he would recognise for what it is.

He smiles too and hugs me. "Long time no see. You look as pretty as ever."

"Thank you, you look good too." If we are going to be working together next week, we had better be nice to each other for the sake of the cameras. "Where is Maggie?" Chuks gestures to her room and I go in. She is loafing in bed with her usual pack of chocolate and flipping through a wedding magazine Segun brought back with him from US. "Let's go baby."

"Would you believe that divorce rate in the US last year was forty six per cent?" She shoves the magazine into my hand.

"So? Do you want to back out now?" I fling the magazine to the bed. "Let's go. What you should be reading now is how to satisfy your man in bed. Go and get Cosmo."

We reach the Church just in time. You can't rely on Oba for an assignment like this. The young Minister is waiting at the vestry and asks the couple to identify themselves after we take our seats. Maggie and Chuks signify with a show of hands, then he asks them if they would use the regular vows or they wanted to personalise it. They said they would use the church vow. Someone knocks and peeps in through the door asking to excuse the Minister. He grudgingly gets up at this interruption and excuses himself, promising to be back as soon as possible.

"Chuks would you believe that divorce rate in the US last year was forty six per cent?" What's Maggie's business with this divorce rate issue?

"Really?" After a short pause and I guess some thinking, Chuks decides to pursue the matter further. "I hope you know I'm Catholic and we don't divorce, so if you are having second thoughts about getting married, just say so now."

Maggie is shocked, serves her right, it's good to know when to keep one's mouth shut. And as my father would say, there's a when and how to say a what. "I just wanted to share what I read with you, why do you have to take it personal?"

Chuks shrugs. "I also just wanted to share what I know with you, in case I'm missing out something."

"The something you are missing out, my dear is that you may have to kill me if you want to get rid of me because I also don't intend to add up to any divorce statistics." That's a nice way of putting it, Maggie.

"Does anyone know the divorce rate in Nigeria?" Chuks' friend asks, trying to calm the fraying nerves.

"Nigeria? Who do you think would compile such a statistics in Nigeria?" I ask. From what we know now, there are several people who claim to be married and put up a good show of answering Mr and Mrs, when indeed they live separately under the same roof. I wonder why old people can't put their acts together. Before anyone answer, another knock lands on the door.

A gentleman peeps in. "Please, who is Tobi."

Moi, I raise up my hand. "I'm the Chief Bride's Maid."

"Please come."

Is there something I'm supposed to do without Maggie's knowledge? Maggie shrugs as Chuks and his friend look on in surprise too. I follow the gentleman quietly.

And right beside the gate is the coolest, tallest, finest guy I've ever seen. His name is Richard! I think my whole system went to sleep immediately because I'm frozen on the spot. The gentleman pales into oblivion even before he starts walking away, leaving only the two of us. Richard runs towards me and picks me midway to break my fall. I don't know for how long he held me, but I can feel my body shaking now.

"Tobi, I'm sorry, I can't ever say enough of that, I'm so very sorry."

What is he sorry about? I'm glad to see him. "Are you okay?" I can feel the dryness in my throat as the words came out. I trace his face, his dimples, his lips and his eyes. This is truly Richard.

"No, I mean yes, I'm okay, but I should be asking if you are okay. I'm sorry. Please will you ever forgive me?"

"It's okay Richard, I …"

"Richie!" Maggie calls from the distance when she sighted him. The three of them are coming behind the Minister to go into the church. Maggie runs to join us and they both hug tightly. "Richard, is this you? When did you get back?"

"This morning. Maggie I'm sorry about everything."

"Sorry? You should be more than sorry. Let me get this wedding over with before I bring out your cane." Typical Maggie. The others have joined us now. Chuks and Richard do the manly half embrace and Chuks introduces his best man to Richard. I'm sure the guy would be wondering who the intruder is. We follow the Minister into the church to start the rehearsal. I'm only there in body, my spirit is somewhere else and I don't know where that is. Unfortunately!

Richard waits through the whole process sitting outside on the pew under the cantilever.

*

"Tobi, you haven't said anything, please talk to me." Richard shakes my shoulders gently. "I need you to forgive me and that's the only thing I ask. You can call me whatever name you want, curse me, kick me and you'd be justified, but please forgive me." He looks pleadingly into my eyes. Why is it difficult to get angry with him?

"Maybe if you had given me notice and time to reflect and prepare for this meeting, I would know what to say, but sincerely words elude me."

He takes one hand and starts caressing it, the shocking waves that pass through it make me withdraw from him. He is shocked at my response and stares long at me when he regained himself. "Just tell me I'm forgiven."

We are in his hotel room and I'm on his bed in my favourite reflective crouched position. After the church rehearsal we had all gone back to Maggie's house the same way. Richard drove alone in his fine sporty open-roof

Mercedes which Monday had mentioned earlier in the day, and I rode in Chuks' car with the other three. Thankfully Maggie made no allusion to Richard in the car despite the fact that she must have been frantically itching to talk about him. "You know you don't have to follow him." She had whispered to me during the rehearsal.

When we got to the house he held me gently, but tight enough to stop me from entering the house. "I need to talk to you." He said and called out to Maggie and Chuks. "We'll see you later guys." He led me to his car and opened the door for me before climbing into the driver's seat. He told me the name of the hotel he was staying and asked if it was okay for him to take me there or if I would rather go somewhere else. Would it make any difference wherever he took me? No!

Confusion rages through my whole mind and body. This is Richard, the guy who taught me how to love and love deeply. He had abandoned me and hurt me in a way only he could, yet I am not angry with him, I never was. So how can I forgive him? I was hurt, but he had a good reason for what he did, all I needed at that time was an explanation and assurance that he would come back for me. And now he has come back. My voices take over. He has come back for what? To fool you again of course! That's not fair, he only wants my forgiveness. Then what? I don't know, I haven't asked him. Remember he's married now? Oh, tell me what I don't know. And remember Oba. Oba, what does he have to do with this conversation? He loves you Tobi! Wow, Richard loves me too. He dumped you, he wouldn't do that if he loved you. You are being judgemental now. What does he want from you? He already said it, forgiveness. Then what? Just leave me and I'll handle it.

"Richard, I forgave you long ago." I leave him on the bed and walk to the window looking out pointlessly at the human activities below. I see a man and a lady holding hands - swinging, talking and laughing - walk into the hotel and I wonder if they thought or knew it would last forever. How unpredictable life can be. I turn back to face Richard, leaning on the TV stand. He still looks astonishingly handsome even with the look of remorse written all over his face. "All I needed was an explanation, an assurance that you would come back and I would have been okay. You hurt me Richard, badly. Why didn't you write me or did she hold a gun to your head seven days a week?" He shakes his head slowly. "But you were with her, do you love her?"

"Love her? Tobi, you are the only one I've ever loved, the only one I want to love."

"Then why did you do it?"

"If I wrote you, she may have found out somehow. There was no other way if I was going to continue to stay in the UK. I needed her to help me regularise my immigration status. It was initially supposed to be a business arrangement, but when we started she wanted more and started threatening me. I couldn't back out because she would have gotten me deported." Then he went on to explain how Nigerians and other immigrants legalised their continuous residence in the UK by contract marriages and how some get unlucky and deported if there's a problem with the contractor's relationship and the only option is to hang in there once you've started because the moment you get your residency, you can walk of that relationship as if you never knew each other. "That's why I had to stop communicating. Any little mistake on my part would have jeopardised the arrangement."

The much I understand about Richard's narrative which is not much really, sounds like a sordid arrangement to me, but I don't want to focus on that right now.

"Are you still with her?"

"Yes, but only for another twelve to eighteen months and everything would be sorted." Another eighteen months of knowing he is with another woman sounds like another eighteen months of hell. I turn my back on him again. There's a woman with two kids, and a man walking ahead of them with a frown on his face. I only realised they are together when the woman stops to pet the younger child who is crying; the man shakes his head, turns back and grabs the second child and continues walking, leaving the woman to catch up with him. The world is full of all sorts.

Richard is behind me now, I can hear him breathing and I feel his gentle hands on my shoulders, he turns me around and stares into my eyes, probing and pleading. "It's going to be alright Tobi, I've lost you once, I don't want to lose you again. Just trust me please." I want to believe him, I believe him. "I can never stop loving you. I love you. I've missed you so much." He draws himself to me and starts kissing me, humming Bryan Adams' *Please forgive me* with the huskiest of voice. This is the Richard I know, the one I miss, and at that instant I forget all my scruples, my hurts and myself; nothing else in the world matters except this moment. I kiss him back with tears building up and trickling down my face. I love you Richard, even when it hurts. Gradually our souls and bodies begin to fuse together and we are making love as if we were never away from each other.

TWENTY THREE

"He's back, who is Richard?" Pause "Oh, Richard. So, what?"

"Lami I don't know what to do, I'm so confused."

"Confused about what? Are you stupid? Don't tell me you are even considering…" His voice trails off. I can hear some background noise and Lami's muffled voice. That's harsh, why would he call me stupid? "I'm talking to my sister please, lay off." Pause. "Yes Tobi, what were you saying?"

"I just needed someone to talk to. I love him Lami and he's asked me to wait for him."

"Can you listen to yourself? And what happens to your relationship with Oba?"

"I don't know, but my heart is with Richard, I've waited for him all this while and now he's back, I don't want to lose him and he wants me too. He had to do what he did to survive. Surely, I can't hold that against him. He said he can divorce the lady in about twelve months and then he would be free for me forever and I can join him in the UK." The words rush out.

"When did you see him?"

Why is he asking me that? "Yesterday. He came back yesterday and he came to look for me and ... Lami I realise I still love him. I never stopped loving him."

"Did you have sex with him?" Why should he ask me that kind of question? "Now listen to me carefully Tobi. If love was enough to hold people together, there won't be as many divorces as we see. You need love, but above all, you need character and sensitivity and someone that would stand with you through thick or thin, not someone that dumps you in the middle of somewhere for whatever reason, I don't care."

That sounds like what Mummy would say, not Lami. "But, you can't judge someone if you've never been in their shoes."

"I'm not judging, I'm only telling you it's wrong to go about hurting people's feelings as if they are not human beings. I don't care what you feel for Richard, what about his wife, and what about Oba?"

"I never made any commitment to Oba. I feel for him, but not in the same way I feel for Richard. And even his wife knew I was there before her. What about the way she hurt me?"

"My little sister, if we all acted the way we feel, the world would have come to an end a long time ago. Do you know how many times I felt like strangling you for doing something stupid?"

"You've felt like strangling me?" This is news to me; he had always been an understanding brother, the one I could never annoy.

"Yes, and exactly how I feel right now. So if you don't have anything better to talk about, you will tell Richard to get lost, and I won't have to strangle anyone?" Lami drops the phone. So much for brotherly advice, not what I expected to hear from him, he had been rather emotional about Richard, if I can forgive him, why can't he?

Parting with Richard yesterday had been extremely difficult and sleep had remained elusive as I continued to relive our reunion and the pleasure I had felt when he held me, sang to me and made love to me, while something that looked like Oba's shadow kept lurking somewhere in a distant background, trying to accuse me of double dealing. But I hadn't felt like I was double dealing, I had felt like heaven and I don't want anything to make me feel guilty for being with the one I've always loved. Even attending morning service in church hadn't exactly cleared my mind.

He had evoked all the emotions and passions I thought I had lost. He had been quite understanding about Oba when I told him and he admitted it was his fault, and it was his responsibility to redeem everything we've lost. He wanted me back; to love him, to give him another chance, to trust him and wait for him to extricate himself from his *arrangee* marriage. He said all the things I wanted him to say, he tickled me, made me laugh and much more, except that I relapsed into my dilemma immediately I left him.

Everything would have been okay, if only I didn't have to contend with Oba. How do I deal with him without hurting him the same way I had felt hurt when I thought Richard had abandoned me? To think that he was just supposed to be a distraction. Phew! Why should being with Richard feel so right, yet so complicated? If only!

There's a knock on the door and with it the trepidation of having to face Oba. When he dropped me off at Maggie's house yesterday, neither of us would have thought that anything would happen to affect our relationship. Yet, between yesterday and now, a thousand things have happened just by Richard showing up. I open the door to let him in.

"Is anyone home?" I shake my head glumly, but not noticing, he sweeps me in his arms and starts to kiss me. Something must be exciting him. "Can we go out, there's something we have to celebrate?" He asks excitedly and I nod in response. What can he want to celebrate when all I'm feeling is confusion? "Are you okay?" He asks when he finally lets go of me.

"I'm okay." I manage to squeeze out a smile for him. "I'm just a little bit tired."

"I know you've had a lot to do with Maggie's wedding and all the planning." If only. "How was the rehearsal?"

"It was short and just routine. It went well." At least until Richard showed up.

"So where can I take you my lady, where can I blow your mind?"

Nice try, but I don't think you can blow my mind even if you tried for a thousand years. That's something only Richard can do, but I keep that to myself. "Anywhere would do." I don't feel up to playing my lady and milord today.

We drive all the way to Allen Avenue, the same ice cream shop we had seen Furo the last time. It's late evening and expectedly it's dimly lit and almost filled up. I hope I don't run into anyone I know again, especially Richard, so I look for a seat at the corner of one extreme where I can see everyone who walks in without being seen myself. After settling down with our ice cream and my popcorn, because Oba wouldn't eat popcorn without washing his hands, I ask him what we are supposed to be celebrating.

"I'll tell you, but you have to tell me what you are thinking about first. You've been unusually quiet. Is it something I did, are you annoyed with me in anyway or is there something I should do that I'm not doing?"

Why does he have to be so sweet? "Oba, it's nothing really, I told you I was tired. Like you said, running around for Maggie's wedding hasn't been as easy as I had thought." How am I going to tell him about Richard?

He shrugs, and then reaches forward, spreading my left eye wildly with his fingers like he was examining me for some ailment. "Or are you pregnant and you don't want to tell me?" Of all the things to think about now.

"No Oba." I almost scream at him, shaking my head profusely.

"Okay, my lady, if you say so. He takes both my hands and looks into my eyes. "I know this is going to surprise you and I hope you won't kick me for it." I smile, raising my brows. Now I am impatiently curious. Has he gotten another girlfriend? That would remove a lot of load from my shoulders, but I'm sure he wouldn't think that called for a celebration. "Could you just close your eyes for a moment?" I do as I was told and shut my eyes tightly and he lets go of my hands for a few seconds. "Okay, you can open them now."

Inside a red, velvet small case is a beautiful cluster of diamond gold ring. I don't know if it's diamond really, but it's beautiful and big, not like the tiny one Richard gave me, which I have refused to throw away by the way.

"Oh, it's so beautiful, very beautiful." He is looking at my face, smiling, waiting for me to pick the ring from its case. But

I know what I said has nothing to do with what I'm feeling. "But, you shouldn't have."

"But I want to, my lady." He removes the ring from the case and makes to kneel but reflexively, I stop him midway.

"Don't Oba, please."

"Why not? Will you marry me Tobi?" I feel like crying, but I don't, I rub my hands on my face and start pulling my cheeks. This shouldn't be happening to me now, God, why are you doing this to me knowing that I can't?

"Oba, you don't have to." I mutter.

"I'm not doing it because I have to, I'm doing it because I want to, I love you my lady and I'd like you to be my wife if it pleases you."

"I wish I could, but not now."

"Is that a no?" No response. He closes the case and puts it back in his pocket carefully and takes hold of my hands again. "What's the problem Tobi?" It's so annoying that there isn't even a trace of anger in his voice, just disappointment. "You know I'm a patient person, I can wait, but I need you to let me know what I can do better." This is not going to be easy.

"You are perfectly okay, you are good just the way you are, it's not about you, honestly. I'm just confused."

"If it's not about me, what's it about then? Tobi, please talk to me." He says gently, continually caressing my hands.

"It's Richard." I blurt out, tears welling in my eyes.

"Richard? Who is Richard?"

"Richard, the guy I told you about, the one that went abroad."

"The guy that jilted you?" I nod, but he didn't exactly jilt me. "What about him?"

"He came back yesterday, he was the one looking for me yesterday. He wants me back." He's still holding my hands but the caressing has stopped.

"He wants you back? How is that your problem?" Silence. He releases my hands. "Oh, you said you're confused. Why are you confused, Tobi? You think you still love him? Or you think he loves you more than I do? But you're not confused about him, it's me you're confused about." He sighs and raises his head up, deep in thought. There's a very loud silence between us, even in the midst of all the background noise. I reach for his hands, but he flinches and gently withdraws from me, bringing his face down. "I thought you said he was married." I can feel his eyes blazing hot, but his voice remains calm.

"Yes, but it's a contract marriage and …"

He cuts into my speech. "And he's going to leave her and come back for you." I nod, coming from Oba, that makes me feel like second best to Richard's wife. "And you don't mind." Another bout of silence from both sides, each lost in thoughts. How can he remain this composed? I would have preferred him to shout at me, even slap me or kick me so I can feel the pain he's feeling. "I don't know what that guy has told you, but I have little respect for someone that would treat ladies like commodities, discard one for another because he wants to live abroad, then swap them all over again because he wants to live with the one he thinks he loves. It's a selfish way to live Tobi and you deserve better than that."

"He said it was a business arrangement. You're judging him Oba, you've never been in his position, and you've never had life so rough like he did. Maybe you'd see the world in another light if you've had to survive on your own without your parents sending you to school and holding your hands throughout your entire life." Will I always have to defend Richard like this?

Oba is shaking his head and biting his lips as if to hold himself back. "If you think I've had it all rosy for me, you had better wake up from your slumber. But I don't toy with people's emotions like you and your boyfriend are doing." That hurts, Obaniyi, nice one. His voice is beginning to rise, I look around, but everyone is busy with their own business. "Give me your hand." That sounds like a command, so I give him my hand, his grip of my hand is very tight and it feels rather hot. "Listen to me carefully, Tobi." That's the second time in one day I'm going to be ordered to listen carefully, Richard you had better be worth this trouble. "I know the pain of losing someone you love, because I've been there. I love you and I don't want to have to bear the pain of losing you if it's avoidable. I appreciate your confusion because I respect your feelings, so I'm going to give you one week to sort out yourself. If you still feel like this after your friend's wedding, then it's over. Forever! I won't look for you and you won't look for me unless you want me in your life without looking back. Is that okay?"

Is that okay, Mister? No, it's not okay, why can't you fight back and tell me how stupid I am, how much you want me and can't live without me? Thank you for your magnanimity, but no thanks. I'm supposed to feel good, but I feel empty. "Can I take you home now?" He asks me coldly, getting up and stuffing his hands in his pocket.

"Don't worry, I'll take a cab home. I'm sorry, Oba."

"I'll take you home if that's the last thing I do. Please let's go."

Phew!

*

She pelts the ball of chocolate in her mouth. "So what will you be doing when he goes back?"

"What do you mean by that? We'll be in Law school, then we'll go for NYSC and he should be through before we finish serving?"

"You haven't exactly answered my question. What will you be doing with yourself here, while he's living in London with another woman he says he doesn't love? He would have to hold her when she's lonely, have sex with her when he feels like, eat the food she cooks, go out with …."

"Exactly what are you saying Maggie?" She doesn't have to taunt me like this simply because I told her I had broken up with Oba, or rather, Oba had broken up with me. The past week had been one of the most terrific I've had in a long time especially with Richard, as we rediscovered each other. Suddenly I felt younger and more alive. When I told him I had lost Oba because of him, he had been overjoyed and carried me up high. "Tobi, you are so gracious towards me. I will always love you." We went to see his father together and went to pick up Faith to take her out, Bibi had been shocked to see me with him, but she congratulated the two of us anyhow, without any trace of bitterness in her voice. She's really more confident now and I respect her even more for that.

I had spent as much time as I possibly could with Richard

from Monday through this afternoon without arousing any suspicion or query from home about Oba. When we came to Maggie's house on Wednesday, she and Segun had joked around with us, implying they were okay with us being together. Segun had teased Richard that he was enjoying the best of both worlds and Maggie had patted my bum, encouraging me to have as much fun as I could. Since the wedding is tomorrow and I had to spend the night in Maggie's house, he had driven me here and only stayed a couple of minutes because Segun wasn't home, kissing me goodbye and promising to see Maggie at the wedding tomorrow if she didn't develop cold feet.

We are lying on Maggie's bed, perhaps for the last time, after sorting the clothes and parking the suitcases she would be taking to her husband's house. Her parents had warned her that the room would no longer be available to her once she says 'I do' to Chuks.

"I am saying that you're very stupid in case no one has bothered to tell you."

I startle and sit up on the bed. "Maggie!" I wish I could slap her right now. "What is your problem with the poor boy? The last time I checked you said I should follow my heart. My heart is with Richard and that's who I want to be with." She tosses in another ball of chocolate before answering me. A lot of brides-to-be would be afraid of touching anything sweet before their wedding so they don't add fat in the wrong places. Not Maggie, I wonder where all that sweet hides in her body.

"I don't care much for your heart now as you can see. Tobi, you deserve much more than Richard is offering you. He's a nice guy and fun to be with, I won't deny that, but he's not for you. Both of you are of different stocks, he doesn't have the kind of values you have and my dear, your heart can only take you so far, you need your head to take you all the way. You don't want to get to the middle of the road and find you are suddenly alone. That is where I see you going with Richard."

"Sage Maggie, it's easy for you to say because you got yourself the man of your dreams. Since when did some nonsensical value become important to you? I thought you were marrying for love." I say sarcastically.

"You know I have more experience in matters like this, even though you are older."

"Thank you for your concern, little sister. As you can see this little girl can take care of herself."

She smiles as she turns back to the mag under her pillow, until she remembered something. "Can I ask you a question?"

"Yes sis."

"Never mind."

"Just like that? I mind."

"Seriously, never mind. I just want you to know that whatever decision you take, I'm with you all the way girl."

"That's good to know, Mrs Okoli. Thank you and get some sleep."

TWENTY FOUR

"Dearly Beloved, we have come together in the presence of God to witness and to celebrate the marriage of Margaret Abolanle Abiola and Mark Chukwugozie Okoli…."

Finally, the day has come. My best friend and near sister Maggie is getting married, but I'm here still as confused as I was on Sunday. It's a beautiful day and I have decided that it would be one of my most memorable days as well, as I dutifully follow Maggie, carrying her train with all smiles and pleasure as she marched and sat majestically in church. The church is filled to capacity with people overflowing to the gallery. Maggie's parents are rich and they are popular socialites in their own rights and a lot of their friends have come out to honour them in various beautiful attires.

Almost every group has their own distinct *Aso-ebi*. The groom's men and the brides' ladies are one set; Chuks' parents' friends have their own traditional *Aso-ebi* in george fabric while the family also have their own fabric in another colour. Maggie's mother's friends which is the group my mother belongs are wearing orange and blue lace, her father's friends are wearing white lace and the extended family's *Aso-ebi* is orange and peach lace.

Four months of planning and one of the most colourful weddings in town!

".... And the blessing of God Almighty, the Father, the Son and the Holy Spirit be upon you and remain with you always."

"Amen."

As we march out with the recessional hymn, people struggle to catch Maggie's attention, waving, smiling and some calling her name. Maggie dutifully continues to wave at everybody. I look out for Richard where he sat and I wave to him as he gives me the thumbs up. He had come to the house to join Segun and the other groom's men. I scan the crowd to see if I would see Oba. After all, he's Maggie's friend as well and he hadn't told me he wouldn't be here. But I don't see him, not inside and not outside too. I try to focus on my duties while the photographs are being taken. Maybe he would show up for the photographs.

The reception is at Muson Centre in Lagos Island because Maggie had insisted that the first thing she wanted to do after getting married is to drive through Lagos in the white open-roof Limousine, so it takes us almost one hour to get to the reception. Trust Maggie's wedding to be a carnival.

By the time we got to the reception, the hall is almost filled up, particularly by a lot of people who hadn't bothered coming to church. Whoever did the decoration must have spent a lot of time and energy doing it and with a high level of creativity. Making such a big hall this beautiful is by no means an easy task, although I guess that is why we call some people professionals. The hall is decorated in Maggie's chosen colours – the colours of royalty, royal blue and purple, yet every table has its own personality.

Everyone dutifully gets up as we dance through the aisle up to the stage. If I am feeling this important, I wonder how Maggie would be feeling, it's a wonderful sight to behold, and I have to humbly admit in my heart that it would be a long time I would be part of another wedding as grand as this. A very long time, if ever! Along the aisle, Biodun is frantically waving at us from her table and Maggie stops to say hello. She is there with, her husband and Oba. Maggie hugs the three of them and I do the same, and I feel Oba's body very cold against mine.

Shortly before we get to the stage, I notice a familiar face where Segun and some of his friends, including Richard are seated and I ask Maggie who the guy is. "That's Tai Coker." She says dismissively.

"Have I met him?" He strikes me as someone I should know, yet I can't quite recollect his face.

"I'm not sure, unless you met him in our house. He's Segun's doctor friend and he claims he has the ability to read palms a while ago."

"Oh, yes, now I remember him. The guy that went to Jamaica."

Once we were seated, the MC takes over and he is equally a quite capable professional, managing the events of the day and making everyone laugh intermittently in the process effortlessly. Seating at the high table behind the couple positions me to see almost everyone as far as my weakening sight would allow and it removes me from the hustle and bustle of the activities in the hall, affording me the opportunity to reflect on my future from here. Maggie and I have spent almost the entire time of our growing up lives together and we've come to the stage where we would have to say goodbye once they leave for their honeymoon in South Africa. I can't even follow her to the airport. After Maggie is gone to Chuks' house, what will I do with my life?

I scan the hall for Oba and Richard again and I see my parents sitting beside each other somewhere on my right. They look beautiful together as they always do on the rare occasions Daddy agrees to go out with Mummy. It suddenly dawns on me that all the people that I've ever loved in my life are in this hall today, except Lami who is in Port-Harcourt. Following my urge to fish out Richard, my eyes fall on Tai again. Tai, the palm reader. And I try to recall what he had said about me when he read my palm at Maggie's house. He had said something like Richard wasn't my husband and I would meet my husband that year. Yes. That is what he said.

Everything is coming to me now! He had said something or someone would hurt Segun. Yes, and that same year the poor boy had lost his girlfriend. That would just be a coincidence. He had said Segun would also move away and that Maggie would get a gift and that Maggie shouldn't leave Chuks and Segun would have something to do with music. Yes, he had said all that. Hold on; is it possible that he had actually read correctly? Yes, Segun lost his girlfriend and moved away to the US the following year. Maggie is marrying Chuks for sure, it's only the gift I'm not sure of. I reflect more on that, but no gift comes to mind. I look at Tai again. Could he have been real? No! It's just sheer coincidence, after all Segun is not anywhere near music now. And Richard is still with me.

I look at him now. My charming Richie, full of life, romantic, the first guy I ever loved, the one who always spins my life inside out, can I ever have enough of him? The unpredictability about him is enchanting and continually draws me to him. Never a dull moment! Yes, he's hurt me, and I've forgiven him and we could have lived happily ever after. But for Oba!

Reliable, careful Oba, gentle and caring, he was supposed to be just a distraction, but I've come to respect and love him. He's a very thoughtful guy, mature, deeply reflective and takes care of me even to the littlest detail. Can he ever hurt me if push comes to shove? Of all the guys I've ever known, only he comes close to the profile I've carried in my head since I was young. Yet…

The MC calls on Maggie and her father to do the daughter and father last dance. And the whole hall goes agog as they collect the microphones and do their own version of Nat King Coles' and his daughter's song, *'Unforgettable'*. When they finished singing, Maggie's father takes her hand and brings her back to Chuks, kissing her on both cheeks before handing her over to her new husband. It's so moving the guests give a standing ovation and I'm almost moved to tears. How can this ever happen between me and my father? It's something I wouldn't mind, but which I know may never happen.

My father, what would he say to this dilemma I've found myself? "Young lady, doing the right thing for the wrong reason is as bad as doing the wrong thing for the right reason." Hmmmmm! At this point, I am perfectly convinced about what I have to do.

I look in my bag for a pen and I begin to recall the lyrics of Whitney's *'I Will Always Love You'*, frantically scribbling it down on the programme.

Soon enough it's time for the couple to dance with their friends as the reception draws to a close. I exhale in relief; I had been itching to get up since I finished writing that song. God help me. Once Maggie and Chuks started dancing, I leave them on the dance floor and go to get Richard for a dance. I don't know the song playing and I don't care, the only song I want to sing now is playing in my head and I lean on to Richard, singing exclusively into his ears. ' ***....but above all this, I wish you love!*** "I will always love you."

My heart feels heavy, drawing me close to tears. I know I have to get out of here immediately before I change my mind and make a mess of my life. Maggie doesn't need me anymore, I rush out of the hall without looking back. I hail a cab and ask the driver to drive as fast as he can.

I greet everyone at the barber's shop jovially and take a position close to the door, where I can see easily him once he comes, through the mirror. Twenty six minutes had never felt so long. I hold on for him to open the gate, thank the barber and bolt out as he starts locking the gate. He's shocked to find me beside him. I ignore the frown on his face and I place my middle finger on my lips to silence him. "Shooooo." He raises his brows, shrugs and lets us in.

"What are you doing here? Why did you disappear from the wedding?"

I pull him to the middle of the living room and start singing in his ears, hugging him tightly even as he tries to protest. It's the first love song I ever learnt by heart in form three when we just started getting attention from boys, sung by Foreigner. I feel his tensed body begin to relax. "...*I wanna feel what love is, I know you can show me ...*"

I've learnt a few things from Richard, but I know Oba is the one for me!

Glossary of words

Arrangee – (Slang) Contract

Aso-ebi – (Yoruba) Festive uniform

Ashewo – (Yoruba) Prostitute, Tart

Effiko – (Local slang) Bookworm

Environmental sanitation day- Every last Saturday of the month, between 7.00 -10.00 am

Fiam – A sound to indicate sudden disappearance

Freshen – (Slang) A new university student

Gbam gbam – Reverberation of musical sound

GCE – Final examination for secondary school students

Gonna – (Slang) Going to

Ich liebe dich – (German) I love you

JAMB – Joint Admission Matriculation Board. University Admission body

Jambite – A year one undergraduate

Je t'aime – (French) I love you

Jor – (Yoruba) Please

Juju – (Yoruba) Charm

Ma Cherie – (French) My darling

Ma fijo yin oba ogoooo – (Yoruba) I will praise God with dance

Mon mari aimant – (French) My loving husband

Moi – (French) Me

Na im – (Pidgin) That's it

Na me wan marry the boy? Abeg o - Am I the one that wants to marry the boy? Please.

NEPA – The national electricity power authority

No dey – (Pidgin) We don't

NYSC – National Youth Service Corps, a national work-experience integration programme for Nigerian graduates

Oga – (Yoruba) The boss

Oyinbo – (Yoruba) White man

Scripture Union – A Christian group usually school based

Sege Bobo – Segun, the dude

Shakking – (Slang) Drinking

Shaks – (Slang) Booze

Toaster – (Slang) Suitor

Toasting – (Slang) Wooing

Tokunbo – Fairly used / second hand

Voila – (French) There it is

Wanna – (Slang) Want to

Wetin gwam – (Pidgin) What's happening?

Wonderfulment – (Pidgin) Wonder

Yonder – (Pidgin) Around

You dey craze – (Pidgin) You are crazy

ACKNOWLEDGMENTS

I would like to thank the following people for their support and encouragement towards making this book possible:
Emmanuel and Bolu, who had to endure every thought and written word and had to sacrifice the laptop endlessly while this was going on;
Members of Angel Writing Group and mates at City University, especially Keren David, for their continuous support and feedback;
And a host of others including; Wura, Seyi, Nike, Ime and IY Afolayan.

ABOUT THE AUTHOR

When she's not writing or working, Tayo Emmanuel is meddling with other people's love lives, trying to set up or fix their relationships. She lives in London with her small eccentric family.

www.rel8ing.co.uk

www.tayoemmanuel.co.uk